THE
BUTCHERBIRD

GEOFFREY COUSINS

THE BUTCHERBIRD

ALLEN&UNWIN

First published in 2007
This edition published in 2009

Allen & Unwin
83 Alexander Street
Crows Nest NSW 2065
Australia
Phone: (61 2) 8425 0100
Fax: (61 2) 9906 2218
Email: info@allenandunwin.com
Web: www.allenandunwin.com

National Library of Australia
Cataloguing-in-Publication entry:

Cousins, Geoffrey.

The butcherbird.

ISBN 978 1 74175 601 2.

1. Entrepreneurs—New South Wales—Sydney—Fiction.

I. Title.

A823.4

Typeset in 10.35/12.68 pt Minion Pro by Bookhouse, Sydney
Printed in Australia by McPherson's Printing Group

10 9 8 7 6 5 4 3 2 1

To Darleen

chapter one

The two Rolls-Royce engines buried in the bowels of the *Honey Bear* fired up with a deep-throated roar as the tangerine light of a late autumn sunset washed the castles lining the shores of Sydney's eastern suburbs. Inside these exquisitely coordinated temples of taste—in the art deco style, or the Gothic style, or the French fifties style, or the French provincial style, or the God knows what style, and even in one, for reasons that none of the other owners could possibly fathom, an attempt at an 'Australian' style, which included such items as a dining table that had once served in a shearers' mess together with a variety of farm implements scattered about the room, none of which were in fact Australian—women were shedding little tennis dresses in order to bathe before dining in some bistro that refused to take bookings, or explaining to friends on their B&O walkarounds why Charles was a wimp in every sense of the word, or rubbing their recently waxed thighs with special rose cream made in Portugal and only sold in one shop with no name, or screaming at their husbands who had arrived home early, for no reason, with no presents, no plans for dinner and a paunch that, in the dim light of dusk, looked even more prominent than it had that morning.

On the *Honey Bear*, all was soft, golden, sweet as treacle in a crystal jar. Indeed, Macquarie James Biddulph, master and commander of all he surveyed—one hundred and eighty-three feet of throbbing Huon pine and celery-top pine and swamp mahogany, all staterooms lined in suede leather tanned from the hides of his own cattle, from the vast properties in the Kimberley where they measured them in millions of acres—Mac as he was known to friends, and Big Mac to the press and to those who would like to be friends but had no chance of stepping across the great social gangway onto the sacred decks of the *Honey Bear*, Mac held a glass of Cristal of another origin in his prize-fighter's mitt as he gazed benignly, patronisingly, at the gaggle of guests being piped aboard. Of course, there was no piper, although the thought had floated through the Big Mac mind more than once before it was dismissed as a touch ostentatious, though only a touch. But there was a bevy of immaculately turned-out crew members of both sexes in pristine white shirts and tailored navy shorts—tight-fitting shorts so the tight arses of the girls and the bulging quadriceps of the young men could welcome the guests with promises and glasses of vintage, and fresh peach juice for those who just drank peach.

Mac stood on the bridge, three decks and thirty feet above this assemblage of bronzed concupiscence, legs apart as if bracing against a rolling sea. The massive torso was bare and golden (waxed in the privacy of his own castle by a maiden who received a great deal more than the standard waxing fee and who would never reveal the secrets of the Big Mac chest). The Big Mac loins were covered only by a triangle of leopard-print silk, and the snowshoe feet with kangaroo skin sandals.

Although Mac was only five feet eight inches in his sandals, the width across his shoulders appeared approximately equal to his height, producing the impression of a solid block of squareness where the sum equalled more than the parts—although 'there's nothing wrong with the parts', as Mac was fond of saying. As if in confirmation, he glanced briefly at the apex of the leopard print, the bulge, the discrete (although not so discreet) mound straining at the Italian silk. Yes, it was there all right. You might not be able to see the Mac prick but you certainly knew it was there. It was a presence at the party and all the guests would sense it when they fronted up to pay homage—all packaged up like department-store boxes in their navy blazers and chinos and neat white shirts and tiny diamond bracelets, while he, Big Mac, a name they would never dare to speak on the *Honey Bear*, stood before them so full of juice, so full of torque, they would have to look away.

He gazed at them now as they came aboard. Talk about a motley crew. What was motley anyway? Whatever it was, this lot was it. God knows why he asked some of them. Because they were all usable in one way or another, he supposed. Look at that old ponce, Laurence Treadmore, tiptoeing across the gangway as if he was avoiding a dog turd—*Sir* Laurence for Christ's sake. Picked up his knighthood before Australia abandoned all that crap for those little lapel buttons everyone clamoured for. The dried-up old prune was even wearing a tie. A tie, on the *Honey Bear*? Never before seen, not even when Prince Charles sailed aboard wearing some sort of cravat. But tie or not, Sir Laurence was the chairman of his board and useful, full of useful qualities. Namely that he loved money and would rationalise almost anything to get it. And a fair chunk of his money, a handsome pile of millions (stashed somewhere, probably up his benighted arse since he never seemed to use any of it, to enjoy any of it), had been provided, directly or very indirectly, by Mac—or rather, if you wanted to be pedantic about it, by the shareholders of Mac's company.

And who was that behind the neat, prissy figure of Sir Laurence? Ah yes, one of the pigeons for the weekend: Jack Beaumont, the property developer. Well he at least seemed likely to enjoy the pleasures on offer. Good-looking fellow, though lacking the power, the charisma, the bulging triangle of a Big Mac, of course. He was only a baby pigeon in the great scheme of things, but nevertheless he had something to offer. And offer it he certainly would by the end of a weekend under the spell, the delicious warm embrace of the *Honey Bear* and all she had to offer. And here came some of that sweet, sweet candy.

God he loved to watch Bonny skip onto the boat. She seemed to skip, literally, she was so supple and full of life and youth and crushed fruit and mung beans or whatever the hell she ate. She was always stretching or bending or clenching her tight little buttocks to make them tighter still, though they couldn't be any firmer or rounder or more perfect, as he knew only too well. There wasn't a hair anywhere on her body except on her beautiful head, not one hair. He knew, he ought to know, since he paid for all those Brazilian jobs and facial mud cleansers and polishing and sluicing and colonic irrigation and everything else that went into keeping that perfect, smooth, taut body exactly the way he wanted it. And that was the point. He wanted it. Why not? Wouldn't any sixty-four-year-old man want a body like that sliding and rubbing and slipping and pulsing its way across his sculpted loins? It was a mystery to Mac why all men who could afford it didn't have a Bonny tucked away somewhere. Sure you had a wife, and kids if you must, but you had a Bonny to keep the juices running. She was his personal trainer in her official capacity, and a fine result she delivered. Look at him. How many men of his age had the biceps, the latissimus dorsi, the quadriceps, the sixpack—well maybe not quite the sixpack, but all the rest, all firm and hard and ready. The odd barnacle here and there, it was true. That's what Bonny called them, his 'barnacles', but that was an honest enough thing on a ship that had sailed more than a few miles. He was still seaworthy, that was the point. Seaworthy, shipshape, ready to voyage. And Bonny helped to keep the engines turning over.

Look at her little friends coming on board. They were all sanded and polished and varnished. Smooth, sweet, happy, grateful little honey pots. He loved every one of them. Which wasn't to say he didn't still love Edith. In his own way. But she was always asking him that: 'You still love me, Mac, don't you?' And he always gave the same answer: 'I'm here, aren't I?'

As for the contrast between these beautifully wrapped little bonbons and the amorphous lump of old political horseflesh following them, well it was almost enough to turn the stomach. Why didn't Harold Wilde do something about himself? Although what that might be Mac wasn't sure. There was no way any of Bonny's medicine ball throwing or shadow-boxing exercises (Mac loved to punch at her) or squats or anything could wear away the rolls of fat that were flopping around under that tent of a shirt. There must be a couple of kilos in the neck folds alone. Disgusting. The huge behind just sat itself on a soft Senate seat and dozed until it was lunchtime or dinner time or some meal time no one had ever heard of, and now it was waddling its way onto his boat behind his collection of sweetmeats, defiling the soft evening air, a great heaving mass of visual pollution. But useful, potentially useful. So feed him up, let him leer and sip and sup. One day, some day soon, it would pay back in spades. Mac gave him a cheery shout as he lurched his way aboard and the great bloated jellyfish almost slipped over as he looked up.

He would have slipped over if it hadn't been for the steadying hand from behind that grabbed at some protuberance poking out from the tent. There was Shane O'Connell, where he always was, lurking just behind someone, ready to pick up any crumbs that fell from a corporate table or grease some grateful politician's way into a sinecure. He was another member of Mac's board, the company that was the great provider, the tree of plenty, the goose of goodness, the cream jar for all these sticky-fingered players and hangers-on and pigeons; the company he, Mac, Big Mac, had created, sired—yes, sired like a great stallion and then given birth to like a . . . well anyway, sired like a great stallion. By sheer force of personality and guts he'd wrenched it into the world, and now it was the largest home-insurer in Australia, a name everyone knew, HOA, Homes of Australia—the name he'd given it, just as he'd given it life and form and air.

But you had to watch people like Shane O'Connell. They were not always unquestioning in their allegiance to Mac, to HOA. They failed to understand that the two were indivisible, that HOA was nothing without Mac and that Mac was—he jerked back from that thought as if slapped with a wet fish. Sure, all his vast, complex, interlocking, tangled fishnet of private companies and Swiss bank accounts and hedge fund investments and trust funds and God knew what else (well he hoped God knew because Mac could never understand it all), sure this stuck-spaghetti mix all lived on the sauce of HOA, but there was no reason ever to assume that sauce would cease to flow. Maybe now and again Mac woke in the night, in the room he'd moved to across the hall from

Edith, or in the apartment, with Bonny breathing softly, evenly beside him, the magnolia scent of her breath mingling with the musk of her mounds and clefts. Yes, he woke sometimes despite his oft-repeated boast, 'I always sleep like a baby'. (Babies woke, didn't they?) But not often. And not for long. If there was a problem, and lately there'd been one or two icebergs in the water, he attacked ferociously and sank them, or whatever you did to icebergs.

But you had to watch the doubters. Shane O'Connell was easy to handle once you knew where he was headed. But he was deceitful and shifty and on the take. At least Sir Laurence's arrangements were all in the open—well, in the open with Mac. There was no need for others to be concerned with them.

O'Connell was one of those lawyers who didn't really practise law and was only on his board because he represented the interests of the biggest foreign shareholder in HOA. Just how he'd brown-nosed his way into that job Mac had never discovered. Anyway, it wasn't O'Connell who had been waking him up in the black hours lately. It was that damn idiot Buckley, a creature of his own making. The man had been a run-of-the-mill accountant before Mac promoted him to chief financial officer and then, only a year and a half ago, to chief executive. And now he'd found religion or something and was scampering around mouthing off about 'corporate governance' and 'transparency' and 'triple bottom line'. There was only one bottom line in HOA and that was the line Mac drew in the sand, the auditors audited, the shareholders knelt before. As they all had and did in the regular, steady rhythm of corporate communion. So why this idiot Buckley was digging around in corners among contracts and 'conflicts' that didn't concern him and hadn't concerned anyone else—because they didn't know about them, because they didn't need to know about them—Mac was at a loss to understand. He was well paid, obscenely well paid. He just failed to understand what he was paid for. Why did he need to know the detail of every consultancy fee? What business of his was it when reserves were released to profits? The actuaries were responsible for working that out, not the CEO. Or, more accurately, Mac decided what was needed and the actuaries signed off on it. It had always been that way. For Christ's sake, he'd hired all these people, and they hadn't been easy to find; flexibility of thinking was required and not many people had it.

Apparently not Buckley. Well, he'd have to go. But in the quiet transition the market appreciated. Which meant a replacement who looked better. Which was what was keeping him awake at night. Still, as his father used to say, 'Macquarie, the solution to any problem is usually in front of your eyes—you just look through them.'

Enough of this navel gazing (though he took one last peek down at the Big Mac chest and stomach and thighs before they had to be lightly covered to greet the guests). The last of them was aboard now and it was time to descend and dazzle them with all his force and power and the trappings of this floating castle. The one he'd really blow away was this last figure, coming aboard in a jacket that looked like tweed—tweed, on a twenty-degree evening—probably with patches on the elbows, and carrying a duffel bag that reminded him of something you found in an army disposal store. Archie Speyne might be the director of the Sydney Museum of Modern Art, he might be used to sauntering around halls jammed with masterpieces (half of them jammed with crap from what Mac could see), but he'd be bowled over when he took the art tour on the *Honey Bear*. Yes, they'd start with that today. He'd been planning to start with the toy tour, all the boats and gadgets and playthings, but this was better. Straight into the art. He couldn't wait to see the look on that pumped-up little know-it-all's face when he saw Mac's Whiteley, better than anything the gallery had, and the Moore sculpture—a small one, admittedly, but on a boat and who the hell expects to see a Henry Moore on a boat in Sydney Harbour? Well, he'd be blown away, and would soon forget about plaguing Mac for whatever it was he'd been manoeuvring for over the past few months. Mac had invited him for sport, so let's have some sport.

Wisps of early-morning fog were burning off the gunmetal Hawkesbury, flocked here and there with shafts of sun filtering through the impasto of clouds and mist. The river was still, tide turning, windless, birdless, fishless, boatless—except for the sleeping *Honey Bear*, resting at anchor in an angophora-lined cove. Its gold standard hung limply at the pole. The deep navy of the hull with amber rails and beading curved elegantly into the sheet-glass water. A fish jumped. The ripples spread out gently from the point of entry and reflected in the eight coats of marine varnish. As the haze swept up off the river, the peeling pink bark of the angophoras was lit with klieg lights and the colours danced and dazzled in a blotchy palette. The great river turned blue in unison with the sky and the world was suddenly awake. A pelican flew overhead, peered down at the floating blue log like a bewigged judge assessing a miscreant, lowered its undercarriage and set down in a foamy wash.

Jack Beaumont's bare feet edged their way onto the deck, stepping quietly, carefully, even though there was no one for the feet to wake. The other guests were three decks above and Mac slept in a separate apartment at the stern that was the size of the average Hawkesbury cruiser. The movement of the feet was almost furtive, as if their owner was afraid to be seen, to be discovered emerging here as early a riser as the mist. The feet arrived at the rail and Jack looked down at the pelican. He knew this river so well, ever since he'd first paddled fifty miles of it in a Canadian canoe as a boy, all the way from Windsor to Lion Island, letting the canoe run when the tide was flowing out and paddling steadily into the incoming stream. He knew it better than the pelican, because the huge bird wouldn't fly into the upper reaches where the grass ran down in a smooth edge to the casuarina roots disappearing into the water. He knew it as it was now, at peace, and he knew it when the storms whipped waves over the sandbars and the outgoing tide was a flood you'd never swim against. He knew the wide mouth into Pittwater and Broken Bay. He'd slept on Lion Island, which was infested with snakes baking on burning sandstone in the furnace of the summer midday, and woken with tiny penguins in their dinner jackets sniffing inquiringly at his swag on the beach at midnight. He remembered blue swimmer crabs boiling in a pot over an open fire and his father poking in the ashes for potatoes in their charred jackets. He'd felt the first stirrings of rising sap in an old Halvorsen on this river, as his fourteen-year-old hands ran over the nearly there breasts of Bobbi Ruwald and the Everly Brothers sang nasally about tearing down goalposts.

But now he felt a vague queasiness, bile in the mouth from a cocktail of guilt, remorse and champagne. Why should he? It was all well and good for the pelican to cast judgement with that great nodding bill of supposed wisdom. What did he know of copper-coloured loins thrusting and sliding in a marble spa? No one was hurt. No one knew. She seemed to demand orgasms for her reward, nothing more. Anyway, girls were like that now. They didn't need love and promises anymore, just orgasms. And Louise wasn't here. She was at a literary retreat, discussing the early novels of Jane Austen, or Tolstoy as a misogynist, or something. The kids were in camp. So who was he hurting? After all, he was still Jack-the-lad to the boys in the group, so now and again you had to play the part. Besides he was bored, life was too easy, business was too easy, money came too easily. You had to look over the edge now and again. But still his mouth was a stale lemon.

The pelican drifted almost to the hull as if to check the alignment of its bill in the mirrored wood, looked up at Jack briefly, then slowly turned and paddled off into the gentle eddies. Jack followed its dignified exit up the river. Minutes ticked away. Nothing moved except the great bird and the sliding clouds.

Crack. Suddenly an explosive sound, a gunshot, a weapon of some sort wrecked the peace and a missile fell into the water not far from the pelican. Jack was shocked into action. There it was again. Crack, and then a thump into the water, closer to the bird this time. Jack was running now, bare feet thudding on the immaculate decks, any thoughts of disturbing sleepers cast aside, running to the stern where someone—who?—was shooting at the pelican. A pelican, for Christ's sake. Who could ever shoot at any bird, let alone a pelican, the most majestic of all birds? Jack had always loved watching them landing like 747s in the bays of Pittwater and waddling onto Snapperman Beach to take the chips he threw from the greasy paper, the hard bits that were left from the fish and chips his mum bought from across

Barrenjoey Road. He loved to watch the span of their wings as they rode the uplifts along the cliffs between Whale Beach and Palm Beach above the wilderness of rockpools where he went to search for shells, or tiny, brightly coloured fish that looked like they belonged on the Barrier Reef, or octopus that sometimes leapt frighteningly from crevasses. He always poked around with a stick in the pools for the octopus but secretly he hoped never to find them.

Now someone, on this boat, where he was a guest, complicit in a way in this barbarous act, was shooting at a pelican. There it was for a third time—another crack, another missile into the water. It was originating from somewhere above him. He looked up. There was a figure holding a rifle. He called out, 'Hey!'

The figure turned in surprise. 'Hey yourself. Didn't know anyone was up and about. Come up and have a whack. I hear you're pretty good at this.'

Jack squinted into the sun, panting from his dash down the deck, confused by his panic for the bird. The voice was unmistakeably that of his host, but what was that he was holding? As Jack scaled the gleaming ladder he could see it wasn't a rifle the man was swinging, but a stick of some kind.

'This is the new Taylor Made. Big bastard, isn't it? Had it flown in from the States, just arrived yesterday. Pretty good weapon.'

Jack peered at the golf club held out to him, still slightly out of breath, unsure how to respond.

'Here, have a crack. You need to warm up for later. We'll have the longest drive competition after breakfast, so might as well get a head start on the others. Not that I think the rest of them amount to much. But you're pretty hot I gather. Single-figure handicap, hey? Anyway, we'll see. Have a couple of swings.'

Again the club was pushed at him. Jack took it, looking around. There was a rack of golf clubs like a billiard cue rack standing nearby and a huge plastic tub of new golf balls, individually boxed, into which Mac was dipping his sizeable mitt. 'Were you . . . were you . . .' Jack began hesitantly. 'Were you aiming at the pelican?'

Mac started. 'Good God no. That'd be worse than killing an albatross at sea and they reckon that's the worst luck around.

Who was that bloke?'

'Ah, the Ancient Mariner I think.'

'Never read it, but heard about it. I don't read stuff like that. No time. I don't read anything, to tell the truth, unless it can be put on one page. Winston Churchill was like that—put it on one page or forget it.'

'But I saw your magnificent library on the lower deck.' Mac chuckled. 'People like books, I have books. People like pictures, I have the best. But you needn't worry about guns; there's no shooting anything on this boat, all fish are tagged and released, all foods organic, all juices fresh—especially mine.' The last comment was delivered with a cross between a wink and a leer that should have been repulsive but, for some, was strangely endearing. 'The only time any of my shots goes near anything is purely accidental, but I hit them a bloody long way and on a river that's what counts. No greens, no fairways to hit, just whack it as far as you can. Have a go.' Jack took the proffered club and swung it easily in the smooth arc of a gifted player. 'Nice swing. I see you'll be a problem. Still, there's no run out here for your top spin, it's all carry. Mac's the reigning champion and not about to give up the belt without a fight, so let's see your form.'

Jack removed the ball from the box, placed it on the artificial grass pad with a built-in plastic tee and, in one easy motion, swept the missile fifty yards past where the last explosions had landed and fifty yards to the right of the pelican. Mac drew his breath in through his nostrils.

'Hmm. That'll do you. No more practice. You don't want to tire yourself out. Come and have breakfast.'

He led Jack by the elbow in a direction the younger man's nose was already following. 'Jack, this is Ernest, the best omelette-maker in the world. Aren't you, Ernest? Of course you are. He gets them almost crisp on the outside but still fluffy and moist inside. Unbelievable. I sound like a damn ad or something, but you've got to have one, Jack. What are you going to make for Mr Beaumont, hey Ernest? Spanish, mushroom—what's your poison, Jack?'

When they were finally seated after a seemingly endless inquisition on number of eggs, whether crisp bacon should be served on the side, whether guava juice should be added to the fresh orange, whether sourdough toast was better than jam and black bread, Mac gazed appreciatively at Jack's full plate.

'It's great to see someone enjoy their tucker. Know what I mean? Enjoy life, really. People who don't eat don't really enjoy anything much I reckon. But you seem to have a bit of fun.'

Jack looked up quickly to see whether this was an oblique reference to his indiscretion of the previous evening, but Mac was concentrating with great intensity on the slicing of a kangaroo sausage, 'killed on the old place'. He felt the need to respond to his host's enthusiasm for breakfast, sport, life, toast, kangaroos, all that lived and breathed and was cooked.

'Well, I've always loved sport and activity and a good feed afterwards, although I don't often eat a breakfast like this.'

'Nor do I. You wouldn't believe the stuff Bonny gets into me. Fruits you've never heard of all blended up with wheat germ and soya beans and curdled goat's milk or whatever. It feels like she pours it down me with a spout. No enemas needed in this household, I can tell you.'

Jack laughed uncertainly. 'Yes, we go the healthy organic route most of the time.' He paused for another mouthful of his four-egg omelette with three types of mushrooms and chorizo sausage on the side. 'Incidentally, you mentioned I had a low golf handicap, how do you know that?'

Mac looked up with a half-smile. 'I like to know about my guests, know what they like, what to avoid. Just common courtesy, hey?'

There was silence and serious eating. Finally, Mac pushed away his plate and it was instantly whisked from the table. 'So, you've had a great run in property, I hear?'

'Yes, the last few years have been remarkable. We've sold just about everything off the plan, which is unheard of.'

Mac poured coffee from the plunger. 'Do you have a formula? The one-sheet-of-paper idea?'

'Pretty much. Always a harbour view or waterfront, always big rooms, huge bathroom somewhere, usually a fireplace, a home cinema, a concierge in the building, forget the gym and the swimming pool since no one ever uses them, always an enormous price. And we never bargain. It seems to work.'

Mac laughed. 'They made you chairman of the Property Council and you were on the shortlist for Businessman of the Year. It seems to work all right. And you love it, do you? It still gets the adrenalin running? You've got to have that, haven't you?'

Jack eased back and looked out across the rail to the river of his youth. He played with his sugar spoon, tapped it on the cup, placed it carefully in the saucer. 'Well, to tell you the truth, it has lost an edge for me lately.' He paused. He barely knew this man and he hadn't spoken of his feelings to anyone, not even Louise. But no one else had asked, and Mac was leaning forward, genuinely interested in him and his life, and he was sated with the warmth of coddled cholesterol and New Guinea Highlands coffee and the memory of . . . what was her name? He would have to find out discreetly before she came up for breakfast. Mac said nothing. He knew the art of a good listener.

'I like what I do and I guess I'm good at it, judging by the results. I suppose this sounds incredibly arrogant, but it's just become too easy. We design those things, I dream up some absurd price, jack it up another twenty per cent and they generally snap them up before they're even built. In a way, I enjoyed it more when we had to struggle.'

'Who's we? You have partners?' Mac's voice was quiet now.

The staff had slid away, they needed no signal.

'No, I'm a lone wolf, I guess. Louise, my wife, used to be my partner. She's still my partner, but not in the business. We have two kids so that's pretty full time.'

'You like it that way?' Jack looked up. 'Being your own boss?' Mac poured more coffee into both cups. The pelican flew quietly away as the boat eased up on the anchor chain. The tide was turning and the Pacific Ocean was running in to meet the fresh waters of the Nepean and the Colo and the Hawkesbury, running down from the Blue Mountains and the Southern Highlands. With the salt water came the schools of red bream and taylor, flathead, sometimes black fish, and the predators that followed—the Port Jackson sharks, the hammerheads, the ferocious bull sharks. The sharks were all saltwater creatures and yet they'd been found more than thirty miles upstream, way into fresh water, and once, when Jack was only about eighteen, a waterskier had been taken at Sackville, which was thought to be impossible. He had hoped all the waterskiers would be frightened off this river. He'd hated their destruction of the tranquillity even when he was a boy.

He chewed at the question. Did he like it that way? Being his own boss, working with the same circle, half-circle, of colleagues and contractors, lunching regularly with the group, using the same ideas he'd lived on for twenty years, dining out on the same stories he'd told for too long. He hated it when Louise said, 'I think we might have heard that one, Jack', but it was always true.

But something made him hold back from opening his cloak to this man. 'I do. I like running my own race.'

Mac gave him the knowing smile of an old python. 'So do I.' He rose from the table. 'Come on, I'll show you a few of the other little toys we have on offer. God knows when the rest of these lazy bastards'll climb out of their pits.'

The two men walked slowly away together, both satisfied with their conversation. Not too much was to be given;understanding would come from what was unsaid. As far as Mac could see, which was further than most, Jack wanted nothing from him except a bit of fun. If so, he was the only person on this boat with such modest desires. And Mac wanted very little from Jack. Sure, he would touch him up for a discount on that penthouse for Bonny and get it, but that was just pigeon shooting. He liked the bloke.

From behind, as they strolled the length of the boat, the contrast in the silhouettes was comic. The one short, square, bandy. The other tall, lean, lithe. The sun was high now above the bridge. The *Honey Bear* was ready for another day.

chapter two

The door to number thirty-two Alice Street, Woollahra was a solid block of stainless steel without blemish or keyhole. Set into the facade of a late 1890s terrace in a conservative, manicured street of immaculate 'restoration', it seemed to be either thumbing its nose at history or promising relief, depending on your point of view. The minuscule front garden was a sea of river stones rather than the ferns and mondo grass or camellias and azaleas of neighbouring terraces. Apart from these two aberrations, number thirty-two faced the world with wrought-iron and Victorian modesty, just like all the other widows in the row.

Jack climbed somewhat more stiffly than usual from the leather seat of his Aston Martin, stretched, looked up and down the street as if checking for observers, and clicked the remote. A dull thump emanated from the stainless steel and he made his way into the house. He still experienced a frisson of pleasure every time he entered. It was his finest work as an architect, from the days when he really practised his design skills. That was the part of property that lifted his soul. And Louise had used all her skills as a negotiator to convince the local council to allow a conversion they'd never seen before and of which they were deeply suspicious. Two terraces joined together, not side by side but from front to back, with a glass atrium between, opening to a sculpture court in the centre—it might comply with the building codes, but was it 'right'?

As Jack entered, great shafts of light fell down through the three-storey-high glass roof and lit the yellow sandstone floor in soft pools. In one of these shimmering enclaves stood Louise, smiling at him, relaxed, willowy, tanned, in jodhpurs or some trousers vaguely reminiscent of horses and a cream cashmere vest that set off her shoulder-length blonde hair and brown skin. She was a handsome woman, that was how Jack thought of her; fit, athletic, strikingly attractive, with an aura of confidence and commitment. And she was his wife and he loved her. She came forward to embrace him and ran her fingers up through his hair in a gesture that always affected him. 'So, the great sailor returns from life on the high seas. Didst thou conquer the waves? Didst thou haul on mighty hawsers and splice the main brace? And hast thou returned to thy safe port and the bosom of a soft woman?'

Jack led her through the sculpture court into the kitchen that ran the entire width of the house. She was always teasing in this way, bringing him to earth or to heel, whichever she deemed necessary, and he loved her for that as well. It had been the same when they were partners together in the business. She'd been a competent architect—not in his creative league, never able to take the leap from a logical solution into the poetry of design, into the shadow puppetry of shapes and light falls—but brilliant in all the practical necessities of contracts and councils. He'd missed her when they started a family and she decided to commit to that. He missed sparring with her when they came together for coffee, when she looked over his shoulder at the sketches on the drawing board, sometimes mildly critical, but more often with, 'Not just a pretty face, are you, Jack?' He fed off her approval and the work was always better when they were in tune with one another. But he'd become the architect everyone loved so much he'd stopped being an architect and become a property developer. He'd moved effortlessly from design to building to financing as he collected people, or more as they collected him and his charming talent. But somewhere along the track, the profitable, seamless footpath of success through Sydney's best suburbs, he felt he'd lost some of Louise's respect. Not that she ever overtly showed this to Jack or anyone else. But he felt it.

'It was a motorboat actually, or ship more likely. Enormous great thing. But not much call for hauling on the mainsails. Anyway, how was the literary event?'

She examined Jack carefully. He was a hopeless liar or dissembler, which was one of the things she loved about him, along with a basically good heart, a sound set of human values—capable of eroding at the edges, but in the main sound. An immediate attempt to change the subject usually indicated nervousness.

'You would have loved it. Locked away in an overheated room in Bowral discussing whether Truman Capote did or did not contribute to Harper Lee's only novel and whether J.D. Salinger actually exists or is merely a figment of his daughter's imagination. Or something like that. But tell me more about life at sea. Who was there? What was said? I stand, or sit, ready to be amazed.'

Jack drummed his fingers on the wooden table, unaware he was telegraphing more signals of uncertainty. 'No one of great interest really, no one you'd know. Oh, except Archie Speyne from the museum. He was swanning about chatting up Mac. And a couple of business people and some broken-down old pollie. You didn't miss much either.'

'Really?' She paused and slowly twisted a strand of hair between thumb and forefinger. 'And no wives? No women at all? That must have been dull. What is Mac Biddulph, a misogynist or gay or something?'

Jack laughed, not knowing it was the wrong laugh. 'Hardly. I don't think he's gay, that's for sure.'

'Really?' Another, longer pause. 'I didn't realise you knew him at all. And no stimulating conversation or even gossip for me to share with the girls at tennis?'

'You don't play tennis.'

'Quite so. But if I did, and I might take it up, I'd need gossip to bring with me or I'd be driven out of the group and publicly stoned as a woman of low morals.' She was smiling broadly at him, no hint of suspicion or condemnation.

'Well, I sold the penthouse in The Pinnacle, so it wasn't a wasted weekend. Mac snapped it up, which pretty much closes off the sales for that one.'

Her eyebrows arched up in surprise. 'That's extraordinary. It's a wonderful penthouse, don't get me wrong, but I wouldn't have thought it was anywhere near grand enough for Mac Biddulph.'

Jack squirmed in the swivel chair, rose and began to pace. 'That's what I said. But he's bought it as an investment.'

Again the eyebrows shot up. 'An investment? Either he must have new ideas on how to get a return on six and a half million dollars that we don't know about or he's prepared for a long wait for a capital gain.'

Jack opened the see-through refrigerator door, peered into its lighted recesses, closed the door again. 'I guess that's up to him. Anyway, I took a bit less than the asking price to get the deal through. No point in being greedy. Bird in the hand.'

She followed him with her eyes, wondering which cupboard he'd open next in his exploration of cutlery and crockery. 'And which bird did we get in the hand—a sparrow or a goose?'

'I took six. It's a fair price and we've made an indecent profit on the whole development.'

'Indeed we have, darling. I'm just a little surprised you decided to grant some of it to Mac Biddulph, who hardly seems a deserving case, when winter is coming and blankets, warm food and thick clothing will be required for less fortunate citizens.'

Jack had reached the atrium and paused as if deliberating whether to disappear into it or circle back towards her. She decided to solve his dilemma.

'You know best, darling. Come on, I'll make us a decent cup of coffee, something not available within a hundred kilometres of a literary retreat.' But as he approached, she couldn't resist one last shot. 'Still, I hope you don't get invited on that boat too often. Half a million dollars makes an expensive weekend.'

A few nights later they sat at dinner together. It was a ritual they all treasured. Considering sixteen-year-old girls were supposed to be rebellious, especially with their fathers, and thirteen-year-old boys to have the attention span of cocker spaniels, it seemed a custom from another time. But any night they were all home, which was often, they ate as a family, with Jack acting as quiz master in another strange Beaumont custom.

'Who was the King of Spain in 1922?'

'That's dumb, Dad. We know they were all called Carlos. Ask a proper question.'

Sarah would be another Louise, he could see that already. She was captain of the hockey team, frighteningly good at maths, and more than capable of instructing her father in the finer points of his behaviour.

'Yes, well, you may know that but a reasonable percentage of the world's population is unaware of these mysteries.'

Sarah tossed her head so her long hair shook from side to side, something she had observed many twenty-year-old girls in the coffee shops of Paddington were wont to do. 'Nonsense, Dad. Everyone knows it. Now ask us something decent and remember you have to know the answer.'

Louise interjected. 'A family rule which has stifled many a brilliant question in former times.'

Jack observed them all with deep affection. This was the family sport, scoring points off Dad, but he knew it was their way of expressing love and that the day it stopped he would have lost more than respect. He looked across to the dog sleeping quietly on the rug, for support, but received none.

'All right then, who's the President of Tanzania?'

'Where is Tanzania?' Shane was always ready to answer a question with a question.

Jack smiled at his only son, the prodigal son he always called him, without really knowing the meaning of 'prodigal'. 'I cannot be called upon to give clues in the great game of life.'

'Meaning he doesn't know and therefore loses the great game of life.' Louise raised her eyebrows at him again.

'A preposterous and outrageous slander. Tanzania is in Africa, situated conveniently near Zambia and Uganda, especially if you live in either of those highly desirable localities. As the atlas will confirm.'

Sarah had already leapt up to fetch the reference books. 'He's right, Mum, it is in Africa.'

'Of course it's in Africa, darling, but it's a hundred to one your father doesn't know who the President is and is relying on the fact that none of our books are up to date. Am I right?'

The phone rang. Jack gestured for Sarah to answer it. 'Why do I always have to get it?'

'Because it's usually for you.'

Louise held his gaze. 'You won't get away with this bluff, you know.'

Sarah called. 'It's for Dad. A Mr Biddulph.'

Jack was startled. Louise watched him. 'Big Mac strikes again. You are popular. Remember, we can't afford another weekend away or we'll go broke—and besides, Shane has rugby.'

Jack took the call in the atrium and they could only hear him mumbling and the occasional word. He returned after a few minutes, running his fingers through his thick hair absent-mindedly.

'You haven't sold the house and left the family homeless or something, have you? You look somewhat addled.'

'I am. More than somewhat.'

'Well, what did he say? We're all agog. And keen to get back to Tanzania and the leader of that great nation.'

Jack gazed around the room, around the knot of his family, apparently not seeing. 'He said all roads lead to me. He said he'd been thinking about me ever since the weekend. He said he wants me to come and discuss running his company. That's about it.'

They were all quiet. The kitchen clock ticked. 'Why would he do that?' Jack shot her a look. 'I didn't mean it that way. We all know you're a genius and an MBA and all, not to mention your ravishing good looks. But he's in the insurance business, isn't he? You don't know anything about that.'

'Or who the President of Tanzania is.' Sarah tried to emulate her mother's arched brows.

'Yeah, it's strange. I assume he's talking about the insurance company. He's in all sorts of things privately, but that's the big public face. I was too stunned to ask. He cut off any questions and said, come and talk. I was the only one, all roads led to me. He repeated that. Don't think about it, just come and talk. That was the line.' Again the fingers ran through the hair.

'Why would you? You run your own company. Quite well we feel, don't we, group? Although we may razz you from time to time, you're a good little earner. Why would you bother to talk to him?'

Jack didn't answer. He looked up. Shifting clouds and a full moon were visible through the glass roof. 'Well, are you going to talk?'

He nodded slowly. 'I'm going to have a chat. Why not? It's intriguing. I'm a bit bored, to tell you the truth, doing the same thing. I don't mean I'm going to do this, whatever it is, but there's no harm in talking.'

'You're late, Jack. Just off the nest, I'll bet. And missing a great story. Start again, Maroubra, this one's a cracker.'

Jack slid into the only vacant chair at the long table and looked around the room. He loved the old beach house and the ritual of the monthly lunch with this disparate group of prominent citizens, knockabouts and larrikins. The creaking timber floorboards, the roar of the Bondi surf, the smell of fish grilling, of chilli and garlic melting in the pan, jugs of beer on the refectory table, Armando in the kitchen yelling his way into any discussion he chose to join, yarns and stories, myths and fables spinning around the table, sometimes raging arguments about politics or sport—never religion. Tales of women they'd known or wished they'd known, good humour and mateship in the old ironic manner. Armando closed the restaurant for them now, even though there were only a dozen or so in the group and the room seated more than double that number. They'd been coming for years and he was proud to have them—judges and heads of companies, people you saw sometimes on television, other characters you thought you should know but couldn't place, a few you felt it mightn't be a good idea to recognise. He just cooked whatever he felt like and served it with his favourite wines; no bill, always the same charge.

'Wake up, Jack, Maroubra's in full flight. What are you dreaming about?'

The voice came from the depths of the great lump of a man sitting beside him. It was a voice said to engender fear in the hearts of witnesses who had something to hide as the withering cross-examination of Thomas Wetherington Smiley QC lashed them from six feet five inches. Tom was slouched beside him, schooner in hand, drifts of froth finding their way onto the signature Zegna suit he always managed to make look like a charity cast-off within a month of purchase.

'Get on with it, Maroubra, or we'll rule you out of order and tell Armando to ration your grog.'

Another towering figure rose from the end of the table and raised its hand slowly in a gesture of silence. 'Gentlemen. As I was saying before Jack-the-lad graced us with his exquisite presence, reeking no doubt of bodily fluids, the nature of which most of us only dimly recall, an appalling and frightening apparition appeared at the door of number four Cross Street, Maroubra, the family home, at one in the morning last Friday.' Maroubra paused for effect, glaring around the table, capturing each eye. 'My son. Yes, gentlemen, the fruit of my loins, my only son, Gordy—rugby player, drinker, rooter—all fifteen stone of muscle and meat, beaten, bleeding. Shirt torn. The shirt his mother gave him for Christmas, five years ago admittedly, but ripped, covered in blood. Gordy, my son. I ask you, gentlemen—' another pause, 'who would dare lay a finger on my son and expect a happy life?'

The group nodded, mumbled assent, took long drafts of beer or wine. There was expectation in the air. Maroubra's stories were always rich with courageous deeds or extreme violence or remote and dangerous locations. Weird characters of dubious origin, often involved in his salvage business, threaded their way in and out of the fabric of the stories. But the pride of the family, beaten by unknown persons in the middle of the night—the wrath of Maroubra (kayak medallist, surf belt champion, mountaineer, stroke of the Olympic Eight), the wrath of this man was terrible to witness.

'I extracted the details soon enough, gentlemen, as you can imagine. A professional job. Bouncers from New Zealand, Gordy in a club, a few beers more than he should, perhaps, but nothing we all haven't done. They could've asked him politely to leave, but no, they smack him around the head. Bad call.' Maroubra swung his gaze slowly around the table again and then lifted his eyes to the roof. 'What was I to do to restore the honour of my family? Sometimes, gentlemen, you receive a sign. I looked up and there on the wall was my most treasured possession. The oar I used to stroke the Olympic Eight. With the crew's names in gold. What could I do?'

Maroubra lowered his head, sighed. 'I took down that oar and sawed it in half.' There was an intake of breath from the table and a shuffling of chairs. 'I took the butt end, comrades, put it inside my overcoat and walked down to that club. Straight in the door. Past those two ugly thugs before they could stop me and yelled as I went past, "If you had a mother she wouldn't recognise you after I say hello." I was in the toilet before they could wake up to themselves, put the overcoat over the stall door, the butt of the oar inside and started to wash my hands. It didn't take long. They came in quietly, cautiously, not sure what was going on. And I let them come, just smiling. I was drying my hands until they were in range. Then I grabbed that oar and belted the shit out of them.'

Maroubra nodded almost sorrowfully at his own story. 'It's a heavy thing, a racing oar. Even half an oar. It did a lot of damage very quickly, so I grabbed the coat and ran and kept running. Straight to Coogee Oval. I always feel at home there, safe.

Straight to the middle of the oval, dark at two in the morning.

Down on the ground, comrades, spreadeagled, nose in the dirt, not moving a muscle. You could hear the sirens pretty quickly. I suppose they were both police and ambulance—they would've needed one. They went on for a long time, lights flashing around for a while, but they'd never see me out there. I didn't move for two hours, and when it was all quiet I got up and went home.' There was nodding around the table. 'I put the oar back on the wall one piece above the other. I like it that way.

You've got to look after your own, hey?'

When the thumping of tables and clanging of glasses had subsided and the great steaming bowls of Sicilian fish stew and rice were set down, quiet fell on the group. Jack had felt it an honour when he was casually invited to come to his first lunch. He knew no visitors were ever invited to this informal club. If you were asked once, you were in. And he'd wanted to be in, to be included in this tangle of flotsam and jetsam that washed up on the shores of Bondi once a month.

When Maroubra had rung him three years ago and suggested lunch, he'd assumed it was merely one of their occasional boozy get-togethers. They'd known one another for nearly twenty years, since the day Jack had first signed on at the surf club for his bronze medallion training. There was the massive frame at the end of the line of newcomers, even then a head taller than the rest. And when they came to the surf rescue training with the old belt and reel, Maroubra had picked him as a partner—although even today he swore it was only because Jack was lighter than the rest and easier to tow as a victim. When the roles were reversed and Jack was required to rescue Maroubra, when little or no headway was being made through the rip, he'd felt the hand on his shoulder and heard the deep voice. 'Don't worry, mate, I'll kick underwater. No one'll ever know.'

And no one ever had. Just as they'd never seen the same hand take Jack's pack when they were portaging in the Franklin River and it was all he could do to scale the cliff, let alone manoeuvre a twenty-five kilo pack. But Maroubra came to him for advice, for support, once for money when he was starting his business.

They were joined, if not at the hip, somewhere near.

The group had been formed this way, all from different backgrounds, not a collection of school friends or sporting mates, just one link binding to the next, but a chain forged from a series of found pieces, each as strong as the next. Over the years they'd helped one another with tragedies and traumas, jobs and joyous occasions, funds and faith.

The only other member Jack had known before he joined that unexpected day was the Pope, who'd been at university with him, but even then was an exotic, distant figure. He seemed to have money when no one had money. It was said he made it by selling fur jackets fashioned from rabbit skins, but this seemed so unlikely it was dismissed by most. When Jack had jokingly asked at his first group lunch if it was true, the Pope had simply nodded and said, 'So what?'

There were people around this table whose intellect challenged him. He looked across at Murray Ingham sitting opposite, dipping a chunk of bread into his bowl. The face was a block of pitted granite with two thick, black slashes above the eyes. How did he grow those brows like possums' tails? Were they groomed and fertilised and cut like hedges? Jack looked away before the hooded eyes could catch him staring. Murray had written two critically acclaimed novels—both of which Jack had tried to read but which were still in the drawer by his bed with bookmarks a few chapters in—as well as a biography of an obscure artist that had won him awards and prizes and a year in some garret in Paris. And then there was Murray's apparent disdain for Jack's facile brain and purposeless life as property developer to the semillon set. At least Jack perceived this contempt from the occasional sardonic remark that was thrown his way.

Beside him was the imposing figure of the Hon. Mr Justice Norman Crosby, Judge of the Supreme Court of New South Wales, connoisseur of rugby and rum, Latin scholar, collector of Picasso ceramics, author of an unpublished play of considerable vulgarity. The Judge, as he was always referred to in the group, was examining

Jack with great interest, much as a taxidermist stares at a potential subject in order to define its precise attitudes.

'Mr Beaumont. Always a pleasure when you grace our table.' For some reason—and it made Jack nervous, as if he'd committed an undetected felony—the Judge always referred to him as 'Mr Beaumont', whereas all the others received their nicknames or given names. 'What news upon the Rialto? What do you bring us from the real world, the world of commerce, of glamour, of intrigue and money and success, of failure and suicide, or indeed of fraud and jail and terrible penalties, of the ruin of families, the dissipation of great fortunes piled brick upon brick over generations and then dashed to the ground in one lifetime of excess, of gambling, of drink, of illicit sex? What of all this, Mr Beaumont? We wait with bated breath.'

Jack tossed off a glib response. He knew he could never strike the right note with people like the Judge. Jack Beaumont, the great salesman, ask anyone, look at his record, look at the money he'd made. Why he could buy anyone around the table, pretty well—except the Pope, perhaps, but then nobody knew exactly what the Pope owned or did, just the way he lived—but all the rest. He could buy or sell them all, but as good as he was at selling, sometimes he felt challenged. There was no reason for it. He'd graduated with honours and been second in the year, tacked on an MBA for good measure. They all liked Jack-the-lad, were always happy to see him, welcoming. But with just a few, like the Judge or Murray Ingham, he sensed another level of activity in their brains that he couldn't reach.

It hadn't been like that with Mac Biddulph when they'd met in Mac's office earlier that morning. There was an immediate rapport. Seated in the vast, gloomy space with two life-sized paintings of brumbies above the desk there should have been an initial feeling of uneasiness. That was the intention of the design, if design was a description that could be applied to a room where the furniture seemed to be built for giants and one unrelenting colour pervaded, a sort of early mineshaft brown that appeared to soak up all the available light.

Mac had immediately asked him to run his company, HOA, the biggest home insurance company in Australia, as chief executive. It was an absurd notion, he'd felt at first, because he knew nothing of the insurance industry except that it was complex and required sophisticated assessments of risk and pricing. But Mac swept these doubts aside.

'And what do you think I know about risk assessment and pricing a book? What do you think I know about coefficients of variation and central estimates and all the other jargon and palaver the actuaries go on with? That's why we have actuaries, Jack, so people who create businesses like you and me don't have to spend our lives crawling around a pile of papers. Did you ever meet an actuary who built a business? And there are the regulatory authorities like APRA and ASIC and the ASX and every other alphabet coven of bureaucratic witches who pore all over the stuff. You wouldn't believe the truckloads of documents we pack off to these leeches. So you don't have to worry about everything being kosher—that's the one benefit of all this crap. But who brings the business in? Who creates the revenue instead of just reporting where it's kept? Isn't that what a business is really all about? And that's where you come in, Jack. You're a genius at selling. Don't tell me you're not. I've checked. And the banks love you; you're the only major property developer who's never missed an interest payment through all the market's peaks and troughs over the last fifteen years. They trust you, Jack. Do you know what trust's worth in this business? Think about it. For ninety per cent of our customers we do nothing every year except send them a bill—only about ten per cent make a claim. They renew because they trust us to pay out if that fire ever comes, or the burglar ever breaks in. Trust. It's what insurance is all about. You have it from the people who matter, the guys with the money, and you'll build it with the customers. And you know everyone in the building industry and all the associated services, and particularly in home finance. We insure homes, Jack. More than half of all the homes in this country. But how do we increase that share, get the new business, the first-time young buyers? Jack Beaumont gets it for us, with his contacts and his salesmanship. You can push us forward, instead of treading water while the weight of regulatory bullshit tries to pull us under. You're a visionary. We need you.'

What words that tug at the core, he thought. Not we want you, but we need you. Jack was already partly lost with those words, he knew it even though he wouldn't yet allow a decision to form. He certainly wouldn't voice one to Louise, to anyone.

'So what've you been up to with Mac Biddulph? Out on the floating girlie palace and all, I hear?'

He started at the stentorian tones of Tom Smiley. How could Tom know he'd been seeing Mac Biddulph? Was this city the glass bowl people said it was, where a thousand eyes watched every time the orb was shaken and the fake snow fell on a different branch? He tried to change the subject, to laugh off the question with a Jack-the-lad response, but if Louise could detect dissembling, the professional antenna of Thomas Smiley caught the false notes as clearly as bellbirds calling in a forest.

34

The barrage that followed pinned him with its forensic intensity and before he was aware of the prising open of his soul, he was spilling details of not just the weekend's capers but the conversation in Mac's office, his initial doubts, even the possibility, the possibility he hadn't admitted to himself, that he might take this challenge. Yes, it was a challenge—a stretching of his abilities, a leap from being the charming property developer to the leader of a major business, a critical business for the average Australian, a business people depended on in crisis, a complex, intellectually demanding exercise that he could drive forward better than anyone else. Mac had said so. Before he knew it, all this had tumbled forth into Tom's waiting arms where so many witnesses had relieved themselves unsuspectingly of their burdens in the past.

'Be careful, Jack.' The shrewd eyes assessed the rush of adrenalin sitting beside them. 'These blokes are tough customers, Mac Biddulph and his cohorts. Have you met the chairman, Laurence Treadmore, sometime member of my esteemed profession? Very subtle character, if I can put it that way. Quite deep. You need to know what you're getting into, Jack, if you're really thinking about this. It would be quite a stretch from a number of points of view. A big stretch.'

Jack flashed him an angry glance. 'Too big for me, you think?' 'I didn't mean that, old fellow. It's just that there are a lot of very complex issues in that industry and you need to work with people you can trust a hundred per cent. I'm not saying you can't with this gang, but how well do you know them?' He paused and saw the resentment on Jack's face. 'Talk to the Pope if you're really contemplating this. He knows a bit about it. Don't rush into anything is all I'm saying. Beware of hubris and flattery lest you slip on their greasy surfaces.'

chapter three

Laurence Treadmore nodded at the doorman of the Piccadilly Apartments without actually looking at him, stepped briskly into the familiar environs of Macquarie Street and commenced the daily triumphal perambulation to his office. He liked to think of the morning walk in this way—'a triumphal perambulation'. Because it was. Every few steps some passer-by would greet him as he wandered by the Colonial Club, the Anon Club, the great office buildings that housed the heads of companies who nodded to him deferentially. The Sydney office of the Prime Minister hidden away in one, hidden but well known to Sir Laurence, the tower of the state government and the Premier—all this a few paces from his home and open and welcoming to him, if not to others; a source of honours and wealth, of comfort and privilege, to him if not to others. For Sir Laurence was widely known for his intellectual flexibility. He could understand and appreciate any point of view, particularly if significant benefits might result from it for a client. And, of course, for the advisor.

Sir Laurence had never been a lawyer in the conventional sense. His was more a 'strategic commercial practice', in the course of which he guided clients through the intricacies of takeover law or contract negotiations or other complex matters of a more delicate nature. This tributary of the law allowed fees to be charged of a very different dimension to those based on the simple hours of toil which the lesser members of his profession received. 'Success fees' and other ripe fruit fell into his basket, the harvest of a merchant banker more than a lawyer. Indeed he would have been appalled to regard himself as a 'lawyer'—the law was merely a useful or annoying reference point, depending on the circumstances.

His small, neat figure in its tailored suit from Savile Row, trademark pink shirt of a certain soft hue, and matching silk tie and handkerchief were familiar to all who were familiar, as it made its way at eight-thirty every morning to the flower stall in Martin Place. Here he purchased a boutonnière of complementary hue, contrast was not a fashion concept of which he approved, before entering his offices and arriving at a desk which would already be laid out with Earl Grey tea and a croissant from La Gerbe d'Or in Paddington. He liked to breakfast alone. In the early years Mavis had often encouraged him to start the day in conversation at their table, but he found it unsettling. After nearly forty years of marriage she'd learned to hand him his briefcase and watch his straight back walk to the lift, as she'd learned so many things. Besides, Sir Laurence was a secretive man in certain ways, and he liked to be unobserved as he took his gilt scissors and cut items from the newspapers about people who might be useful or might need his arcane skills, or deals or possibilities, or scandals and indiscretions that could cause alliances to crumble and crumbs to fall. All these clippings were pasted into albums and filed in a tall locked cupboard in the hallway leading to his office—decades of the detritus of social and business life, discarded by all except him. It was remarkable how often he fossicked through these files and turned up a nugget.

He had a deep and productive relationship with certain sections of the press. Whereas most of his colleagues and most business people he knew were cautious and wary in their dealings with journalists, if not downright hostile, Sir Laurence had a passing affection for those who fell within his sphere. These were business journalists of a serious bent, columnists of a gossipy disposition and one or two editors who saw a future role in management. The relationships were deep, in the sense that they were hidden from view, and no public hint of the source of information was ever given by those who received his calls—they were never to call him. Productive, in the sense that the chosen ones would receive information that was not otherwise available and frequently should not have been so, while Sir Laurence or those he represented would be depicted as champions of all that was right and just. It was surprising what could be achieved in this way. People could gain positions of importance, people could lose them. Government ministers could change their minds on vital issues (after all, their job was surely to represent public opinion). Institutions who'd planned to vote one way at a public meeting might vote quite differently. Productive, and no fingerprints.

At one time or another, Laurence Treadmore had been chairman of trustees of the Museum of Modern Art, chairman of the Australian Opera and the New South Wales Public Library, and president of the King's School Foundation. Many other institutions tried to woo him to their causes but he no longer accepted simple directorships. And as to charity boards, he preferred to send a cheque. Occasionally he went to a major charity auction and made a spectacular bid or two, in which case the press contacts would be alerted beforehand. A detailed examination of his custodianship of these appointments wouldn't reveal a record of great success—Sir Laurence was fundamentally lazy, and the hard work of planning or fundraising was not to his liking—but no such examination was ever made and his timing was always impeccable. He'd gone, moved on, leaving the next incumbent to patch up the holes.

His secretive nature was revealed in a number of almost furtive habits. While he was obsessive about order and cleanliness, he had a strange desire to observe people who lived in other ways. He would park his car near the City Mission where the derelicts and street people came to feed from the soup kitchen. He liked to watch, just watch. Or the lanes where prostitutes touted. If any approached the car, he would drive off immediately. Sex, or at least the practice of it, seemed not to be uppermost in his mind. Mavis could attest to this. And their home life was closed to public view. Few people had ever visited the apartment, although he'd owned it for decades and was intensely proud of its purist art deco décor. When the Treadmores entertained, which was seldom, it was always at the club. Mainly they were entertained by others. Besides, Mavis was nervous of people she didn't know well and sometimes of those she did. Frequently she found her husband frightening, a fact which frightened her more when she registered it.

Mrs Bonython entered the office as Sir Laurence was picking the last crumbs of the croissant from the plate. She had never fully overcome her unease in his presence despite nearly twenty years of service. 'Mr Beaumont is here, sir. Shall I show him in?'

The pale eyes glanced up from the newspaper. 'Not just yet, Lois, thank you. I'm rather busy. I'll buzz in a little while.'

It was an uncomfortable conversation that ensued when Jack was finally ushered into the beige-on-beige office. Sir Laurence rose briefly then resumed his seat behind the desk, eschewing the relaxed offering of the sofa and lounge chair by the coffee table. Indeed no coffee was served. He sat with suit jacket fully buttoned while Jack, tieless, immediately removed his blazer and slumped casually into an easy chair.

'I know you've indicated to Mac that you're keen to sign on with us as CEO, which is welcome news, but you and I must conclude the matter between us. That is only right and proper in a publicly listed company, I'm sure you'll agree.' No pause was allowed for the agreement as Sir Laurence ploughed on. 'The relationship between the chairman and the chief executive is a vital one in the success of any company. I'm sure you agree. And it must be clear that the CEO reports to the board through the chairman. That is clear. In this company, of course, we have a significant shareholder who is also a director and, in some ways, the founder or perhaps foster father of the business. This can raise certain complications. These are best left to me to solve as chairman, so that you may be free to manage the business side of things. I'm sure you understand. If any such matters arise, simply raise them with me and worry no more about them. That's what I'm here for.' An attempt at a thin smile flickered across the grey lips. 'Now, as to your contract and its details, I understand you have a basic agreement with Mac. I will incorporate this into a formal document and execute it with you.'

Jack shifted uneasily in the chair that had looked comfortable but was designed for no more than looks. This meeting was the opposite of his discussions with Mac.

'Don't bother, Laurence.' There was a slight flinch at the lack of the Sir. 'I don't need a contract, a handshake is fine. If we're happy together, I'll stay. If we're not, you don't want your shareholders having to pay me out.'

Laurence Treadmore's mouth tightened as if he'd just eaten a particularly sour fruit. In a couple of sentences Jack had sneered at the three fundamental principles on which his life was based. The first was a love of money. The man appeared to be dismissive of the potential gain that might accrue to him. The second was a basic distrust of all persons except those who were bound to you by necessity. And the third was the absolute requirement to, and vicarious enjoyment of, drafting, honing and redrafting a legal document that would deprive the recipient of rights that he or she assumed to be self-evident, without this being evident. He coughed unnecessarily. 'I'm afraid in corporate life these days it is common practice to document these matters. Indeed good corporate governance suggests we advise shareholders of the details. I'm sure you can understand that the description of a handshake'—the word was almost chewed as it emerged—'would not sit comfortably in an annual report.'

The meeting edged from topic to topic as the manicured finger ran down the embossed notepaper. Sir Laurence was contemptuous of all forms of modern technology, even the cell phone—the public use of which he regarded as a particularly invasive form of bad manners—so when Jack's BlackBerry appeared from his pocket, buzzing and vibrating in an obscene display of uncivil interruption, their antipathy towards one another was complete.

'I'm sorry, Laurence, I'll have to dash. Didn't realise we were going to be so long; thought it was just a quick hello. But I hear what you're saying and, of course, I'm new to public company life. I'll certainly think about it all.'

The farewell handshake sealed their pact, leaving one gently massaging an imaginary bruise and the other hoping to wash away the clamminess.

When Jack strode with relief into the sun and clean air of Sydney's mildly polluted streets, it was Mac Biddulph's name that flashed up in his message window. He didn't return the call but went back to his office in the old Pyrmont warehouse and sat staring out at the incongruous collection of public amusements spattered over the former railway yards. He'd loaded goods trains there as a part-time job in the university holidays when he was nineteen and remembered the area as ugly but honest. Now it was full of shops selling sweaters that looked like Jackson Pollock's worst nightmare or cute marine artefacts that had never seen a ship. Why was he even contemplating leaving the familiar, safe harbour of a business he liked, was successful in, and was handsomely remunerated for running with a modicum of effort? He looked around at his team of bright, attractive, talented, likeable young people working away happily in the huge space flooded with natural light and salt-filled air. He'd be crazy to leave. He'd ring Mac right now and tell him so.

The direct line rang on his desk. Only Louise and a couple of close friends had the number, but when he answered it was Mac's voice on the line.

'G'day, Jack. Hope I'm not bothering you sitting down there counting your money. How did you get on with my chairman? He can be a bit of an old woman sometimes.'

Jack cautiously began to express his reservations, but Mac broke in.

'Don't you worry about Laurence Treadmore. Known him for years. He may be a bit pedantic at times, but he crosses all the tees and dots every other letter. That's what you want in a chairman. As far as running the business goes, you talk to me. We speak the same language.'

'I'm not sure, Mac. Laurence says I report to him. I'm sure he's an excellent chairman, don't get me wrong, but I was a bit uncomfortable with the discussion.'

Mac chuckled. 'Everyone's "a bit uncomfortable" with Laurence. Part of his charm. Don't give it a thought. He's good on detail and harmless on everything else and owes a fair chunk of his good fortune to me. You and I stay in tune and I promise you there's no problem. Now the good news is I've been chatting off the record to a few fund managers we know intimately and your appointment's going to be well received. You're a growth story, just like I said. And the analysts who cover insurance all know the whole financial services market. So they checked you out with the banks. And who loves Jack? So we'll probably see a kick in the share price. It's always nice to know your value.'

Jack was stunned. 'But we agreed there'd be no announcements or public discussion until I finally committed.'

'My friend, you've got a bit to learn about the market. This is not an announcement or a public discussion, it's just Mac having a little chat with a few people who treat us well because we treat them well. No decision's been communicated, just flying a kite. But they're going to love you, Jack, that's the main thing.'

She was the only woman he'd ever loved, he was certain of that.

He looked across the table at her now and there she was staring straight into his eyes, as she had the first time they met. It was at a party in the surf club at Bondi when he'd just graduated as an architect and was pondering the shape of life, usually with a beer in each hand. He'd seen her around the university campus but they'd never spoken. She came towards him, holding his gaze. 'So you're Jack-the-lad? Do you like that name? Or does it embarrass you just a bit? Do you lie awake on hot summer nights thinking "How can I live up to this?" You can tell me the truth, everyone does.'

In truth, he hated his nickname, but he tried to banter with her as he did with any woman, to hold the high ground and keep her off balance, but she was too nimble and slipped away from any thrust, so he seemed to find himself on the defensive, teetering between enjoyment of the contest and discomfort at the result. And then she was leaving as suddenly as she'd arrived. 'I'll see you in about five years, Mr Jack-the-lad. It's a little too early in the cellaring for me. But we'll talk again. I did enjoy your spontaneous sense of enthusiasm.' She turned away with that wonderful warm but slightly quizzical smile and disappeared into the crowd.

He saw her often after that, at parties or friends' flats, and asked her out a couple of times, but she never came. It was about five years later, maybe a little more, that they'd started to work together and, not long after that, to make love and to love.

She'd never directly approached his colourful reputation but once, when he was reminiscing about his father, about how he loved Jack's mother but couldn't resist wandering, she'd interrupted his relaxed flow.

'How did your mother survive?' He'd paused and examined her carefully. 'I think either she never really knew for sure, or chose to ignore it.'

She'd laughed, a humourless laugh. 'Women know, Jack, they know even when they don't know for sure. Did they argue?'

'Not that I remember. He was sweet and loving to her, it seemed to me. It was only later, much later, that I learned he was famous for being sweet and loving to a few other women as well.'

She'd let it go at that until a few months later when, unexpectedly and unrelated to their earlier conversation, she said, 'I can understand your mother ignoring your father's affairs—up to a point. But there must have been a boundary beyond which the relationship would break; there'd have to be. Self-respect isn't infinitely flexible.'

When, after a couple of years, he'd asked her to marry him, she'd said, 'Yes. I can't think of anyone else I'd care to live with or have children with or make love to, anymore, and I don't want to die alone, an old spinster wearing a knobbly cardigan while an obese cat eats my meals-on-wheels dinner, so I guess it'll have to be you.'

And she'd watched his shocked face with amusement before reaching one hand to his mouth and letting a finger caress the line of his top lip. 'Besides, you're the sexiest man alive, a moderately good provider and will never let me down. So, yes.'

As he looked at her now, he could say he never had. Not really.

'Okay. We're at our favourite restaurant, with our favourite wine, eating our favourite pasta. And you have something to tell me. So tell me.'

He poured the Curly Flat and smiled. 'Can I ever have a secret that's not immediately obvious to you?'

'Darling Jack, what secrets could you possibly want to have from me?'

He laughed and a slight flush deepened the tanned skin. It only happened with her, this tendency to redden slightly in the face at difficult moments.

'Now I've made you blush, darling. Why don't you just get on with it and tell me what's bothering you?'

He paused, ran his finger around the lip of the wine glass and hesitantly started to unwind his dilemma. 'I need your advice. I want to do this thing with Mac and I don't want to do it. I talked myself into it a week ago because it's a monumental challenge, way beyond anything I've ever contemplated. Twelve thousand employees—not just me and twenty kids; hundreds of millions in premiums, vital to the country's wellbeing, and so on. But I'm worried about the people, particularly the chairman. You're always the wise one, so what do I do?'

She'd never seen him so uncertain, openly at least, about anything, even though he turned to her for advice frequently. But usually the advice sought was how to do something he'd already decided to pursue, not this wallowing in the ultimate dilemma. 'You're bored, darling, and a bored Jack is a dangerous thing. It's not so much whether you're sure about this, but more how you're going to be if you don't do it, spending the rest of your life wondering how good you would've been, whether you were up to the job, whether you could have mixed it with the big boys. That's it, isn't it? You want to know if you can run in the Olympics?'

She was always right, always knew him better than he knew himself. 'Yes, I guess so.'

'Then do it. Cast aside your doubts, don ye mighty armour, ride thy great steed across the moat of indecision—and pour me more of that lovely wine while you're about it.'

chapter four

Jack felt the adrenalin pumping through him in a way he hadn't for years. The boardroom was packed with journalists and photographers and he'd finished his last radio interview as fresh as the first, even though he'd said the same things twenty times over. He was very good at this, he knew it. Everyone in the room knew it, you could feel it. The public relations people hadn't liked his concept of posing the questions about the company's results before they were actually asked, but he'd insisted it would allow him to present the material in a contained, logical flow, and it had worked beautifully. When he opened the forum for additional questions, there were very few and they were mainly follow-ups from the ones he'd flashed on the screen in his own presentation. It was a virtuoso performance. Journalists didn't clap, but he'd felt they'd wanted to.

He loved performing in public, always had. Speech-making was easy, selling a message was a gift. Why, he'd even developed a groundbreaking communications package for the staff. Each month a live video was transmitted on closed circuit to all HOA offices via satellite. Jack was the star of the show, true, but so were the employees, in a lesser way. There was the 'hero of the month', someone who'd made a unique contribution. A camera crew surprised this individual at his or her workplace with Jack presenting an award—like 'This Is

Your Life' without the relatives. There were questions and answers, and graphs and charts, and every other device anyone could dream up. The staff loved it—and they loved Jack, almost ran from their workstations to shake his hand when he wandered through a call centre, to no great purpose, just so they could see him, just so they had the opportunity to run from their workstations. But this was the big time, with radio and TV and every major newspaper in the country. HOA had a massive retail shareholder base apart from insuring half the homes in the country. Its performance was an indicator to the economy's performance; its results were real news. Even though they weren't really his results, yet, but he was the head of the company, he was the person they wanted to see.

Yesterday he'd been in Canberra visiting the Minister, massaging perceptions, ensuring when the results were released there wasn't a spin that the profits were excessive, explaining the return on equity was still only fifteen per cent—low considering the risks, and the regulatory regime, never forget the regulatory regime, the impact on the business of filing all those reports, of copying all those board papers. And as the Minister was escorting him out—yes escorting him out, a good sign the company's handler said, an excellent sign—who did they meet as they strolled through the corridors of Parliament House? The Prime Minister. Just like that, in the corridor. The Minister had simply stopped the PM as he hurried past with a couple of minders. 'Prime Minister, good morning. I'd like you to meet Jack Beaumont, new CEO at HOA. Giving us some of his valuable time.'

And the Prime Minister had stopped in his tracks and seemed genuinely pleased to meet Jack. 'Welcome to the people's house. Heard a great deal about you, Mr Beaumont. Keep up the good work.'

What would he have heard about him? Jack couldn't imagine, but it was obviously positive, that was the point. He wasn't impressed by meeting important people; he'd met plenty of important people. Half of them lived in residences he'd built, for goodness sake. But this was the Prime Minister of Australia, who lived in a relatively modest late Victorian house on the harbour in Kirribilli, a house Jack had never been in but now would probably be invited to because—because he was who he was. And this was the Prime Minister.

As the last of the press packed up their gear, Jack saw Mac Biddulph wave from the doorway and give him the thumbs-up sign. It was one of the qualities Jack had come to appreciate in Mac. He was supportive, but let him get on with the job.

'Mr Beaumont. Could I have a word before you go?' He turned to find a woman he'd noticed during the presentation because she'd been impossible to miss. At least, impossible for Jack to miss. She'd been seated in the front row but had asked no questions. He knew the PR people were careful to allocate seating positions based on rank, so she had to be a journalist of some substance, but he'd no idea who she was. In truth, it wasn't her stature as a journalist that had caught his attention. She was an extraordinarily attractive woman in a severe sort of way. There was nothing overtly sexual or flirtatious in the way she was dressed or looked, quite the contrary. She appeared to be wearing a man's suit, but it wasn't cut like any man's suit Jack had ever seen. There was some subtlety in the shape that made it completely feminine, despite the fact she was also wearing a collar and tie. The collar on the shirt was spread somehow, the tie was knotted lower; whatever it was, the effect was captivating, compelling, almost heady as she stood smiling at him with a wry, challenging smile.

'I'm Prue Patterson from the Australian. We haven't met. Very impressive presentation. You must be pleased with your results.' She gazed at him from clear, blue eyes behind the oversized, black-rimmed glasses of a librarian or a school mistress.

'Thank you, but they're not really my results, you know. I'm the new boy on the block, so I'm just putting the shine on other people's hard work.'

'Indeed.' She smiled again. 'But you polish up so well. I'm not a business journalist, which is why you may not have seen me before. I used to write for the business pages but I get bored by figures.'

'So do I. But don't tell anyone.'

'I'm very good at keeping secrets—unless, of course, they'd interest my readers. I write mainly profiles and opinion pieces these days, and I'd like to write a personal profile on you to run in the feature pages. You're very important to a lot of people now, Mr Beaumont, and we don't know much about you.'

She observed his dismissive shrug with amusement. He seemed such an unlikely person to be connected with Mac Biddulph, who she knew well. Her profile on Mac had won her a Walkley Award and a trip on the *Honey Bear*. Both sat on her mantelpiece, one way and another. There was a certain naivety about Jack Beaumont that appeared deeper than just natural charm. Not that there was anything wrong with natural charm. 'I'd very much like to interview you in a relaxed setting—over lunch, for example.'

Jack had flirted with too many attractive women not to recognise the undertones. But despite the heady injection of adrenalin from the morning, he was in control.

'I don't have lunch these days. I mean, I eat lunch, but usually at my desk or a sandwich in the park or something. I'm not really a luncher anymore, if you know what I mean.'

Her mouth curled up at the corners in an extremely alluring way. 'How interesting. You see, we've just discovered you're not like the average run of businessmen who move from club to restaurant to boardroom on a regular lunching cycle, and we haven't even started the interview. So it's dinner then?'

'Well I'd rather it was just in the office, if you don't mind. If I could get my assistant to call you . . .'

'I don't deal with assistants. It'll be quite painless, the dinner, I promise you. It's a well-established format I've used many times. You might even enjoy it.'

Jack handed over his card with his direct line number and found himself in the restaurant before the week was out. She was extremely professional and businesslike in her approach to the interview, as they sat in a booth at the back of a fashionable restaurant in The Rocks. She ordered the wine and the food, after asking what he'd like, told the waiter to leave the white wine out of the ice bucket, was in control from the moment she arrived fifteen minutes after he'd been seated. Her research was extraordinary. She knew details about his life he'd forgotten himself. When she asked about his competitive streak he'd tried to shrug it off with an 'Oh shucks' line, but she brushed it away with facts.

'You won the eight hundred metres open championship in the GPS athletics in one minute fifty-four point two seconds which, although it wasn't a record, was only nought point five seconds outside; you play golf off a single figure handicap, you blitzed the top end of the

Sydney property market for ten years, you're the CEO of a major corporation. Don't be coy.'

The restaurant was nearly empty, and half of the second bottle of wine sat between them. She'd switched off the tape machine ten minutes ago and put the notebook into some extraordinary handbag that appeared to be constructed from rusty nails. They sat, relatively silent after the steady rhythm of her questions. He wasn't entirely surprised when she carefully removed her glasses and, looking him straight in the eyes, said 'I don't normally sleep with the people I interview Jack, but in your case I might make an exception.' It was two days later and the buzz of press interviews and chance meetings with the Prime Minister had worn off. Jack sat at his desk with stacks of documents arranged across its surface. He'd asked Renton Healey for a summary of the company's financial position, key performance indicators and potential cost savings, but this trolley-load of unbound papers had arrived. When he'd complained that he was drowning in detail, Renton had replied, 'Let me know what you feel is irrelevant and I'll have it removed immediately.' The implication was obvious—you won't know enough to sift the gold from the dross.

But he was sifting: painstakingly, excruciatingly slowly, Jack was working through the piles. And the nuggets were there. Sometimes they appeared to be fool's gold and raised more questions than answers, but he was determined to grasp the essence of this business. He would not be a once-over-lightly presenter of someone else's work—a show pony of a CEO. And if any of them thought he'd ever operated that way, they were wrong. Sure he'd been the creative force in his own business, but he'd always understood the detail, even if it was managed by others.

He was struggling with the detail, or lack of it, in a thick pile of contracts Renton had dropped on his desk. He'd wanted to examine the quantum of HOA's payments to outside contractors, but instead of an analysis he'd been given all the legal contracts. His initial browsing had been disturbing. The monies involved were way beyond what he'd expected, and some of the contracts were vague in the extreme; the description of the services to be provided was so broad as to be meaningless.

The further he dug down into the papers the more alarmed he became. Some of these matters he would raise at the board meeting next week. Others would require more intense scrutiny. But he wasn't going to let it go. He'd sell the story better than anyone, but it was going to be his story.

'Thank you, gentlemen. The hour is past. We have a quorum so let me call the meeting to order.'

Sir Laurence's prim tones relayed antiseptically through the next-generation German sound system, bounced dully off the silk-lined boardroom walls and fell mainly on deaf ears. As he glanced around the U-shaped table, he was reminded that the 'gentlemen' was no longer entirely appropriate. His slightly bloodshot eyes fell on the brightly coloured plumage of Rosemary Stipple, the headmistress of the private school that one of Mac's daughters had attended. She'd recently joined the board at Mac's insistence, despite Sir Laurence's strong objections that she had no business experience of any kind and had never been on any other board except that of the Sydney Symphony Orchestra—and only because her husband was a major benefactor. The market would see her as no more than a sycophantic supporter of Macquarie James

Biddulph and a sop to political correctness and would deride the appointment. So said Sir Laurence. Mac had just laughed.

'The market follows me, Laurence. They couldn't care less who's on the board.' Sir Laurence's lips curled slightly at the left corner at this remark. 'All that corporate governance crap is just for the annual report and the regulator. Anyway, Rosemary is a woman.'

On this last point Sir Laurence wasn't entirely convinced. She appeared to be dressed at present in the plumage of a rainbow lorikeet. He'd always understood it was the male bird that wore the brightest colours. In any event, she might not be a man but if she wanted to be a member of his board she would have to do her best.

'Gentlemen. If we could please.' He tapped the small microphone in front of him with his silver pen. The sound reverberated through the fifteen miniature speakers in the ceiling and finally penetrated the consciousness of his distinguished board members. They were all in their customary places. It had always fascinated him the way some process of natural selection caused people to occupy the same seats in a meeting room even though there were no allocated places. It was a ritual dance, a pecking order. As far as he was concerned, so long as they all understood that the chairman's seat was at the head of the table, they could scatter where they liked.

'The minutes of the meeting of February the fifteenth. Any comments?'

There were never any comments on the minutes. The directors were acutely aware that at least four or five drafts would have passed across the antique partners' desk in Sir Laurence's office in a flurry of neatly pencilled corrections before they were finally allowed, reluctantly, into the voluminous bound volume that comprised a set of HOA board papers. This document was delivered by courier to the office or home of each director in a sealed security pouch and had to be signed for by the recipient before it was released. Sir Laurence had considered locked and chained red boxes in the tradition of Westminster, but had rejected this as perhaps too governmental. Nevertheless, he insisted on the intricate sealing device which required a tough plastic tab to be broken—often at the expense of Rosemary Stipple's fingernails or Justin Muir's temper—just as he did on the sweeping of this room for bugs before every meeting. You could never be too careful.

'Shouldn't we wait to get Mac on the line, Laurence?' To the casual observer, Jack's question was a harmless observation. To Laurence Treadmore it contained a quiver of sharp insults. It failed to address him as chairman—the proper appellation in a boardroom. It then failed to recognise his everyday title, a title conferred on him by the Queen of Australia. It came from someone who, while purporting to be the chief executive of a major public company, wasn't even wearing a tie let alone a jacket in his boardroom. He'd already discussed the question of the tie with Mac but he'd just laughed it off, saying, 'We all have our own style, Laurence, even you. Who cares so long as the market loves him?'

He refused to look directly at Jack as he answered—but then he never looked directly at him or addressed him by name.

'I understand we're having difficulty establishing a connection to the Kimberley. Perhaps the secretary could ask our technician to step in.'

The rest of the board resumed checking their diaries and phone messages in a series of electronic beeps, despite the chairman's clear ruling that no such devices were to be switched on during a meeting. Only Sir Laurence noticed the totally inappropriate exchange of 'G'day Tom' and 'Hi Jack, how are you?' between the technician and the CEO. This type of familiarity between management and workers could only lead to trouble.

Crackles and static began to emanate from the doughnut-shaped speakerphone in the middle of the table and finally they heard the unmistakable tones of Mac.

'We have him now, Sir Laurence.'

'Thank you. You may leave us. Good morning, Mac, we have you now, although I must say the line isn't particularly good, there's still a great deal of static. Is there stormy weather in the Kimberley?'

Mac laughed from the gut. 'Stormy weather? It's the dry season. It doesn't rain for months. I'm in the shower, Laurence, that's the noise you can hear, and a bloody good shower it is, too. Biggest head on it you've ever seen. Had it brought over from England. How are you all?'

The distasteful nature of this exchange caused both corners of the Treadmore mouth to curl—usually a dangerous sign. This constant failure to attend board meetings in person, no doubt a complete absence of any attempt to read the papers and now to attend in a state of undress, even by phone, was beyond any pale Sir Laurence could conjure. How could two such distinctly opposing personalities survive together? The answer, as both were acutely aware, lay in the bonding power of money. It was the Araldyte of their relationship, whose unique properties could cause any two surfaces to adhere, no matter how uneven.

Mac, wrapped in an outsized white bath towel, sprawled in a massive colonial wicker armchair in the shade of the double-width verandah. Everything at Bellaranga was enormous. You could fly over its million acres in a helicopter for a couple of hours and still be on the property. The views were infinite—from the beginning to the end of the world in time and space was how Mac phrased it when he was in a lyrical mood. Some of the oldest artworks in the world were on this place, painted on the walls of rock caves by peoples unknown; some said the Australian Aborigines, some said not. To Mac it was irrelevant. They were graceful, elegant, tasselled figures with extraordinary headdresses, painted with exceptional skill, as alive on the rock face now as they would have been over twenty thousand years ago. One of Mac's prized showpieces was a small Matisse oil with dancing figures. He reckoned Matisse must have been to Bellaranga.

How he wished his old dad could see him now, the lord of this domain and the other world on the end of the telephone. He'd never believe it. One of the European migrants who'd brought their skills to help build the Snowy Mountains Scheme, his father became more proudly Australian than any native born. He named his son after Governor Lachlan Macquarie and added James, as English a name as he could imagine. Mac still saw him sometimes, walking away from him down a Sydney street or cupping his hands to light a cigarette in a pub doorway. He remembered the line into the small church in Auburn and the crowd stretching away under the trees at the graveyard. He'd never seen half these people before, yet they all knew Ja.

Suddenly he was brought back to the present by some discordant note from the telephone. His mind worked that way. He could half listen to the conversation and hear a clear bell ring in the middle of the hubbub.

'I'm sorry, Chairman. I missed some of that. The line's not too good. Would you mind summarising for me?'

Sir Laurence was only too happy to oblige. 'The chief executive, in the course of presenting his monthly report to the board, was highlighting the well-known fact that we run a negative profit on our insurance operations with an insurance margin of one hundred and three per cent. While this is common in the industry it is apparently of great concern to him. He was directing his remarks to the twin questions of pricing and costs in addressing this issue. I trust this is an accurate summary?' Sir Laurence gestured vaguely in Jack's direction.

'Yes, Mac. I know some insurance companies lose on every policy they write and make their profit on investing shareholders' funds, but to me it's a dangerous way to run a business and I'm not comfortable with it. We've got to look more closely at how we price risk. There might be a percentage of our book we want to discard because we can never make money on it and some business we want to keep but reprice.'

Mac's voice echoed from the doughnut. 'Hang on, my friend, you've got to tread carefully here. The market won't like us writing less business just because we think we're going to make more profit somewhere down the track. They want growth. But I thought I heard you talking specifically about the cost side.'

Jack's enthusiasm began to rise. 'Absolutely. There's so much we can do there. Not just with internal costs, although I'm convinced already we can take eighty to one hundred million out of those, but on the education side, with our policyholders. If we can teach them how to better secure their homes, we reduce the incidence of burglary. And more, if we can work with local communities and the police on drug rehabilitation, we can help to treat the cause. If we can convince local councils to use our rating information and rezone likely flood areas, or change the building codes for hurricanes and severe storm areas, we can reduce claim costs and help our customers at the same time. Because that's what insurance is all about, as I see it. Just a spreading of risk across the community so one family's disaster is shared by everyone else.'

There was silence in the boardroom and from the speakerphone. Finally, Sir Laurence spoke. 'Are you still there, Mac?'

'Yes.' A short cough. 'Yes, of course, Laurence. Chairman. Just thinking about Jack's comments. Very commendable sentiments. Very much in line with my own thinking. Of course, you have to balance these long-term aims with the short-term interests of the shareholders. As directors, I think that's where we have to look, is it not, Chairman?'

'Indeed. The Corporations Act requires us to represent the interests of shareholders at all times.'

'Just so. I've heard you say that many times. So, Jack, it's quite right of you to raise these matters and commendable that you should get on this track so quickly, but we must plan carefully and slowly to strike the right balance of interests. Everyone agree?'

There were murmurs from around the table of an indeterminate nature, as there usually were when Mac put this question. No vote had ever been taken in this boardroom, no clear dissent ever expressed.

'Excellent. So I think we're all agreeing with you, Jack, just expressing a note of caution. But didn't I hear you mention specifics on the cost side?'

Jack drew a deep breath and coloured slightly. 'I'm not sure you are agreeing with me, Mac. It's clear as day to me we need to move ahead on all this immediately and in the absolute interests of the shareholders. Our investment returns have been behind the market lately and I'm still trying to understand how our profits are increasing at such a pace.'

Now it was very quiet and still in the room. No one shuffled papers or fiddled with pens. Even Shane O'Connell, who was usually prodding at his electronic organiser with a stylus, sat with his palms flat on the table. Jack continued.

'Frankly, I see the cost side as the easy part. For instance, we seem to spend a fortune on consultants. I'm certain we can slash that in half. I don't even know what they all do yet, but I'll have a detailed analysis for you by the next meeting. And the other example is this company called Beira. We appear to pay it between thirty-five and forty million dollars a year, yet no one seems to know what it does precisely. So there's a ton of potential for cost-cutting and I plan to get on with it.' He paused and counted to ten in his head. 'In the interests of shareholders.'

It was really no more than a rock jutting out of the Mediterranean. The vegetation, such as it was, consisted of a few scrawny olive trees struggling for survival in a thin layer of wind-blown soil trapped in the rock's crevices. There were donkeys to carry supplies from the boat up the hill to the village, chickens in the yards, depression in the air. He only ever went there once with his father. It was enough. Enough to remind him where he came from, more than enough to know he wasn't going back. He'd searched for it in the index of his atlas but there was no Beira listed among the Bs. But Ja was proud of where he came from and grateful for where he'd landed. They were different in that way. Mac felt he'd wrestled what he had from opponents who would have turned him over in a crocodile roll given half a chance. His father saw life with a softer palette.

He walked stiffly down the verandah steps to the lush green lawn under the poinciana trees, the only expanse of soft green anywhere in the Kimberley in the harsh dry season. When he woke, alone, in the early morning after a day of riding, his body always felt like a rusty old car that needed a grease and oil change. He loved being alone up here. It was strange, because in the city he hated to sleep or eat alone and rarely did, but he'd never brought Bonny or any other girl to Bellaranga and Edith had only come twice. It was too hot for her, too wild, too far from the bridge club. A few times a year he flew major clients or investors in for fishing and shooting but, unlike life on the *Honey Bear*, this was bloke's stuff, men's business. Huntin', shootin', drinkin'—but no rooting. And a great tax deduction.

This last thought brought him back to the subject of the board meeting with an unpleasant jerk. What possessed these people, given a huge salary and the chance to make a fortune from options, to go digging in holes full of snakes? First Buckley, with all his pompous crap about corporate behaviour, and now Jack Beaumont sounding like he was preaching a sermon. He'd have to learn. There were some holes that had big snakes in them with very nasty bites. Hopefully it wouldn't come to that. Let Renton Healey sort it out. He could confuse anyone in three easy lessons. He'd been promoted to CFO and given a whacking pay increase thanks to his loyalty and ability to show flexible, creative thinking on tricky issues; now was the time to bring those qualities into play.

Louise entered quietly through the open hatch, her bare feet making no sound on the wooden steps. It was one of Jack's flights into whimsy, this study in a loft with a narrow staircase and a trapdoor. It was a wonder he hadn't included a pole to slide down into the bedroom.

'What are you doing, lover boy? It's three o'clock in the morning. What's happened to the digger who sleeps under gunfire?' She was holding his head in both hands now and he was grateful for the warmth and comfort. He nuzzled into her body. 'This is a worry; you've either fallen in love with another woman, in which case tiny parts of your body will be lightly sautéed with onions and garlic, or you're more concerned than I've seen you since your daughter was born breech. Which is it? Be quick lest I ready the pan.'

Where had his 'values' come from, that's what Jack could never figure out. His mother was a classic snob who revered all things English, all persons of a higher social order, as she saw them. His father's principles were elusive. But somehow Jack had developed a black and white view of some issues that wouldn't leave him. His behaviour might wander at the margins but he believed he'd never walk away from his basic principles. On the other hand, he hadn't really been tested before. And was he being tested now? That's what was waking him in the night. If he knew for sure something was wrong he'd attack it, but these issues seemed to slip and slide, ripple and flatten like wind on a river. He couldn't even explain them properly to Louise.

'So are you saying you think they're running the business inefficiently or recklessly or acting fraudulently or breaking the law or what?'

'God no, not breaking the law. Well, I hope not. I mean, I'm not saying that. I don't understand enough I suppose. The issues are very complex but I'm trying to make them simple.'

She rubbed the back of his neck again. 'And that's part of your talent and the value of fresh eyes. And part of mine, remember? So simplify them for me.'

It was like the old days when they'd sit together in their first ramshackle office above the delicatessen, the smells of cheese and salami and fresh bread drifting up the fire escape. He'd explain the brilliant design concept that short-sighted councillors couldn't fit into the local codes and she'd tear it apart with logical precision, put it back together in almost the same order and make it fit. But she always left it as his idea.

He tried to lay out the shapes in his head now as lines on a plan, but they weren't as straight, the corners weren't as sharp. It had all started brilliantly. Mac had been right, the market loved him. The shares had jumped two per cent in three months despite his lack of major company, not to mention insurance industry, experience. He was a great story, just as Mac had predicted. 'They love growth, son, and that's what you represent. You're a salesman. You know about increasing our share of new homes, forging bonds with property developers, driving the top line. That's what matters. Let us worry about making the profits, managing the balance sheet, all that stuff that's unbelievably complex in an insurance company. Leave it to the accountants and the actuaries. That's what I do. You bring the business in the front door, the profits will fall out the back, I promise you.'

But would they? That was the part he couldn't see. When Jack sat through the briefing with his CFO, Renton Healey, and later with the head actuary, he could see the policies marching in the front door in ever greater numbers—but at prices that left no margin for any profits to fall out the back. And when they gave the argument he'd heard so many times now—that most insurance companies don't make money from their underwriting operations—he'd replied, 'I know that. But the best ones do. They have insurance margins below one hundred per cent, not at one hundred and three per cent like us. And sure, they make the bulk of their profits by investing policyholders' funds when the sharemarket's performing well. But at least they won't go broke when it isn't.'

Renton Healey had just remained calm and grimaced, you couldn't call it a smile, not in that squashed pumpkin of a face with a shock of pumpkin red hair above it, and looked at him in that paternalistic, slightly pitying way adults do with children who are struggling in their lessons.

'Jack, isn't it a bit early in the learning curve to be trying to reconstruct the entire insurance industry? We've been doing things this way for quite a while. The market fully understands the nature of the insurance cycle, the concept of the smoothing of profits, the orderly flow of releases from reserves. They're fully aware of the swings and roundabouts of investment returns and the sophisticated systems of collars and caps we implement to assist in smoothing. And of course the very effective but complex reinsurance arrangements we have in place to limit risk and, to some degree, to protect financial returns. I think it's fair to say, without wishing to be patronising in any way, this is an area you are still grappling with.' Here the pumpkin crumpled again. 'The point is, Jack, unless you have a clear overview of how all these factors come together, how all the levers are pulled, you can't be expected to understand how the bottom line is derived. Or how the balance sheet fits together. They're very difficult concepts for anyone from outside the industry, I grant you, but we'll do our best to explain.'

He shifted his sizeable posterior in the expensive Italian chair.

Exercise and Renton Healey were not as close friends as cannelloni and a Margaret River pinot noir. Possibly a little cheese. At lunch. Despite the new CEO's edict, banning alcohol for the management team during working hours. The new CEO had a great deal to learn, and not just about reinsurance contracts. Healey chuckled to himself. Indeed, he was unable to learn anything on that subject.

As Jack tried to explain now to Louise, if HOA was losing money on underwriting its policies, and their investment returns were below those of the previous year, how could they keep announcing record profits?

'Well, maybe they're right, darling. You said yourself this business is more complicated by a mile than anything you've done before. As much as one is loath to suggest that the boy genius is incapable of getting his Scouts badge for insurance basics, maybe you just don't understand. Yet.'

He'd thought about that a lot, wondering if he wasn't up to this challenge intellectually, but as he discovered more about the business his confidence was growing, not diminishing in awe at the majesty of it all. It wasn't that difficult. He believed in his simple analysis—just people sharing risk to protect one another. All the rest was gobbledygook. But maybe this was something Louise couldn't help him with. Maybe he needed an expert this time.

chapter five

The beds of red canna lilies waved softly as the nor'-easter gradually picked up its afternoon velocity. It was Wednesday, so shortly the eighteen-foot skiffs would come rocketing out of Careening Cove and the Royal Sydney Yacht Squadron's more dignified fleet would be gearing up at Kirribilli for a sunset race. Men with knobbly legs, white football shorts and salt-encrusted boat shoes would be rubbing their chests and peering aimlessly at their expensive boats, while younger crew members skipped about being genuinely useful. In the Royal Botanic Gardens, joggers, lovers, derelicts, old male backgammon players of vaguely European origin, gay boys suntanning, public servants in navy suit trousers with white belts and synthetic shirts, businessmen in earnest conversation about events of shattering importance walking very purposefully, politicians from nearby Parliament House walking more purposefully, old ladies in wheelchairs, gardeners in khaki with leather pouches on their belts hiding in the shrubbery, more lovers loving on rubber-backed blankets—all this gallery of Sydney's humanity presented itself to the lunchtime spring sunshine. The harbour sparkled and jazzed as a few whitecaps flecked the deep blue and the sails of the Opera House stood stiffly against the breeze.

Jack found the seat as described (under the Moreton Bay fig, opposite the Bronwyn Oliver sculpture), set down his brown paper bag and waited. It was peaceful beneath the massive spread of the old ficus with its gnarled aerial roots snaking down to the earth like some tropical growth from a rainforest or a Tallahassee swampland. He watched the carefree throngs jogging and pacing by and wondered if anyone was 'carefree'. It sounded like something from an Enid Blyton novel or a shampoo commercial. But he had been, pretty much. And now he was in the swamp, without any roots.

Before these black thoughts congealed, the lean figure of the Pope strode into view through the water glare. To Jack, the Pope always looked like Clint Eastwood on holiday—spare, rather taciturn, relaxed, yet in total control of all around, knowing something he might tell you on a good day. Because the group always used the nickname at their luncheons, he'd forgotten that the Pope's real name was Clinton Normile. It seemed an oddly formal name for this good-looking character who no one knew much about. He'd had to ring Tom Smiley to get the phone number and was amazed when the Pope had answered the call himself, rather than some secretary or personal assistant. The Pope was fabled to be wealthy beyond counting but the origins of this wealth, if it existed, were the subject of wide speculation.

'I see you found my office.' He glanced at the paper bag. 'And Vera's, I trust. Leg ham on the bone and the rye bread?'

'Exactly as ordered.' Jack laughed. 'Although I must say this isn't quite the venue I expected. Do you always hold meetings here?'

The Pope took a sandwich from the bag. 'As often as possible and as little as possible. I don't like meetings, but if I have to "take one", as the Americans say, I might as well take it here.'

They munched silently for a while. The Pope was outstanding at silence. Finally Jack started. 'I need your advice. Tom Smiley said you might be able to help.' He paused. 'What should I call you, by the way? "The Pope" seems a bit out of place here.'

'Nobody calls me that except in the group. John will do fine.'

'But I thought your name was Clinton.'

'Nobody calls me that either. Try John.' Jack shifted around on the park bench and recrossed his legs uneasily. He couldn't explain why he felt so in awe of this man. He was the chief executive of one of the largest listed companies in Australia, while the Pope was—what? Maybe wealthy? Yet somehow he seemed to have taken immediate control.

'So?' Just the one inquiring word as the last sandwich disappeared and the Pope drained off a bottle of juice. Jack laid out his concerns—precisely, he felt, and much more succinctly than he had with Louise. The response was laconic in the extreme. 'Facts. Documents. Where are they?'

Jack hesitated. 'Well I'm just seeking your initial guidance, in a general way. To see if you think there's really an issue.'

There was a long silence. Finally the Pope turned and looked Jack straight in the eye for the first time. 'Of course there's an issue.

You're dealing with Mac Biddulph and Laurence Treadmore. Two piranhas in a fish tank full of money. What did you expect?' Jack made no response. The Pope shrugged. 'So you didn't ask.' He paused. 'I owned a small reinsurance company for a while. HOA was always looking for what we call "financial reinsurance". Unlike normal reinsurance, which all legitimate insurance companies have, financial reinsurance can be just a way of making the balance sheet look better. There's no real transfer of risk involved. It's probably illegal most of the time, and most legitimate operators won't touch it. If you're in the market for this stuff, you're in the market for all sorts of other rotten fish. And you're going to come up smelling, Jack.'

Neither spoke for a while. Finally, the Pope stood and stretched. 'You need to know the right questions to ask. They'll slide around you otherwise. I'll draw up a list for you. Meet me here in a week.'

Jack laughed. 'What if it's raining?'

The Pope ignored the question. 'You're going to need legal help when you get the answers. But first get the facts, the documents. Then we'll talk about that. I know the man to help you, if we can get him.'

He turned and loped off into the gardens before Jack could stammer out his thanks. Jack's gaze drifted over all the unconcerned citizens of Sydney contentedly enjoying the smell of fresh-cut grass, the wafts of jasmine in the salt-filled air, the intricate beauty of the coves and bays of their lyrical city. His lyrical city. Except he was smelling old fish heads. He walked slowly through the mix of exotic and native trees, the great groves of palms, and then on to the rose garden that seemed like a remnant of the colonial past. In front of the regimented beds of the rose gardens, next to the Macquarie Street exit, was a large green board listing the directors of the Royal Botanic Gardens Trust. At its head, as chairman, was the name Sir Laurence Treadmore.

Popsie Trudeaux smiled knowingly at the attractive man standing in the bay window of the old stone mansion on the edge of the Botanic Gardens. As far as she knew, she'd never seen this person before in her life, but she always made it a rule to smile knowingly at attractive men, whoever they may be. You could always sort the wheat from the chaff later. She practised this smile in one of the many mirrors in her Double Bay penthouse. She thought of the penthouse as hers, even though her husband nominally lived there and the title was in both their names. But Angus knew it was better to spend as much time as possible travelling on business and give plenty of notice before arriving home. He also knew it was much cheaper to let things drift on as they were rather than try to seek a resolution. A lot more than the penthouse would go in those circumstances.

Popsie looked around the room with considerable satisfaction. She could see at least a half-dozen 'well-known Sydney business identities', as the press called them, from where she was standing. She'd had affairs with all but one, and she wasn't an especially beautiful woman. But she had life and electricity and a great love for fucking, which was all they wanted and weren't getting at home. She'd even thought of fucking that old fart Laurence Treadmore once, years ago, just because he was who he was and looked as if he needed it, but then she decided the trophy phase was over and they had to be good looking or they could fuck themselves.

Popsie eased over to Sir Laurence anyway just to give him a thrill, if there were any nerve ends left to respond. 'Lovely night, Laurie—as is anything you're involved with.'

Sir Laurence peered at her with considerable distaste. He regarded her as a sort of female pirate who'd been doused in heady perfume, her blowzy charms were vaguely repulsive. 'Yes, thank you, Popsie. Very kind of you to come along. Angus not here tonight? What a pity. Still, we're very grateful to get anyone to fundraising events these days. People seem to have other priorities, do they not? But thankfully there remains a core of generous citizens who are always prepared to contribute. And the cactus garden is in desperate need of refurbishment. Have you considered adopting a plant?'

The thought of having a particularly spiky plant that flowered once a year in the middle of the night named after her had not in fact occurred to Popsie Trudeaux, and she adroitly continued her drift towards more interesting quarters. It was a vital social skill, the ability to move on at a cocktail party without appearing to do so or causing any offence, but never being trapped with some bore or ugly lump. The attractive man was no longer in the bay window. No matter. There were plenty of other windows.

Laurence Treadmore sensed her departure from the periphery of his wide vision with some relief. Talking to Popsie Trudeaux for more than a few moments was a substantial risk for a man of his impeccable reputation. Besides, she never gave any real money despite vague promises. Ah, here was more worthy company. Rupert Littlemore, on the other hand, did give substantial sums almost on request and furthermore, or hence, depending on your degree of cynicism, was also the president of the Colonial Club. The Colonial Club's premises were located behind an unmarked door not far from Sir Laurence's residence in Macquarie Street, and contained his favourite luncheon venue as well as quiet lounge rooms and libraries where he conducted many useful chats in peaceful seclusion.

'Rupert, it's wonderful of you to come. Is there any good cause you don't support? None that I know of. How is Beryl? Any better? Ah, it's a great burden to you, old chap. We all think of you, you know.'

Rupert Littlemore was a well-presented septuagenarian with a fine mane of silver-grey hair and a very ill wife. He looked like, and was, a retired naval commander, but was also a successful businessman with a considerable fortune derived from his family's rural properties. He spoke in a clipped, direct manner, but when he smiled—which was, unusually, when he was genuinely pleased—his face came alive with joyful creases.

'Very nice party, Laurence. Cheque's in the mail. How's that new CEO of yours? Up for the club. Name's just gone on the board. Assume he's a great fellow, otherwise you wouldn't have him.'

Sir Laurence raised his thumb and forefinger to his chin in a gesture that a few people knew particularly well. It seemed to indicate deep thought but in fact was equivalent to a cobra eying a small rodent. 'Really? I'd missed that. I usually check the board. I see.' He withdrew the hand and checked the alignment of his pocket handkerchief. 'Well nominated is he?'

Rupert Littlemore took half a pace back. 'What? What do you want to know for? Of course—Stockford's put him up. No problem, is there?'

Laurence Treadmore seldom answered questions of this nature directly. 'You just took me by surprise, old fellow. Let me think about it. I only really know him in business. I've never even been to his home. Let me make some inquiries.'

Rupert's thick black eyebrows shot up. 'Not at all. Not necessary. I only asked because he's your chief.'

'It's no trouble, don't give it a thought. Now come and meet our new director. She's the first woman ever to run these great gardens. You see how we're moving with the times.'

Later that evening Sir Laurence sat in his study on the second floor of his two-storey apartment in The Piccadilly. He looked out over the Botanic Gardens, past Stone House where the party had recently wound up, to the black harbour beyond. The sky was lit only by a quarter moon but he could still see the thousands of birds wheeling in the neon lights of the city buildings. His was the antithesis of the book-lined study. There were no books. Sir Laurence found the reading of novels a great waste of time, there were few biographies that appealed since they rarely contained the type of information he was looking for and historical tomes, by definition, failed to deal with the most important moments in history. Sir Laurence was interested in the present and the future, particularly his present and future, and those of persons who might make these a little brighter. This was not, as he saw it, selfish thinking. If everyone took care of life with this focused view, there would be no need for welfare payments, charities, church raffles, soup kitchens and other annoying lead weights hanging from the sturdy belt of society. Let people look after themselves, keep their noses in their own business, and all would prosper.

Which brought him back, unpleasantly at this late hour, to Jack Beaumont. He reached behind him to a wall of panelling studded with silver knobs, pulled open one of twenty-two filing cabinet drawers concealed in the wall, and took from it a fresh folder which he spread on the desk. He examined its pristine whiteness with some pleasure. There was always the slight shiver that caused his spine to flex when he wrote a name on a new file. It was incredible, even to him, what events could overtake people's lives, alter the smooth flow of their previous even currents, just from the notes he would make in the peace of this small room. He wrote the name BEAUMONT on the file in neat capital letters. There was no need for this. The man could have made a great deal of money and played polo or golf or rafted rapids or whatever he did for pleasure. It was bound to be something active and mindless. The thumb and forefinger of the left hand rose slowly to his chin, while the pen started to write. Of course, he could record a little of what Jack did for pleasure already and, in time, expected to record a great deal more. There were files and there were files. Sir Laurence liked order; otherwise there was chaos, and chaos was only in the interests of those who had nothing. Namely, those who didn't apply themselves. It was late. Even the birds had stopped flying. Edith would be asleep. He would go down now.

'What the hell is this, Jack? I'm not asking you if it's true, I'm not some weak little lamb of a wife bleating about her ram fucking everything in the paddock. I'm asking you how it got in the fucking newspaper.' Louise stood over him as he blinked in the shaft of early morning light and threw the newspaper down on the bed.

'What? For Christ's sake, keep it down. You'll wake the kids.'

'Don't fucking tell me to be quiet when the whole of Sydney is sitting down to their bowls of low-cal yoghurt, imagining you screwing some juicy little bimbo.'

Jack jumped up from the bed in an attempt to hold her, but she backed away. 'Christ, go easy on the language, darling. Whatever it is, it's just a newspaper story, just a piece of gossip. No one pays any attention to this stuff.'

She snorted. 'They pay more attention to it than they do to people starving in Africa.' And then, very quietly, 'Do not break the line of my trust.'

She stared at him for a moment and left him with the newspaper. It was only a couple of paragraphs in a column that purportedly covered the business affairs of prominent citizens but was in fact a daily outlet for bile and vengeance. And it was accompanied by a caricature of Jack wearing a nautical cap standing on the prow of a large boat with the name *Honey Bear* on the stern, incongruously carrying a riding whip. The caption 'Jack-the-lad rides again' was more than enough. The innuendos in the story were sufficiently subtle to skirt the defamation laws, but clear to the discerning reader nevertheless. He sat on the edge of the bed with the paper half-crumpled in his hand and looked around the room. It was Saturday morning. They'd slept late. Usually there'd be scrambled eggs and coffee with the kids before sport in the afternoon. It was his favourite time, slipping through the many sections of the brick-thick weekend paper, reading about the lives of other people. But not today.

It was a huge bedroom, the way Louise wanted it. A room they could almost live in, except for the lack of cooking facilities. The entrance was through a narrow corridor, opening out into a vaulted space with armchairs and couches, sun streaming through the skylight above onto the wooden floor, and then three steps up to a podium with the oversized bed and carpet your feet disappeared into. Louise had even sketched the concept drawing for this room, something she seldom did, including the bathroom with a big stone bath they could lie in together.

He crossed to the window and looked down on the normally quiet street. On Saturday morning it was lined with parked cars and families walking to the Temple Emmanuel at the end of the street, the men and boys in their black yarmulkes. The old lady from number twenty-three was walking her small, decrepit poodle on its customary toilet outing. She held the plastic bag prominently in one hand, ready to remove offending objects, but as he watched, the poodle painfully left its droppings on the neatly mown grass and the old lady, after glancing surreptitiously around to see if she was being observed, walked on with a smile of satisfaction. A young woman from the flats on the corner jogged by in a pair of shorts he loved to watch because they seemed to have a life of their own. But this morning he turned away to face the music in his own house.

He hated the idea that his carelessness was causing her pain. It was months since his weekend on the *Honey Bear*. Who would plant a story like that after all this time—and why?

He dressed carefully in faded blue jeans and a white linen shirt Louise always loved against his brown skin, combed his hair and then ruffled it again so it looked as casual as possible, and slowly walked downstairs.

'Mr Beaumont, there's a Mr Stockford on the line. He says it's a personal call. Will you speak?'

Jack sighed at the 'Mr Beaumont' and the query about whether he'd take the call. He reminded Beryl every day to call him Jack and to put calls through whoever they were from, unless he'd specifically instructed otherwise. He'd wanted to bring his own PA from his old firm, but Sir Laurence had told him that was inappropriate in a public company and he should use the person already in the job. He was probably right, but God she was painful.

He picked up the phone and said, 'G'day, Bruce, it's nice to hear a friendly voice at the start of a new week.'

There was a nervous cough before, 'Yeah. That was a nasty little piece, Jack, but what can you expect from a rag like that? I wouldn't worry about it, mate, it all adds to your colourful reputation.'

'That's not quite how Louise saw it.'

'No, I guess not.' Again the short unnecessary cough came down the line. 'Listen, Jack, I know you're swamped with work, but I was wondering if we could get together today, just for a coffee or something.'

'Sure. It'll be refreshing to get away from here for a while.

How about three o'clock at your club?'

'No, it would suit me better to come to you, if that's okay. What about the coffee shop under your building?'

It was not a place Jack often frequented because it was always full of HOA staff and he was usually relieved to be anonymous rather than being greeted from every second table, as he was now. Nor was it the usual haunt of Bruce Stockford, who preferred wood panelling or framed boat pennants to stainless steel and hissing Italian coffee machines. Nevertheless, he sat in the hard-backed chair that seemed designed for anything but comfort, and was as uncomfortable as he'd ever been.

'Jack, I really don't know how to start this. I'm terribly embarrassed by it all.'

Jack looked at him in surprise. 'Well, we're old friends, Bruce. Whatever it is, just spit it out, mate.'

Bruce Stockford ran his hand over his eyes. 'I've never encountered anything like this before. Your name is on the board at the club, as you know. That means your membership application has been through all the initial approvals and it's there for the members to be aware of.' He paused. 'And here's the thing, Jack. I've been asked to withdraw your nomination.'

Jack was stunned. His face was ablaze, and he reached for the shirt button and loosened his tie, so much heat seemed to be emanating from him. 'I see.' His mind was whirling. 'Christ. I'm terribly sorry to put you in this situation, Bruce. Is it to do with that bloody article?'

Bruce shook his head. 'No. The president spoke to me on Friday, before that ran. I've been mulling it over all weekend, trying to work out what to do about it.'

Jack grabbed him by the forearm. 'Listen, old fellow, I won't have you embarrassed one minute further on my account. Christ, it's hardly a big issue, I'm already a member of just about every other club in Sydney. I don't even particularly want to be a member, it's just that you asked me. But it's bizarre. I mean, half the people in the Colonial Club are good friends of mine and the other half I've certainly never had any problems with. To be blackballed just seems so—I don't know—somehow low and vindictive.'

Bruce nodded and shook his head almost in one motion. 'You haven't actually been blackballed. I've been asked to withdraw your nomination and told the application won't be successful if I persist. It's as odd a thing as I've ever heard of. I can tell you, Jack, it's left a taste in my mouth like a dead rat.'

They rose, shaking hands and looking one another in the eye, then parted.

Jack didn't return to his office. He strolled down to Circular Quay and leaned against the railing near the ferry wharves.

Fishermen were trailing lines from old cork rolls into the slightly oily water near the wooden piles. These days the harbour was alive with fish and you could see the stubby prawn boats at night, trawling only a few metres from the Walsh Bay wharves where the theatregoers were sipping wine of undetermined origin. Behind him a swarthy, weather-beaten figure in a cloth cap was seated at a table patiently constructing a model of a Spanish galleon. He sat there most days and had done so for as long as Jack could remember, and slowly the majestic little ship had grown from the pile of matchsticks. Jack had watched a passer-by stop once to admire the work and light a cigarette. He remembered thinking to himself, 'I hope he doesn't throw a spark too far.' But he wasn't thinking that now. The sun was finding merging rainbows in the watery oil slick and he peered down into them as if looking for an equally shifting truth. What was happening to his orderly, comfortable, easy life? It seemed the plates were sliding under the earth that had always been solid and stable before, but the force was invisible. There was no cause, no reason, no noise, no shaking, no molten material to gape at. Just a queasy, empty feeling in his gut that he was no longer in control of his life.

chapter six

At about one p.m. each day, as the flow of people through the garish doors of the Australian Rugby League Club's dining room gradually increased, it was customary for many of the diners to nod to the heavyset figure with the rough-hewn face of a Gallipoli veteran seated at the table to the right of the doors.

There was a certain deference in the attitude of the few who approached to shake hands and chat briefly. He ate alone, with a book as his companion. There was no aura of holding court, and yet everyone in the room was somehow aware of his presence.

There was certainly nothing in his manner or dress to warrant particular attention. The suit was a nondescript blue and appeared to have been purchased from St Vincent de Paul, the tie was a narrow strip from the 1960s, held in the middle by a faded silver clip with a Returned Serviceman's badge in the centre. His slab of a face was capped by a thick full head of hair, remarkable for a man of his age, but shaved up at the sides in a fashion no longer seen. There was a forward slope to the whole face, with a jutting chin, huge ears like a prize fighter's but without the scars, and rectangular glasses that, along with the hair and the tie, stated clearly that he regarded fashion as the first sign of moral decay.

Those who summoned the courage to stop by his table as he chewed slowly on his cutlets, chips and peas or, on Fridays, fish, chips and peas, were a rich stew of harbour creatures. Book-makers, rugby league footballers and sometimes those from other codes—businessmen, politicians from state parliament or from local councils, a judge or two (although they mainly nodded from a distance), and others on the make. He was happy to talk about sports or politics or events of the day, but cut off any attempt to discuss legal matters by returning to his book. He was said to be a formidable powerbroker in the right of the New South Wales Labor Party, but how and through what channels this power was wielded no one seemed to know.

His chambers were nearby in Phillip Street, and there a very different stream of supplicants passed through. It was rare for Hedley Stimson QC to appear in person in a courtroom these days, but he still rendered opinions of great force and clarity for others to plead. As he spoke, the body was slumped back in the chair but the face and the attitude leaned forward, intent, alert. His hands waved slowly with the words like a conductor, and they commanded mesmerising attention because they were enormous, out of proportion with the rest of his body, like the ears. But with his final opinion about to be delivered, the hands ceased moving and one finger came up with the words 'therefore . . .' No solicitor who had ever briefed Hedley Stimson had failed to learn that once the finger was raised and the 'therefore' produced, the meeting was concluded.

When Jack and his solicitor entered this inner sanctum he remained seated. 'Good morning, Kemp. And this is obviously Mr Beaumont, about whom I have been reading with such interest.' Jack stiffened, thinking of the newspaper articles, of which there'd now been three. 'I refer, of course, to the documents you have provided and the brief from Mr Kemp, which is, as always, succinct, but in this case slightly mysterious. You have no court case on foot, Mr Beaumont. No one is suing you; you are suing no one; you are not being pursued by any of the authorities for heinous offences;you have not, apparently, for I'm sure Kemp would have noted it, murdered anyone. In short, none of the driving forces which usually herd people into this small, but I hope you agree, distinguished room appear to be in play. So how can I help you, Mr Beaumont?'

Jack felt he presented his case with force and confidence.

Facts and documents were in the brief and he, with the Pope's help and analysis, understood most of them. Sometimes the linking patterns between one factor and another slid away from him when he re-read them at night in the study at the top of the house. This business was unlike anything he'd ever encountered before. You could produce almost any profit, legitimately, just by changing a few assumptions on risk or by tweaking a judgement on reserving policy or turning a dial on 'smoothing'. The line between right and wrong was shrouded in grey mist on a distant horizon. Just when he held it clearly in sight, it merged and shifted and slipped away from him. But it had to be there—somewhere. And he was holding it firmly in sight now as he laid out his concerns in logical sequence to the impassive, watchful figure of Hedley Stimson QC.

The eyes of the old lawyer never left him throughout the nearly forty minutes of his exposition, the meat-pie hands were motionless on the desk. At one point Jack nearly lost his train of thought as he focused on those hands, rough and black under the nails, the hands of a working man, not a lawyer. It was in the workshop at the back of the house in Wahroonga, where he'd lived for the past twenty-five years, that Hedley Stimson formed the opinions that were the foundation of his legendary reputation, as the lathe whirred and shavings and sawdust flew onto the cracked concrete floor that was never swept.

Finally, Jack puttered to a halt. The lack of any visible or verbal response other than that unrelenting stare was too much. The old lawyer nodded at him. 'Most impressive, Mr Beaumont. You have garnered an understanding of a series of most complex issues in a relatively short time. I'm sure you would greatly impress any jury if, of course, you were permitted to address them uninterrupted for a mere half-hour or so. But we have no jury, do we Mr Kemp? A great pity, it is true, for I have ultimate faith in the wisdom of juries—if only we could extend this excellent system into the world outside the sterility of courts. Fewer arguments, less war, more justice? What do you think, Mr Beaumont?' Hedley Stimson paused briefly but in such a way as to block any response. 'Regrettably, however, we must deal with the conventions of our time. You've raised a number of interesting concerns, but it's unclear to me what actions you expect to flow from your inquiries. Are you seeking to raise these matters with the regulatory authorities, take civil actions against distinguished citizens, to terminate your contract or to alleviate your conscience?'

Jack stared back into the pools of the deep-set eyes but didn't flinch, as so many witnesses had over the decades. These were the same questions Louise had put to him when the ice had finally thawed between them. He'd been faithful always—almost. Their fights, and there were few, were about him arriving home late without a call, or disappearing at a party for longer than a drink. No more than that.

She'd sensed a conspiracy immediately when he had told her about his exclusion from the Colonial Club, about the greasy slipperiness of it all. 'These things don't just happen, Jack. We've never before had an article about us in the press that wasn't complimentary, and then you get blackballed. There are no coincidences. Someone is out to get you.' And then, as her focus shifted to the perpetrators of this evil, so did her anger. She was there to defend him, to fight for their world, to attack. Louise on the hunt was as relentless a beast as he'd ever seen. So when he wavered about taking his worries to Hedley Stimson, as the Pope had suggested, she stiffened his back in minutes. 'Darling, there's a link between these attacks on you and all the questions you've been asking at HOA. There has to be. You know in your heart these people are up to something, and you have to pin the bastards, whoever they are—or you're not the man I know you to be.'

What was the answer to the question being put to him in this book-lined room? What actions did he expect to flow now that he'd summoned the resolve to introduce legal opinion into the equation? He looked back across the desk for what seemed like minutes before answering.

'I don't know. That's what I need your advice on. It's certainly not about protecting me. I haven't done anything wrong and I don't want anyone's money. But what we do at HOA affects people's lives whether they're shareholders or policyholders. We're not selling baked beans or a night at the movies. I'm concerned that if the company gets into trouble through improper practice, or even mismanagement, if that's what it is, we could hurt thousands of people. And if it's being done to profit someone else, then yes, I want to bring them to justice.'

The gnarled hands remained flat on the desk, the eyes held his.

'I see.' Hedley Stimson closed the folder in front of him. 'In order to prove what you suspect, you'd need not only the primary documents—and we're talking about dozens of confidential company documents, not just the few you have here—' he tapped the folder, 'you'd also need deep actuarial and accounting assessments from the best practitioners. The support you could expect from the regulatory authorities, despite all kinds of comforting statements, would amount to very little. The forces brought to bear against you, on the other hand, would include a barrage of legal manoeuvres, and the most damaging attacks on your reputation and credibility—not only during the course of any proceedings, but continuously for the rest of your professional life, should you have any, as well as concerted and probably successful attempts to ruin you financially, aided in part by the extraordinarily high fees you would have to pay me and Mr Kemp here, over a very long period, a period we could extend almost indefinitely, given a chance. Therefore...' there was the slight raising of the brow and the one hand was slowly lifted with the raised index finger, 'I must advise you in the strongest terms not to consider proceeding with any of these matters in a formal legal framework. You may choose to handle them by negotiation and discussion within the company and its board, or to resign your position. That is a matter for you and not within my purview. This is the advice I must give you.'

Jack stood and began to pace the room. He had to move when he was uncomfortable, it had always been like that. But now at least he was not uncertain. Some of Louise's anger had transferred itself to him.

'But there is stuff here that's wrong, isn't there? Some of this could be a monumental fraud, couldn't it? Are you saying there's no breach of the law here, nothing to pursue? Are you saying—' Jack stopped in mid-flight to scrutinise the books on the shelves. 'These aren't law books.' He took one down. 'They're all novels.' He turned to the old lawyer with the book still in his hand.

Hedley Stimson smiled at him gently. 'Yes, Mr Beaumont. Every student clerk and second-rate solicitor has read the law books. You're not going to win cases by seeking wisdom in their dry pages. Sooner or later the law's about human behaviour, about motive, about greed, about lust and power and love and violence, about trust and the breaking of it. That's all in these books. If they make any new laws, I read about them. Otherwise, I stick to life.'

Jack nodded. 'And the people you admire in these books, they just give up, do they? They don't question or probe or struggle? They just turn their backs and walk away? If you tell me I'm being paranoid and I've mis-construed all this, okay. But is that what you're saying?'

He felt a hand on his elbow and the voice of Godfrey Kemp say quietly, 'Come on, Jack, Mr Stimson has given us his opinion, and it's good advice so—' But before the sentence was finished the gravelly voice broke in.

'Yes, it's good advice, Mr Beaumont. However—' He paused. Godfrey Kemp dropped his hand from Jack's arm in surprise. Never, in twenty-five years of briefing Hedley Stimson, had he heard a 'however' after the 'therefore'.

'However, Mr Beaumont, the advice I've given you is the best advice anyone could give you. It's not necessarily my opinion about what is the "right" course of action morally, legally or from any other point of view. It's not necessarily what one of the heroes in those novels you've been gazing at so intently would do. But this is not a story we're discussing, Mr Beaumont. We are discussing your life, and whether you'll be able to enjoy it with some degree of normality or whether you'll be chewed up in a legal mincing machine. Do I make myself clear?'

Jack looked at the book he was holding in his hand. 'This is one of my favourite novels.'

Hedley Stimson smiled at the battered old paperback. 'Mine also, Mr Beaumont. When I find the human condition slightly repulsive, I read it quietly with a strong cup of tea.'

Jack was still standing in front of the desk, legs slightly apart, challenging something—he wasn't quite sure what. 'Then what is your view? Are there laws being broken here? Can people be damaged? Are there corrupt persons at work who should be brought to justice? How do I fight this? How do I look at myself in the mirror if I crawl away?'

The face seemed to be hewn from stone, so fixed was the gaze directed at Jack. 'Sit down, Mr Beaumont.' Slowly he eased the chair back slightly from the desk. 'They'll chew you up, son. Do you understand that? Chew you up, spit you out; win or lose, your life will never be the same again. Do you see that?'

'I see part of it.' Jack's shoulders were hunched forward with concentration.

The minutes ticked away. Gradually the enormous hands rose from the desk and began to conduct words in the air. 'In my opinion there are likely criminal and civil proceedings of a serious nature which might result from substantiation of the concerns you have outlined to me. These include breaches of the Corporations Act in respect of the conduct of directors, failure to disclose conflicts of interests, possible falsification of accounts by management condoned by the auditors, possible fraud charges arising from the conduct of the chief financial officer in respect of documents filed with the Australian Prudential Regulation Authority and the Australian Securities and Investments Commission, as well as the Australian Stock Exchange. There are also probable causes of action for shareholders arising from these misleading documents, not to mention other potential actions under Section 52 of the Trade Practices Act. These are merely my preliminary views.'

Jack didn't look away or shuffle in the chair. At last he asked very quietly, 'Then how do I fight?'

Hedley Stimson turned to his colleague. 'Mr Kemp, I know you have a meeting. Please feel free to leave. Mr Beaumont and I have concluded our conference and are merely chatting to no great point.'

Godfrey Kemp departed, surprised and confused. He'd never left a client alone with Hedley Stimson before, or indeed any other barrister. It was bad practice not to have a witness to a discussion in chambers.

'So you admire the hero in that book, do you? Well, Mr Beaumont, no doubt you'd like to fight injustice in the courts and emerge victorious, having protected the interests of all the widows and orphans who live in the humble dwellings insured by your large but probably unscrupulous company, run by a gang of thieves but presented to the world with your own brand of polished salesmanship. Thus you are established as a man of true substance and ethics by these heroic actions and spend the rest of your life smiling admiringly at your burnished image in as many mirrors as you can find. Is that your idea?'

'Something like that, but just the one mirror will do.' The old lawyer chuckled quietly at Jack's response. 'Have you ever been in a war, son?'

'No. I'm one of the lucky ones who's never held a rifle except in the school cadets.'

'They're not good, the little I know of them. I was in Korea, which was no picnic, but my father was killed at Gallipoli. God knows what that was like. This might be your Gallipoli. Why would you want to bring that on yourself?'

'I didn't bring it on myself. I just happened to be there. But I can't walk away and turn my back on it, can I?'

'Thousands would. And do.' There was silence again. The eyes stayed fixed on Jack, but no longer with the searching stare. 'I've waited a long time to meet you, son, a very long time.'

He stood and walked to the window, looking down into Phillip Street, where all the other lawyers and their clients were scurrying off to sue or be sued. 'If you want to fight, you'll need troops. Not just lawyers, they're easy. Analysts, strategists, actuarial advice, communications advice—God knows what. And money, lots of money.'

'I can get all that.' Jack was still holding the book in both hands. He put it on the desk. 'But will you help me?'

The hand that reached forward seemed larger than the book.

'You realise the point of *To Kill a Mockingbird* is that sometimes it can be right to remain silent?' Jack said nothing. 'But not this time, I hear you say?'

The book was placed carefully on the desk and the old lawyer sat, just as carefully, as he always did when advice was about to be despatched.

'Very well. We won't meet here again. I'll write an opinion confirming my initial advice to you not to proceed. Somehow these matters seep through the walls and become known. You will appear to follow my advice. We don't want our opponents marshalling their resources until we're ready to fire the first shot. You'll get your team together and report to me using only this phone number.' He took a card from the holder on the desk and wrote on the back of it. 'You're not to communicate with Mr Kemp again except to inform him that you have decided not to proceed with the matter. I trust Kemp more than anyone I know, other than my wife, but his walls are also porous. When we meet we'll meet only at my residence, and in the manner I instruct. Is this clear? Do you begin to understand the nature of your folly?'

Jack spoke immediately. 'Yes. I'll call within the week.' Hedley Stimson walked with him to the door, opened it and said in a slightly raised voice, 'Goodbye, Mr Beaumont. I'm sorry I couldn't give you more encouraging advice—but best wishes in any event.'

• • •

There had never been a meeting of the group before for any reason other than for lunch. They were a club with no name, no rules, no aims, and their only premises were the wooden-floored rooms in the restaurant at Bondi. This was Monday and the restaurant was closed, yet they sat at the long table looking down on the distant surfers sliding and dipping and cutting back across the face of the breaking waves. Today there were no rich smells of garlic and grilling meat or pungent aromas of chilli and shellfish drifting from the kitchen. The room smelled musty and dead. All the other tables had chairs standing on them. The vases were upside down on the old carved sideboard and somehow the atmosphere was equally inverted.

The Pope sat at the end of the table and spoke in a clear, calm voice. 'Forgive me, friends, for asking you to come. I realise it's entirely against what we stand for—namely nothing. We've been the club without a cause. We meet just to meet, nothing more. But now we have a friend in great need. My question is simply this, is it appropriate for us to unite, to use our strange and disparate resources to help in these circumstances?'

The members looked around the table, unsure who would respond first. Finally Murray Ingham spoke. 'I assume you mean Jack Beaumont since he's the only one not here?'

'That means nothing, he's probably on the nest again,' Maroubra called from the end of the table, but the resultant laughter was uncertain and muted.

The Pope smiled. 'He may well be, Maroubra, but this time it seems to be a nest of crocodiles our friend has stumbled into. But I stress that he hasn't asked for our help.'

Murray Ingham peered out from beneath his bushy brows.

'Why don't you tell us the story and we'll see if we like the plot?'

'I'd like to be able to do that in detail, but part of the deal would have to be that we each agree to do our part without seeing the whole picture. I'd deal with Jack and coordinate things. It's a big ask, I know, and the prudent response would be for everyone to say no.'

Maroubra's voice boomed out again. 'Prudent? Now you're challenging us, you cunning bastard. Since when has anyone in this group been prudent? There was nothing prudent about that swim a few of us did at

Coogee with cartons of beer on our backs—in a ten-foot surf. Remember that? And they had the helicopters out looking for us. Thought we were goners. Remember how I came out of the water and asked some bloke in a uniform what was going on and he said, "Some mad buggers have tried to swim out to the rocks with beer on their backs." I just said, "You're joking," and left him to it. Poor bastard's probably still there looking out to sea.' Now the laughter was genuine, almost relieved. 'So don't give us prudence. Tell us what you can and we'll make the call.'

'Thank you, gentlemen.' The Pope took out a small notebook. 'These are the facts I'm able to give you at this time.'

He began to read slowly and clearly. When he was finished there was a long silence. Again it was Murray Ingham who responded. 'It's an interesting tale, although not one I'd write. It's got everything but sex, which is extraordinary considering the hero.'

The Judge cut in. 'There's considerable potential for serious legal consequences to flow from even the little that's been said. I, for one, am ready to help—with a proviso that if proceedings are commenced in any way, I may have to withdraw for obvious reasons. I imagine one or two others would have similar potential conflicts.'

Maroubra chipped in, parodying the Judge's slightly pompous tones. 'I could state that while my salvage business doesn't appear to bear directly on the issues at hand, should ethical or legal questions relating to the recovery of sunken boats or used bricks arise unexpectedly, I also may have to pull out. Otherwise I pledge my troth.'

The Pope grinned at him. 'Thank you, as always. You might be surprised, Maroubra, but there are many reasons we could call on you. Quite a few of the contacts you have in sections of the police force and insurance investigators and so on could be very handy.' Eyebrows were raised around the table. 'Yes, it could get very nasty, comrades. We'd be proceeding on the basis that if anyone has a problem at any time, they just let me know. Since we don't exist, except as individuals, there's nothing to bind us together.'

'Except one thing.' It was the courtroom voice of Tom Smiley that interrupted.

'Yes. Except one.' The Pope looked around the table, holding the eyes of each person for a moment. 'So. We go forward together?' He opened the notebook again. 'Here's how you can help.'

chapter seven

Red dust disturbed by the helicopter blades drifted over the emerald Bellaranga lawn and the passengers waited for it to settle before disembarking. There were only four, and Mac stepped out from the homestead to greet them as the last figure emerged.

'G'day, g'day. Great to see you, Max. Henry, how are you? You look ready for anything. Jason, how's the golf? That's the one thing we can't do for you in the Kimberley, but a little barramundi fishing, some great tucker, some amazing rock art, a bit of rough riding—it might do the trick, eh? Ah, and here's the boss.'

The last greeting was directed at Jack in the slightly broader Australian accent that seemed to overwhelm any veneer of polish once Mac was in the bush. He was herding them about like a kelpie, pressing them to take a cold beer from the silver tray that the housekeeper had placed on the wicker table under the poinciana trees, telling them to forget their bags, that sunset would be upon them in an hour, that they could catch it by the billabong where he, Mac, on his own, no servants, would cook dinner over an open fire and they could sit together in the blackness and hear the thump of kangaroo tails on the hard ground. He appeared almost excited and nervous to have guests in this remote place, the opposite of the calm commander of the *Honey Bear*. It was always like this with visitors to Bellaranga, but now there were other reasons for his edginess. They were the black thoughts that woke him in the night when the homestead was empty and the only sounds were the rustles in the dry bush from nocturnal animals and his own feet on the old, wide floorboards as he paced about from room to room. The staff slept in another building a couple of miles away on the property. He'd always liked being completely alone at night up here, 'sleeping like a baby'—but not anymore. The black dog was upon him, with sharp teeth. He'd always sneered at people who suffered from depression for no apparent reason, who couldn't pull themselves together and just get on with life without running off to shrinks or counsellors or social workers or other charlatans. Just get on with it. He wasn't one of those. He just got on with it. The problem at the moment was how to get on with it. What to get on with.

There was a tangle of strings knotted up in a ball inside his head and he couldn't see which one to pull. You had to keep them loose. That was the secret of untying knots. His father had taught him that when they went fishing together. 'You don't pull, son. Never tighten. Loosen, loosen. Just tweak a little here, thread a little there. But always loosen, and the knots disappear.'

The biggest knot, the one that was causing him pain in the stomach or the chest so close to the heart he wondered in the night if he was having some sort of attack, if the indestructible, invincible Big Mac was somehow vulnerable like ordinary beings, this dark cloud was the tumbling share price of HOA. When people asked him about it he just shrugged and tossed off his standard line: 'It's only paper money. Markets go up, markets go down. We just get on and run the company for the shareholders.'

But what the market didn't know, what no one knew except his bankers, was that he was a mortal being, that he was vulnerable, that his entire shareholding in HOA was subject to margin calls and all his other assets, at least according to his accountant who spoke an infuriating language Mac struggled to understand half the time, that these assets were so locked up in trusts and nominee companies and other complex corporate structures that they were difficult to access quickly. And it looked increasingly as if speed might be vital. He'd always relied in previous situations like this, and there had been some, close to the wire, kneeling over the edge, you had to look over the edge sometimes or you weren't a real man, in those times he'd always just brought funds from Switzerland and held the dogs at bay. But now the authorities were all over that, too. Sniffer dogs they were, scenting every last dollar a man might have worked hard for, trying to grab it just because a bit of tax hadn't been paid or some currency regulation hadn't been complied with. And the problem now wasn't just potential fines; there were criminal sanctions in place. Why they weren't out catching the hooligans who broke into people's houses or stole cars or dealt drugs instead of hounding honest citizens was beyond him. Not that they were hounding Mac, or even had a whiff of anything, but they would if he started shifting big lumps of cash around, his cash, the cash he needed to get the bank off his back. He either needed the cash or he needed the share price to rise, it was as simple as that.

And that's why he woke in the night. And why sitting beside him on a dusty car seat was Maxwell Newsome, CEO of the biggest stockbroker trading in HOA shares, and sitting either side of Jack in the rear were Jason Little of Bankers Trust, who held virtually no shares, and Henry

Hurst of UBS Warburg, who earned enormous fees from HOA for handling all its market placements.

A barbecue by the billabong. A Kimberley sunset. Steaks from his own beasts, killed on the old place, cooked by his own hand. The best wine. A gentle word here, a little excitement there. It wouldn't be enough on its own, but it kept the knots loose. It helped you to discover which string to pull. It'd never failed him in the past.

And then there was Jack. God, he'd held such high hopes for that boy, built him up to the market as if he was a messiah. And they'd bought it for a while; everything was looking great. But now he always sounded like a bloody preacher. It seemed as if Renton Healey had successfully thrown him off the track he'd been on, but even so Mac was uneasy. Suddenly there were these strange items in the paper about Jack. Weird rumours about something to do with the Colonial Club were floating around the business world, suggestions he'd acted unethically in some property deal. It sounded like bullshit to Mac, but it was odd. Mac was the one who might have the real reason to shut him up, but he didn't poison water. If you wanted to knife someone, you stabbed them in the stomach.

'You see, just a few stones for the fireplace, a few sticks for the fire and away we go. Did you ever see a sunset like this? Now here's the wine, but where's the opener? Still in the truck, I'm afraid.'

Jack stepped forward. 'I need the exercise after the flight.' 'Thanks, Jack. I don't want to leave the fire at the critical moment. Much appreciated. It's in the glove box.'

Jack wandered off with a torch, relieved to be walking the half-mile back to the vehicle alone. He always felt better when he saw Mac face to face. It reminded him why he'd taken this job in the first place, apart from the mental challenge. Mac might be a buccaneer, he might be larger than any life most people would want to live, maybe he did cut a few corners here and there, but Jack couldn't believe he was fundamentally devious or dishonest.

He didn't make your skin crawl like Laurence Treadmore or Renton Healey. Even if some of Jack's concerns were proven, maybe Mac didn't know about those practices. He didn't seem to pay much attention to detail. Maybe the Pope was wrong and he should just sit down with Mac and ask him about all this.

When he reached the truck it was still light enough to see the eerie silhouettes of the rocky outcrops looming out of the dusk as scarlet splashes turned to magenta then grey then black in the night sky. The stars were suddenly bright in the clear air but there was no moon. He rummaged around in a glove box full of rags, repair bills, vehicle registration papers, rings full of keys. There was no bottle opener, but eventually he found a Swiss Army knife with a small corkscrew in its innards, and he stuffed the other contents back into the compartment. As he did so, the torch shone on the registration paper and a familiar name caught his eye. The truck was registered to a company: Beira Pty Ltd.

Mac and Maxwell Newsome stood by the fire away from the other two, beers in hand, gazing convivially into the flames, as men do and have done since fires were first lit. Things could be said by fires that might not be said elsewhere.

'So, I know you love fishing, Max. Are you up for an early start?'

'Absolutely, Mac. Wouldn't miss it for the world. I love it up here, you know that.'

Mac did know that. Maxwell Newsome saw himself as the financial market's Ernest Hemingway, without the writing. He'd never read the stories, but he'd read everything there was to read about the man's life and loved it all—the hunting, the African adventures, the drinking, the women—maybe not the end. Maxwell had a wardrobe full of khaki clothes with strange patches and pockets and zippers which detached parts of them. He could never look at these garments without wanting to fill them with bullets or compasses or folding knives, since he also had a drawer full of these. But he could never figure out which pocket was for what. And besides, he feared he might look faintly ridiculous. Indeed he was concerned there could be a touch of the ridiculous about him now as he stood, legs apart, in a pair of brand-new safari pants and a shirt with a leopard embroidered in green silk on the pocket. He'd shot a leopard. It wasn't something he was proud of, not something he'd tell Mac, not even by the fire. Especially since he hadn't killed it. The white hunter had told him, 'Don't shoot unless you're sure you can kill. A wounded leopard is the most dangerous animal in Africa and I'll have to hunt it.' But his hands had been shaking more than he thought, even though they were in a hide with a kill placed in the fork of a nearby tree. The hunter had given him the option of 'a real hunt' or 'the tourist method', obviously trying to shame him into a hunt in the open on foot, but he'd come to kill an animal, not be killed, paid a great deal of money to kill a leopard, so he could say he'd killed a leopard. But he'd never been able to say that, not even that he'd shot at one, because of the shame, not of the poor shot, but of the fact that when the hunter had asked him to come with him to track and kill the wounded animal—the animal he'd wounded so he could tell people in the living rooms of the Darling Point harbourside mansions how he'd killed the leopard and hear their gasps at meeting not just a corporate killer, which he was, but a real killer, which he wanted to be—he'd told the hunter he'd stay in the hide. He'd never forget the look of distaste on the man's face as he walked off into the shadowy light with a torch strapped to the barrel of his rifle.

In order to regain his sense of control, away from these demeaning thoughts, he turned to Mac. 'So, my friend, the market's been a little unkind to you lately.'

Mac, who with a couple of beers under his belt and the thought of rare steak and Grange Hermitage in close proximity was just drifting into a state of semi-euphoria, jerked up as if slapped in the face. 'Yeah, well, you know better than anyone, Max—markets come and go, we just run the company as best we can.'

'Yes.' Max Newsome swallowed a long draught of beer. 'Still, I think there's some work to be done, Mac. You don't want things to drift too far off course, do you?'

Mac was locked in now, antennae picking up static all around. 'No way, Max. But the business is in great shape, that's what I don't understand. What's happening out there? Why aren't people buying the stock? We're doing as well as we ever were.'

He felt Max's hand on his arm and was suddenly even more concerned. 'You shouldn't worry too much, Mac, there's just a lot of confusion around. Some of it to do with your new CEO.'

Mac tried to read his expression in the flickering light but the long face was turned away from him. 'Worried? I'm not worried by a few analysts who haven't bought their first pair of long trousers yet. But what's this about Jack? You don't mean all that gossipy stuff in the press, surely?'

Max laughed. 'No, the market doesn't care who he sleeps with.

They're probably all jealous, truth be told. Although that rumour about the club's a bit odd, isn't it? But no, it's more that people don't understand the HOA strategy anymore. You're a growth stock, Mac, that's always been your story. Not a defensive play like the banks. Growth. You've sold that very successfully and, for the most part, delivered. Now Jack's sending out different signals.'

Mac knew it was true. Despite all his coaching and cajoling, he couldn't convince Jack to stop talking about 'profitable growth', about insurance as a 'concept of mutual protection'. All that stuff about making neighbourhoods safe and plotting flood areas and God knows what was fine on Sunday, in church, but it sank like a stone in the river of commerce. The market wanted growth, Max was right. And that's what they'd get.

'So a little good news wouldn't go astray, Mac. You see what I mean. We've a lot of our clients' money invested in HOA stock based on your growth story—I don't have any reason to change that, do I? Not that you can give me any information that's not generally available to the market. Nor do I want any. But a small dose of good news—that's the tonic.'

Mac smiled. 'You know the story, Max. No news is good news. If there was a problem I'd tell you. And, without breaking any goddamn stock exchange rules, I'd also tell you if there wasn't good news coming.'

He felt the hand on his arm again. 'Excellent. You always perform, Mac, that's what we love. And the fishing and the fire and the excellent wine. Speaking of which, here comes your man with the opener. Maybe a quiet word, eh?'

It was exactly the sort of function Mac hated. Why in heaven's name had he come? There were the flamingos tapping and preening all over the room in a display dance of social pretension that turned his stomach. And he was part of it, he'd joined in the polka without being dragged, which made it worse.

When Archie Speyne had ushered him into the partly finished gallery and directed his eyes upward with a dramatic flourish of his velvet-clad arm, Mac knew he was in for an evening of relentless agony. There, high on the rough plastered wall in discreetly stuck-on lettering, were the words THE BIDDULPH GALLERY. He was unable to stifle a groan, which clearly was not the reaction Archie was seeking.

'But Mac, it would fit so well. A new home for our masterpieces and the Matisse we're bidding for, if only, if only we can get it, and you, Mac, you, you're the one, you're the only one who fits it all so perfectly. Homes, Matisse—you see it, you must see it.'

Archie Speyne had a curious habit of repeating phrases when he was excited. It was one of many curious habits, several of which were gossiped about in the bars of Oxford Street and Potts Points and none of which, other than the repetition of phrases, would be on show this evening. There was a touch of desperation in the air around Archie. He'd made promises he couldn't keep and his whole career, his carefully manicured reputation as the darling of the art world, threatened to erupt over him in a flood of molten lava. He could end up like one of those frozen bodies in Pompeii, trapped in a river of disaster and found centuries later, fossilised, featuring on a little stand on the desk of some future director of this very museum. On the other hand, there were some things in Pompeii he wouldn't mind being trapped with . . . Archie recovered to renew his assault on Mac, who had wandered out of the half-finished extension to where the drinks were being served. It wasn't fair, not fair at all. When Archie had made the commitment for the works, when he'd assured the trustees he had the money, the money was there. Rudolph Steinmann had promised it, shaken hands on it, delighted to see THE STEINMANN GALLERY on the wall. It was only when the contract had been drawn up for the gift that things had come unstuck.

'What is this, Mr Speyne? Twenty-five years? For twenty-five years you put my name on the gallery, then somebody else's name? Is that what you say? You rub my family name away like so much chalk on a blackboard?'

Archie had grovelled and knelt and bent every which way, explained it was the policy of the museum never to grant naming rights in perpetuity, a policy of the trustees, not his policy, but the crotchety old bastard wouldn't budge.

'No. You want two million dollars of my money. I want immortality. That's a bit longer than twenty-five years. You can't deliver, someone else will.'

And they had, and the money was in their bank account, and the Steinmann name was on their wall. And Archie was up shit creek without a paddle. He hated crude expressions like that, but he was. So there. He hurried after Mac into the main gallery where one long table for twenty-five guests glittered with glass and silver and tiny candles placed next to tiny vases, each holding a single chrysanthemum placed precisely by Archie's own hand. Attention to detail was everything, especially when you were asking people for money.

By the time the guests were seated, Archie had regained his composure, if he could be said to possess composure, and was ready to perform his much-loved party trick of introducing everyone at the table with a brief, flattering but amusing pastiche of their social significance.

'Friends—because that's what we all are, friends of this marvellous museum, friends of art, friends of our beautiful city and just wonderful friends, because we like you all, we don't invite anyone to special functions like this that we don't enjoy—we are gathered here for a very special purpose that I and Arnold Shaw from London will speak about a little later. But I feel I must pique your interest even at this early hour with a name.' He paused and looked archly around as if an indiscretion of some bizarre nature was about to be revealed. 'Matisse.' Another coy pause was made available for the intaking of breath, which did not in fact come. 'Yes, a name to conjure with. The painters' painter. We've all seen the great works in the Centre Pompidou or the Tate. Can we ever expect to see one in our wonderful extension next door?'

An inappropriate thought—'not unless we can get a roof on'—passed fleetingly through Archie's consciousness before he ploughed on. 'We must enable our fellow citizens to view works like this, uplifting works, whenever they wish. And particularly those less fortunate persons in our community who cannot travel to Paris or London.'

There was general murmuring of approval at this. The concept of cold or hunger was difficult to grasp, but the inability to travel to Paris or London was real and terrible to contemplate.

'We want these pictures of beauty and wonder on our own walls.' He cast his hands around the walls in a circular motion. 'Although there is one among us who already has that privilege, as I shall mention in a moment.'

There was a general exchange of inquiring looks at this remark. The burly figure at the head of the table stared mournfully down at the pink cloth and wondered how on earth he could extract himself from this torture. Bonny was spending the week at some sort of retreat to 'find herself' or something. God knows why. She was easy enough to find. He'd been on his own in the Kimberley for a while and he wanted company. He supposed he could have had dinner with Edith, which would have been novel, but she was always asking him how things were. 'How are things, Mac?' she would say in that earnest voice, as if the end of the world was nigh. Even when it wasn't. Not that it was now. Anyway, maybe he should have had dinner with Edith.

At least he would've escaped this lot.

He felt a hand on his lap and turned in surprise to the woman next to him. He'd never met her before and peered at her place card, trying to make out her name in the gloom.

'It's Popsie, darling, just Popsie. Such a pleasure to be with the famous Mac Biddulph again. Unbelievable our paths have crossed so seldom.'

In truth their paths wouldn't have crossed this starry evening had Popsie not carefully examined the table while drinks were being served and surreptitiously moved her name card from near the kitchen entrance to its present cosy and prominent position next to Mac.

She pouted at him in an unusual pursing of the lips that seemed to presage the application of lip gloss, but was merely the prelude to a whisper. 'I hear you're about to become a benefactor of this wonderful museum. What a marvellous man you are. How lucky we are to have people like you.'

She patted his arm in a gesture that Mac found offensive. He turned away from her to listen briefly to Archie's round of introductions—anything was better than this posturing pantomime beside him.

'And now our dear friend Vera North who, with her dear late husband Alec, has helped the museum in so many ways and continues to do so. Where would the arts be in this great city without people of taste and sensibility like Vera? We can't rely on governments, can we?' As Archie's eyes swept around the table for confirmation, they suddenly lighted on the Premier's chief of staff. 'Alone. We cannot and must not rely on governments alone. Because they have other important responsibilities, like hospitals and roads and other things.' Archie sensed he was drifting slightly from his planned course. 'And we're incredibly grateful to this government for more than twenty million dollars in recurrent funding. But we must also help ourselves. From our positions of privilege, we must contribute where we can.'

Mac wondered exactly what privileged position Archie Speyne was referring to in his own case, unless it was the close proximity to the twenty million that allowed him to travel the world in modest style in the interests of art. But his mind was more occupied with how he could escape before Archie sprayed him with his own dose of flattery and cologne, and before the strange creature next to him devoured him with her extraordinary expanding mouth. All eyes were now on

Archie as he was introducing, with urbane wit he felt, the chairman of a large concrete company who was fond of saying, 'Half this country is covered in our product and the other half in red dust.' Gently, unobtrusively, Mac eased his chair back and made his way to the rear exit of the gallery. Only a few noticed him leave as all waited their turn for attention. His rubber-soled shoes made no sound on the terrazzo floor. He always wore rubber, no point in slipping, and God was he glad of it now.

The cold night air was a blessed relief after the claustrophobic atmosphere of those cloying remarks and clinging people. Christ. He'd give anything to be out on the *Honey Bear* whacking golf balls into the river. Come to think of it, he wouldn't mind having Archie Speyne's head printed on them. He waved to his driver to wait for him and set off at a brisk pace towards Mrs Macquarie's Chair. He'd have loved to see Archie's face when his circus act finally reached Mac's empty chair.

A disturbing thought flitted across his vision like a bat through the night sky. There were a lot of well-placed people at that table, apart from poseurs like Popsie whatever her name was, including the heads of three major banks. They wouldn't think he'd slipped away to dodge making a donation, would they? That wouldn't look so good. After all, he had accepted the damn invitation—if you're not going to give, don't go. And the only way to defend was to attack. He turned and hurried back to the museum, fumbling to find the cell phone in his pocket as he tapped Archie on the shoulder and drew him into a corner with the words, 'Sorry, had to make an urgent call, but I've some news for you.' He thought the poor little bastard would piss his pants when he told him, and watched with contempt as Archie almost ran to the table to tap his wineglass.

'Friends, dear friends, I have the most exciting news. What a wonderful evening, made so special by one of those people who contribute so much to society in so many ways. Our godfather here, Mac Biddulph, has just allowed me to reveal the name of the exceptional space behind you that will, on completion, house so many of our treasures and hopefully, with your generous assistance, our new Matisse. I am proud to announce, following a wonderfully generous gift of two million dollars, that this new space will be named the Biddulph Gallery.'

As Popsie Trudeaux drove home in her Mercedes 55 AMG she had mixed feelings. Strictly speaking, she wasn't driving home in a 55 AMG, although the car carried those numbers and letters on its rear. Actually it was a standard model costing about a hundred thousand dollars less. It hadn't been easy acquiring those badges either. The dealer had been outraged when she'd offered to buy them. 'We sell cars, madam, not badges.' So she told him to fuck off and found someone who could get them for a couple of hundred, God knows where from. Just because Angus couldn't even bring home the bacon like he used to didn't mean the whole world needed to know. But that wasn't the cause of her mixed feelings. She'd managed to seat herself next to Mac, which was a plus, but despite her ample charms being on full display and all kinds of electrical impulses being directed his way, there'd not been a flicker of response. It was enormously frustrating. To be so close to a man like that, so rich, so well known for screwing around, so much the star of the night, and not even to score a lunch date or a leg tremble. Nothing. She'd ring her doctor first thing in the morning.

Certainly more Botox was required, perhaps something more radical, although her tits were perfect. Maybe the bottom. He was probably a bum man, that was it. Although she'd been sitting down all night. Certainly a new wardrobe. Angus would just have to pull his weight for once.

chapter eight

Jack parked his car two streets from Hedley Stimson's house, as instructed, and walked through the piles of wet leaves left unraked from last autumn on the footpath under the arch of a liquid-amber. It was drizzling lightly and he had no coat or umbrella. He shivered as he walked, whether from the chill or in nervous anticipation of the clandestine meeting he wasn't sure. It was probably all a mistake. Sure, it looked like Mac was creaming off millions of dollars of HOA profits for his own personal gain, or at the very least failing to report benefits in filed documents. But what business was it of his? Why not let the auditors and the lawyers sort it out?

As for the big issue, well, he was no closer to pinning that down. HOA was reporting record profits, had just issued a market guidance—despite his objections—to the effect that it expected a substantial increase above expectations. His objections had been swept away in a landslide of factual argument from Renton Healey, Mac, the auditors, the actuaries—in fact everyone but the chairman. Sir Laurence had stated his position in a terse telephone conversation that added little to the knowledge bank and nothing to global warming.

'It is not appropriate for a non-executive chairman to become involved in a discussion of this nature. It is a matter for the executive team, in conjunction with the auditors, to make a recommendation to the board. Please advise me when you are in a position to do so.'

And the recommendation had finally progressed, under Jack's signature as CEO. Substantial releases from reserves due to favourable underwriting conditions, together with certain one-off gains, led the company to advise an upgrade in its full year outlook. The share price had reacted immediately. Not only was the slump arrested, but the shares had added three per cent in a week and were still rising. All under his name, with his brilliant salesmanship.

As he approached the lichgate that opened into the garden of the rambling federation house, he could hear the whirr of machinery and the scream of metal on wood emanating from the workshop at the rear of the house, hidden away in a grove of birches, and he could just make out the shape of a man's head bent over in the lighted window. He knocked on the wooden door and the whirring stopped immediately.

When they were seated by the potbelly stove with mugs of tea, and Hedley Stimson was holding forth on the intricacies of lathe work and its contribution to the welfare of mankind, Jack relaxed, forgot about the documents in the briefcase alongside him and examined the studio in detail. It was one large room, roughly built with exposed beams in a vaulted roof where the corrugated iron sheeting was visible, a concrete floor obscured by a coating of sawdust and curled wood shavings. There was a long bench by the only window, with vices and a lathe set in, and a wall of tools meticulously arranged by size and use—chisels of every gradation and type, saw blades, routers, hammers and other tools of less obvious application, at least to Jack's untrained eye. As the gravelly voice warmed to its passion, Jack felt, after a couple of sessions like this, his expertise on woodworking matters, if not on the legal implications of potential HOA misdemeanours, would be complete.

'But I can see I may be boring you, Mr Beaumont. Wood-turning and its subtleties are not to everyone's taste. More's the pity.' He placed his heavy mug on the floor beside the chair and its base and half the sides disappeared into the layer of sawdust. 'It's a lovely, quiet night for anything, Sunday night. Walk around the streets and you'll barely hear a sound. Just the flicker of light from the great god in the living room as you pass each house. The churches are empty and we're all crouched low before the god of light. Football, then the movies—a perfect Sunday. What more could you seek as the rockbed of true belief?'

'You're crouched low in front of a workbench.'

'Not at all, Mr Beaumont. I am uplifted by the joyful experience of releasing useful creations from the fibre of God's work. Under my hands a tree becomes a chair, a table, a rocking horse for my grandchildren. You see the difference?'

'Do you have grandchildren?' It was very quiet in the studio, apart from a faint hissing from the potbelly stove as the thick offcuts slowly turned to ash. The old lawyer spoke without looking up. 'My only son died a long time ago.'

Somehow Jack knew he'd touched an undressed wound, but he asked the question anyway: 'How did he die?'

Now the hooded eyes were raised to him and the big hands lifted slowly and began to circle as if to tell the story, but then fell back on the arms of the chair. When the voice finally came it was flat, empty.

'He was only ten. Perfectly healthy. Bright little fellow. Short for his age—I don't think he would ever have been a big chap—but full of courage. On the rugby field he'd tackle anyone, didn't matter what size they were, and bounce up like a rubber ball just when you thought he had to be injured. Great little half-back, quick hands, clever with the play. I used to love watching him.' He paused and looked away to the window where there was nothing to see. 'I was in court. They handed me a note. By the time I got there he was gone. Just like that. Overwhelming virus of the heart. A virus—and gone.'

He continued to stare through the window into the night garden. 'Have you ever been to a child's funeral, Mr Beaumont? The coffin is white, for some reason. It looks like it's made out of cardboard. Incredibly small and fragile—like a child's life. That alone is enough to break your heart.'

Jack heard the tremor in his own voice as he spoke. 'Did you never want to have more children?'

The square face swung to him and the eyes stared fiercely into Jack's. 'As you will certainly discover in the coming weeks, what you want and what you receive in this life are frequently worlds apart. Now, we're not here to discuss the history of the Stimson family, so let's get on.'

It was difficult to get on, Jack felt. He handed across the file of documents and waited, not speaking, for ten minutes or more as each was read carefully and placed aside, in order, on the floor. When the last document had landed in a puff of sawdust, the grilling began. There was anger in the questioning and heavy sarcasm, rather than irony, in the commentary.

'This is flim-flam, card houses, walls made from woodchip, not a solid beam anywhere. Look at this reinsurance contract that you opine, in your ultimate wisdom, may breach some regulation, law, you know not what. Which clause in its labyrinthine depths do you wish to direct my attention to? Which specific aspect of its cover proves your case?'

Jack stood. 'I don't know. The Pope said it's a financial reinsurance contract that probably doesn't have any real transfer of risk involved.'

'Probably? The Pope? You are communicating with God's representative in Rome?'

'Clinton Normile—we call him "the Pope". I thought you knew him.'

'Yes, I know Mr Normile, but not by any ecclesiastical appellation. You can tell Mr Normile that in these matters his infallibility is not accepted. "Probably" cuts no mustard in this room, Mr Beaumont. If there is no transfer of risk, there must be some accompanying document. Find it, or forget it.'

And so it went. The contents of the file were metaphorically shredded one by one. At the end, Jack felt his ego lay with them. But the hammering continued.

'And here we have your suggested list of experts. Some of whom are worthy of their title. But this woman you recommend as the communications person. A gossip columnist, a manicurist who sends out press releases and does lunch. We want street fighters, maulers. This is not the judging at the annual dahlia festival, at which I'm sure you have won any number of prizes.'

'Fine. Do you know someone?'

'Of course I know someone, Mr Beaumont.' The words were nearly spat at him. 'I know everyone. The point is do you know someone. If we start using my contacts, the jig is up. I am not involved in this, remember. I am a semi-retired old dodderer who told you to slink off into your corner and forget the whole thing, so I could get back to making those rocking horses.'

Jack knelt and began to pick the documents from the floor, shaking each to remove the sawdust. When he replaced the first one in his briefcase, the gruff voice came, tired, dead flat. 'Leave them. Leave them where they are. I'll read them again. Perhaps there is something there. It's late, I'll look at them in the morning.'

They walked to the door. It was raining heavily now and gusts of cold air and a few wet leaves blew in. Jack hadn't spoken. He turned as he felt the hand on his shoulder.

'You would have liked him.' They shook hands and Jack walked slowly back along the slippery path to his car, not caring much that the rain was soaking through his thin layers of clothing.

'I want it to be huge, Larry, enormous—the best goddamn party this city has ever seen. And I want everyone there—not just the business people, I can take care of them, but the pollies and all the art wankers, the lot. That's where you come in.'

Even Sir Laurence's formidable skill as a concealer of true feelings couldn't help to hide his distaste at this remark. Mac was quick to make amends. 'I mean you were the head of the thing, weren't you, the museum? A very distinguished head, from all I hear. Archie Speyne speaks very highly of you . . .' and then, observing the reaction to the mention of Archie, 'and others, I mean others speak very highly of you. Not Archie speaking—you know what I mean.'

Sir Laurence drew himself up slightly in his chairman's chair. They were in the HOA boardroom, where he preferred to hold meetings, rather than his office. The subject of Mac's party, whatever form that may take, was not the subject he'd intended to discuss when the meeting was requested by him. But clearly his topic wouldn't reach the table before this was dispensed with.

'I'm not sure I do know what you mean, Mac. Is there some way I can be of assistance?'

'Exactly. You can. That's what I'm saying. When I open my gallery, the Biddulph fucking Gallery, I want a real blow-out, a sensation, not some boring corporate function. I want the party to be a fucking artwork, do you see? And that means all the art people and hangers-on and social A-listers and whatever have got to be there. You must know all these folks, or how to get them, from when you were mixing with that lot. So I need you to help bring them all in.'

Sir Laurence was now completely attuned to the conversation. His help was needed. These were words of opportunity, never to be ignored. 'Of course, Mac. Whatever I can do. Such a wonderful gesture of yours.' He paused. 'And especially in times like this.' Mac shot him an inquiring glance, but the face was completely opaque. Sir Laurence continued, 'Who's going to organise the party?'

'Well, Archie Speyne, I suppose. Or his people anyway. Strictly, it's their party.'

'I see.' Sir Laurence's thumb and forefinger rose to his chin. 'I'm not sure that's such a good idea. It is your gallery, after all. It should be your party.' Mac nodded, so he pressed on. 'Would you like me to arrange for someone to organise it? It might not look well for you to intervene, if you see what I mean. Better that the party is given for you, since you have already given, yes?'

Mac smiled. 'You're a cunning old bastard, Laurence. I forget just how clever you are sometimes.'

'What a charming compliment, Mac. I'm quite swept away. But I'd be more than happy to oversee everything, and you can rest assured everyone who matters will be there. Who do they have opening it?'

'Archie is going to ask the Premier.'

'I think not. The Prime Minister would be more appropriate. The state may have responsibilities for the museum, but the federal government regulates the insurance industry.'

Mac slapped the table. 'My chairman. You're worth every penny, Larry—and I'm not talking about director's fees.'

Sir Laurence moved on quickly. 'Speaking of money for a moment, is there a budget for this event? We'll need professional event managers.'

'Whatever it takes. Fly the fucking tulips from Holland for all I care. Hang Nicole Kidman from the Harbour Bridge by her knickers. Just so long as all those wankers go home remembering there's only one Mac Biddulph. Now what did you want to talk about?'

Jack had driven straight to Palm Beach, rented a canoe from the hire shop, ignored the instruction not to go beyond Barrenjoey, and set his course for Lion Island. It was foolhardy, he knew, in many respects. The craft wasn't the kayak of his youth, that beautiful wooden-hulled bullet with fitted canvas covers to keep the water out and a balanced offset panel that, in skilled hands, swept the little boat along even into the wind. This was a moulded fibreglass clunker with a gaping, unprotected opening and a heavy, cumbersome paddle. He'd taken the day off, needing to distance himself from the greys of corporate life, to feel the sunlight and drink in the deep blues of the real world. But it was a perfect day, just the faintest feather of wind on his face, even the sea flat like a lake. As he let the canoe run to the edge of the rocks on the headland, he could see the water heaving gently onto the beach, barely shifting the threads of weed on the yellow sand. He loved the colour of the sand on these peninsular beaches; it wasn't the whiter, finer material of the city beaches, or the even more intense white of tropical beaches in Queensland or the Northern Territory, but a coarse salmon from the sandstone cliffs of Pittwater and the Hawkesbury River. The water lapped benignly against the boulders at the base of the headland where the lighthouse kept watch. Even though he knew there'd be a swell the moment he edged the canoe beyond the point and into the open waters of Broken Bay, if there was a day to complete his adventure this was it.

He wanted, needed, to find the natural world again, even for a few hours. When he turned the car onto the access road to the headland car park, he was dismayed by the litter of signs and ticket machines, council barbecues for the tourists, neatly planted trees in rows with huge wind guards around them because they weren't indigenous to the area, seats with concrete pads and metal arms, all the paraphernalia of suburbia in what had been the wild place of his youth. He counted fifty-three signs in the half-mile from the main road to the car park before giving up in disgust.

But on the water, his spirits lifted. They couldn't kerb and gutter Pittwater. As he let the canoe drift in the light breeze, he could see schools of fish darting about under him, seagulls floating quietly, a pelican gliding through the air currents, a sea eagle hunting on the cliffs. His was the only craft in sight on this mid-week day, other than a white sail barely moving in the distance near Mackerel Beach.

He paused at the point for a moment, as if to turn back, then let the canoe drift on the wind until it was hidden from sight behind the rocks and struck out for the island with long, smooth strokes. For the first half-hour he felt exhilarated, euphoric, to be in the sea, low down, almost nestled, in the water, as the gentle swells rolled through the opening into the bay. Lion Island was further away than he remembered, but he paddled without a break and the rhythm was even and the stroke strong and he was eighteen again. Soon the muscles in his shoulders began to ache and his back was cramped against the back of the canoe, so he paused to let the wind take him for a while and to stretch his arms and back. He looked up, hoping to catch a glimpse of the white belly of the sea eagle, but the great bird had either caught its prey or moved on to other hunting grounds.

When he glanced back at the island it seemed more distant than it had before. The swell was bigger now, and when the boat dropped down into a trough he could barely see the land at all. The wind was shifting. The sea had turned to deep green from its turquoise blue, and when he looked up at the sky, there were dull grey patches overhead. He lifted the paddle and drove the canoe forward into the chop, but after another half-hour of increasingly difficult paddling towards the island, with the wind and the sea conspiring against his advance, he began to doubt his judgement. He'd forgotten how quickly the weather could turn here, how exposed the waters were beyond the protection of the headland. The island would have to wait for another day.

He turned the boat and gritted his teeth for a tough paddle back to safety, for the wind was from due south now. The spray from the wave crests whipped into his face and his cap blew away into the sea behind him. His teeth were literally grinding against one another as he strained to make any gain against the superior force. It was cold. What had been a balmy day had turned cold with a blustery, troubled sky, and the sweat and spray cooled on his bare head and under his wet shirt. As he rested for a moment, he felt his body begin to shiver uncontrollably and the dryness in his mouth became extreme. He hadn't bothered to bring any more than one small bottle of water, long since drunk, on such a pleasant day. He recognised the first signs of hypothermia and suddenly he was afraid.

The boat wouldn't sink, that was no concern—but he might. If the swell continued to increase and a real southerly buster blew in, there was no way he could keep the canoe upright. Then the question was how long he could hang onto it. He'd given up any hope of making a landfall this side of New Zealand. The important thing was not to lose his nerve, not to panic. Panic in the sea was death, he knew that, had told people that. But he wasn't eighteen; his body felt spent and feeble, and he ached and shivered as light rain began to whip across the white caps. Visibility was only a hundred yards now—and who would look for him out here where he wasn't meant to be?

He heard the voice before he heard the engine. 'Hello over there. What the hell are you doing out here, having a picnic?' It was a battered old fishing boat, but the most beautiful craft Jack had ever set eyes on. 'G'day, mate. We don't pull many fish like you out of the water. You'd better climb up here before the sharks get you.'

He'd forgotten about the sharks. The area around Barrenjoey where the fish came in to feed was notorious for sharks. He was hauled into the boat, wrapped in a blanket, handed a flask of tea. The canoe was tossed onto the deck like a discarded banana.

'You'd probably rather have a whisky, but no grog on this boat, mate. Not while we're at sea anyway. Make up for it later. What, did you get blown around the headland by the southerly?'

Jack was still shaking despite the warmth of the blanket. 'Something like that. I feel a real idiot, I must say. Thank Christ you came along.'

'No worries, mate. Still, there was no one else around today so you might have been pulled out by the Maoris if we hadn't found you. The yellow canoe, that's what saved you.'

The fisherman stood in a pair of shorts and a T-shirt as the rain beat under the canopy, making Jack feel even colder.

'You want to get home, mate, into a hot bath, have a couple of beers or a scotch, into bed with a good woman, hey? Stay away from the canoes for a while.'

When they dropped him off to shore he left them with profuse thanks—they'd accept nothing more—and drove off with the car heater blasting, home to the safety of Louise. He just wanted to hold her, to nestle into her back, to breathe into her hair while she slept. He wouldn't roll away as he usually did once she was asleep. He would stay, locked against her all night, not sleeping. He would stay, now, locked against her, always. Or at least until he had to face Sir Laurence in the morning.

Sir Laurence gazed contentedly around his room. He loved the silk on the far wall, the discreet patterns of flecks and circles woven into the texture. He loved the majestic space of it all, the sweep of the horseshoe table, the rich quality of the mahogany colour, the deep comfort of the upholstered chairs. The only artwork, an oil by Sir Arthur Streeton, was worthy of a place in any public gallery—indeed the museum had wanted to buy it.

But he preferred it here. Two knights together.

He thought of this room as his own. It might belong to HOA, technically, or to the landlords more technically, but it was his in every other sense. He was not just the chairman but the conscience of this company. Yes, that's what he was. The conscience. He'd never thought of it that way before. Mac might have created the business in the raw sense, but who steered it away from the follies and indiscretions and crude manipulations that people like Mac and Renton Healey were capable of committing? Even his own special arrangements were poor recompense for the value he added. And of course, his contributions were not evident, so he received scant public recognition. But he bore no grudges. The work was sufficient unto itself.

The great bronze door to the boardroom swung open, cutting short these pleasant thoughts. In fact, it was not only the opening of the door but the person entering that reversed his mood. Jack appeared to be even more bronzed than usual. It was revolting. He looked like some sort of native more used to scrabbling around in the soil for roots and tubers—although perhaps it was the women who did that. No doubt Jack would be lounging around in a loincloth, doing nothing but waiting to remove the loincloth. Disgusting. And now here he was in this beautiful room, decorated by Sir Laurence himself, coatless, tieless, probably with a loincloth under the trousers.

'Jack, thank you so much for coming. Very good of you. I know how busy you've been with the results. And the media.'

Two things in these opening remarks caused Jack to pause. It was the first time Sir Laurence had ever used his name—and with warmth. And the reference to the 'media' had just a hint of an edge to it. But perhaps he was imagining it. He'd never seen Prue Patterson after the dinner and nothing had appeared in the press. Probably she was offended by his rejection of her offer. But Jack-the-lad was no more. He'd never be able to live without Louise, he knew that. This whole HOA mess had brought home to him how much he relied on her.

'So I must say you're looking wonderfully well, Jack, despite the pressure of the job. It doesn't bother you at all, the dimension, the intricacy? You take it all in your stride? I must say your public appearances seem to be virtuoso performances.'

Jack wondered how long the web of flattery would be wound around him before the sharp end of the meeting was revealed.

'And I must commend your major initiatives within the company. Particularly, I refer to your efforts to reduce costs and your concentration on the soundness of our P&L and balance sheet. I understand you're also looking into the precise nature of the company's reinsurance contracts?' He waited for some affirmation, which wasn't forthcoming. 'As chairman, I am formally requesting you to report any concerns or irregularities on any of these matters directly to me. I want you to pursue all of them relentlessly and, if possible, to redouble your efforts. We must adhere to the highest standards of probity and fiscal certainty, so if any evidence, no matter how flimsy, should surface which gives you cause for concern, you must bring it straight to me. I'm sure you see the importance of this.'

Alarm bells were ringing in Jack's head, but to what purpose was unclear. 'Of course, Laurence. I'm just doing some preliminary work, particularly on the cost side.' Hedley Stimson had warned him to be circumspect with Sir Laurence when he informed him of the impending meeting.

'Watch him, son, he's a twisted vine that one. See if he takes notes in the meeting. He's probably trying to get something on the record to cover his own back. If he takes notes, you take notes. He can't use a recording without you knowing and without your permission, but watch him.'

There were no notes taken. Sir Laurence sat very still in his chairman's chair, which was upholstered in the same beige material as the other nineteen chairs around the table, but with a higher back. The suit was immaculate as always, the tie perfectly knotted, the shirt pink as always.

'My suggestion, Jack, is that you form a committee to investigate these matters, should any of them crystallise as real issues. Such a committee might comprise yourself as chairman, Renton Healey on the financial side, and perhaps our internal auditor. Something of that nature. You could then report directly to me. We must be proactive at all times, yes?'

'Yes, of course, Laurence, and thank you for the suggestions. It may be a bit premature for that, but I'll certainly bear it in mind.'

'Excellent. That's agreed then. You will alert me immediately if anything develops. You have my complete support in all your efforts. Proceed without fear or favour.'

chapter nine

The sky was ablaze with weird geometric shapes in brilliant colours, vaguely reminiscent of a cubist painting. Somewhere in the Domain or the gardens surrounding the Museum of Modern Art, lasers or other devices of illusionists and magicians were creating shifting pictures on the clouds, as the human interest swarmed in through the portico. The women were in full plumage. The invitation had read 'Party', not 'Cocktails' or 'Reception', and the starting time was eight, rather than six-thirty or seven. There weren't so many real parties nowadays—maybe there'd be dancing, mixing, darkness, happenings, scandals, gossip . . . In the forecourt, beautiful young women in dinner jackets were strolling about with peacocks on leads and a tall, muscled black man, also in a dinner jacket but with no shirt, just a bare chest and a white bow tie, stood motionless with a brightly coloured parrot on his shoulder. Strange, discordant, but not unpleasant, music wafted through the evening air from time to time as the guests queued to enter, and there was a disturbing, musky, vaguely sexual fragrance around. Waiters flitted about the queue with trays bearing champagne flutes and martini glasses filled with a milky viscous substance. When they were asked what the cocktails contained, they just smiled their pretty smiles and shrugged, as they'd been trained, and watched the women take the cocktails anyway, giggling nervously.

By the time the guests had entered the Biddulph Gallery there was expectation, almost danger, in the air.

The new gallery was pristine. Not a single picture interrupted the stark white walls as they swept up to the domed roof with massive skylights. The only adornment was the inscription THE BIDDULPH GALLERY on the entrance wall, not quite as high as it had been when Archie Speyne had made his pitch, and not in the black lettering of the dummy run. The bold sans serif script was built up with gold leaf—less obvious but so much more elegant. Although wisps of smoke whirled lazily through the vast space from time to time, not like the substance from a theatre smoke machine but more ethereal, almost like breath on a cold day, the gleam of the Biddulph name glinted always above the carefully groomed heads.

Everyone was here. Seven hundred and fifty people, everyone hand-picked, the crème de la crème, a perfect potpourri of business and political leaders, arts scions, artists, socialites, actors, a sprinkling of legendary sports figures—not too many because they never dressed well—and just the right dash of wankers. No one had declined, no one. Well, those who had were nobodies now. When the invitations went out—unusual in themselves, just a card with the whole of one side covered with a full-colour depiction of a strange painting labelled 'The Tiger, Franz Marc 1912 (Städtische Galerie im Lenbachhaus)', and on the other, in gold, the briefest details of the party, people were clamouring to get on the list, ringing Archie Speyne, the chairman of the museum, Mac, anyone who'd ever been connected with HOA. Women were berating their husbands with, 'I'm telling you, John, if you can't get us to that party, after all I've done for this city, after what you've done for—whatever, we're finished. I'm not helping anyone anymore, I don't care who they are, they can stick all their charities and museums and whatever wherever they want. That's it.'

It was difficult to find a target to aim all this venom at. Archie said, truthfully, that he wasn't in control of the list. Mac said, mainly truthfully, that it was the museum's party, not his. The invitees smiled, smugly, and refrained from asking friends and acquaintances if they were attending until at least two minutes into any conversation.

Mac stood at the far end of the gallery, champagne flute in hand, and gazed around with deep satisfaction. Who would have thought old tight arse Laurence Treadmore could get together a show quite like this. Sure he'd hired someone, but at least he'd known who to hire. Mac would have to look after him. Christ, he was already looked after well enough. Probably even creaming something off the top of this event. But no—he was too smart for that, was Sir Laurence. His arrangements would be buried deep where no one would ever find them.

Mac winced inwardly as he felt Edith's hand on his arm. Not because it was Edith's hand, but because it reminded him that Bonny wasn't here. There were occasions and there were occasions. One didn't hide these things but nor did you flaunt them when the conclave of wives was in session. It would cost him plenty. So what. He was already enjoying his night immensely. He had no idea what was about to unfold and he didn't care. It felt right. It had the makings.

Mac felt a hand on his shoulder and turned to find the wide smile of Maxwell Newsome a few centimetres from his face. 'Fantastic, Mac, absolutely brilliant. Betty was just saying she hasn't had so much fun for years and the party hasn't even started yet.'

Mac shrugged a humble shrug. 'Evening Max, Betty. It's not really my party, you know, I'm just a guest. Ask Edith.'

There was little point in asking Edith, as everyone knew, since Edith seldom spoke at public functions other than to laugh and nod, which had to count as speech. Maxwell Newsome smiled a knowing smile. 'Sure Mac, we believe you. If the museum board could stir themselves to put on a show like this, we'd be here all the time. It's usually cheap wine and sixties-style savouries, not all—this.' He gestured at the myriad waiters sliding in and out of knots of people with trays of tiny morsels. Everything was tiny, Mac thought, even the waiters. The lamb chops were barely the size of a forefinger. The bloody lamb must have been slaughtered three weeks after it was born. Bastards. Still, they were terrific lamb chops. There were tiny hamburgers barely bigger than a thumbnail, tiny lobster pieces on tiny blinis, delicious wee morsels dropping down surgically tightened throats all over the Biddulph Gallery.

Mac drew Maxwell Newsome to one side, leaving the wives to chat. 'Max, a moment if you don't mind.'

'On a night like this, Mac, no one could deny you anything.' He winked. 'And with the rising share price, why would anyone want to?'

'Yes, that's what I want to talk to you about. I'm thinking of selling a few shares, to balance up the portfolio.'

'Hmm. It never looks good, Mac. A director. A major shareholder. Tends to spook the market a bit, just when everything is back in splendid order. You see what I mean.'

'That's why I'd prefer it wasn't public—to protect the interests of the other shareholders.'

'But you know the ASX rules. As a director, you have to advise the market immediately when you buy or sell. You don't even get much grace these days. They're very strict about that. And the newspapers publish those trades each week. There's no way around it.'

'I know the goddamn rules, Max, but how does that help anyone? They're stupid rules, made for shonky types and start-up companies. This is HOA, one of the biggest companies in Australia, and I'll only be selling a small percentage of my holding. The shares aren't even in my name—some company owns them. We don't want the share price to drop for everyone else just because I've sold a few shares, do we?'

Maxwell Newsome stroked his chin thoughtfully. 'It's really not a question for me, Mac. The individual director is responsible for reporting the sales. Of course, if you don't control the company that owns the shares, you're not required to report. I'm sure Laurence could advise you.'

'Naturally I always value his counsel. But I wouldn't want any leaks from any other source.'

'I'll handle the matter personally, Mac. No need to worry there. But I must stress the responsibility to report is yours.'

'And I'll stick to the letter of the law, Max, you know that. Come on, let's join the girls before they get completely smashed.'

It was a night for intimate and productive conversations. Jack and Louise stood quietly in a corner on their own watching the passing parade. 'It's rather nice to be out, lover boy. Invitations have been rather thin on the ground lately.'

It was true, Jack thought. They used to sit together after dinner with their diaries open comparing dates, deciding where to go, where not to go. There was still a wad of corporate invitations to boxes for sporting events or nights at the opera, but few to the real society bashes. Louise hated business commitments, hated being invited by strangers who she knew had no interest in her, or Jack really, except to fill a space at a corporate table and try to grease their way into some HOA contract. A tall good-looking man in a beautifully cut dinner jacket approached.

'Good evening, Jack. And this must be Louise.' Jack shook hands. 'Darling, this is the Pope—I mean Clinton . . . ah, John, Normile.'

Louise raised her eyebrows. 'Good heavens, Mr Normile, you are a man of many names. Are they aliases, do you change them by days of the week, or were your parents just a little confused?'

'I think it's Jack who's confused. John is fine and it's a great pleasure to meet you.'

She liked him immediately. The room seemed full of people with angles, with Janus faces and cubist poses like the shapes projected on the walls. This man stood straight and square, looked her in the eyes when he talked, not away to see what he was missing somewhere else, and his smile was distributed evenly across the mouth, unlike the lopsided smile of sarcasm or contempt. Jack was called away by a beefy, red-faced business type, leaving Louise and the Pope together.

'I understand you've been a great help to my husband.'

'Not yet, I'm afraid, but we're hoping to be.'

'Who's we, Mr Normile?'

'Just some friends. We're trying to keep it all low key and anonymous.'

She looked at him with her direct, uncompromising stare. 'You need to understand we work as a team when the chips are down. Sometimes I step forward if he steps back, you understand?'

He held her gaze and, without realising it, reached out one hand to also hold her arm, as if to steady her. 'I do.'

'Then there might come a time when you or someone else will need to call me. And I'll need to know everything. Play your Boys' Own games in the meanwhile, but not when the time comes.'

They could see Jack returning to them and the Pope released her arm gently and moved away. She watched his tall spare figure weave its way through the crowd with a nod here, a wave there, as Jack reached her side. 'He's a good man to have on your side.'

Louise smiled. 'Yes. When this is all over, I'd love to have dinner with him and his wife. Does he have a wife?'

'I think so. At least he had one. He's always been a bit of a mystery. And in the group we don't really talk about our personal lives.'

They moved from their corner into the melee, arm in arm. As they reached the centre of the throbbing mass, the unusually excited voice of Archie Speyne could just be heard over the hubbub. 'Ladies and gentlemen. Friends. Ladies and gentlemen.'

It was to no avail. Silencing this crowd, fuelled with adrenalin cocktails, would require more than Archie's entrails. A cell phone rang in someone's pocket. Then another, and another, and within a few seconds scores of tones and tinny music grabs and feeble fake bells were bleating all over the room. People began to laugh and fumble to switch off the offending gadgets, but the number added to the cacophony outgrew the few that were stilled, and as conversation ceased and at last subsided the buzz of the electronic locusts grew louder. A spotlight now framed Archie and the small round podium he was standing on rose a couple of metres higher. Suddenly, a massive amplified bell tolled and, as it did so, all the cell phones stopped their buzzing simultaneously. There was silence for a moment, and then scattered applause.

'Who said you can't silence an art crowd?' Archie waited for more applause and laughter and, unusually, it came. 'Are we going to ruin this night with speeches and auctions and other boring function features? We are not. This is not a function. This is a happening. This is the Biddulph Gallery.'

As the last words rang out in Archie's most dramatic tones, he disappeared into blackness. The spotlight and every other light in the space was extinguished. There was complete darkness for a few seconds and only the weird music swirled louder and louder around the bodies packed together in their designer gowns and La Perla underwear. Lasered shapes reappeared on the walls, merging and drifting apart and then, unexpectedly, coalescing into the image vaguely recalled from the invitation. The crowd could feel rather than see the wisps of smoke thickening around them as the music morphed into more natural sounds, birds perhaps, or the wild calls of some unknown beast, or running water, or was that a roar or the snarl of a predator close by, in the room almost, disturbing, almost frightening, and yet amusing, because this was a party.

A shaft of light strobed into a section of the gallery where, strangely, there appeared to be no people. A shape moved into the flickering light, a human shape, a female shape surely, almost feline in its careful stepping, but difficult to decipher in the gloom. There was something in its hand, a rope, a lead of some kind, yes it was leading something, an animal perhaps was slinking in behind. My God what was it—now, you could see it, see the great black stripes, see the eyes, almost the whiskers, some said later they saw the whiskers, but it was there, the tiger, there was no doubt. There were gasps, squeals, nervous laughter, no screams, yet, but they were coming, they were building—and then a second of complete blackness followed by a blinding light. The dresses and dinner jackets almost stumbled into one another for a moment as dazzled eyes tried to refocus. There was no woman, there was no tiger. Just dresses and dinner jackets. But there had been, hadn't there? They'd all seen it—or had they? Applause and laughter and chatter broke out around the room and slowly they began to focus on the small but brilliantly illuminated painting in the middle of the main wall. It was only about a metre square but it was unmistakably *The Tiger* by Franz Marc.

Mac was as stunned by it all as anyone, maybe more so.

People were wandering by almost shyly, as if he were holding court, saying 'How amazing', 'Congratulations, great party', 'No one else could do it', and he was nodding modestly, not speaking, just letting the parade of supplicants pass by. He felt a hand on his shoulder and turned to find the Prime Minister of Australia standing beside his knight of the oblong table, Sir Laurence Treadmore.

'Great night, Mac. Wonderful gesture of yours. We need more of this sort of thing. Philanthropy, I mean, not parties—although a few more like this wouldn't go astray. Beats rubber chicken at the bowling club, which is what I usually get.'

The scent of power and success, of perfumed women, of the perfect white gardenia on Sir Laurence's black silk lapel, the musk of rising sap—it was a heady potion Mac knew well, usually used to his advantage, but tonight he was reeling from its effect just a degree or two. He was about to click into gear with a witty response to the Prime Minister who, although he'd never had a real job, had risen effortlessly through the political arm of the labour movement and then into local government, state parliament, and on to his present comfortable seat, who was a crass idiot in Mac's view, a hostage of the unions, committed to taking from hard-working successful people and giving to layabouts who'd never worked a day in their lives, but was nevertheless the Prime Minister. Before Mac could fashion his witticism, the crass idiot spoke again.

'Was that really a tiger? Might get me in terrible trouble with the animal liberationists or women against fur coats or something if it was.'

The Prime Minister peered down at Mac, smiling, but not so much. He was a tall, handsome man, especially in his own opinion, with a dense shot of crinkled black hair that gleamed unnaturally in the harsh lights.

Mac stammered a response. 'I'm honestly not sure. It's not really my party. I mean it is, but I didn't organise it. Well not all of it—not that bit.' How to take credit for the great night without accepting responsibility for any difficulties had Mac's stick cleft very deeply. 'Laurence did some of it. He might know.'

Sir Laurence dodged this pass as neatly as if it had never been thrown. 'Mysteries of the night. I'm sure no one will ever know the answers. Everyone here will be much more interested in your new foreign investment policy, Prime Minister.'

There was, in fact, no one in the gallery who was even vaguely interested in such a policy at this moment, other than the Prime Minister, who was always fascinated by his own pronouncements and assumed a similar reaction from other citizens, and Sir Laurence, who never raised any issue without a clear purpose. It was, he believed, discourteous to do so. Mac knew he should be interested, but was still struggling to remember why as the Prime Minister spoke again.

'Yes. Could strengthen our hand enormously. Financial markets don't like it so much, but how many votes do they control? What do you think, Mac? Good for the insurance industry?'

It was coming, the cogs were turning and clicking, he just had to stall for a moment and it would be there, Mac knew it. The answers always came, it just took a few seconds longer these days.

'Mac's probably too polite to say it, Prime Minister, but it has always seemed unfair that some of our leading competitors, being foreign companies, do not have to comply with all the regulations we do.' Sir Laurence turned to Mac as the novice turns to the guru.

'Well, that's true. I'm not one to complain. We're happy to take on anyone. Certainly not afraid of fair competition. And happy to comply with all the regulations the government thinks are necessary to protect people. After all, that's what we do in insurance, isn't it. Protect people.' They all nodded wisely. 'But everyone should be subject to the same rules. You know, a fair go. That's Australia.' Mac wondered fleetingly if he had gone too far with the 'That's Australia', but he'd forgotten he was talking to a politician.

'Absolutely. We all want the old cliché, the level playing field. I like old clichés, actually. People understand them. So Mac, why don't you get your people to put something together and send it to my chief of staff. We don't want our honest citizens at the mercy of foreign pirates, do we?' A wink accompanied this remark and then, immediately at its disappearance, a frown. 'Private remark, not to be repeated. I must go and do my duty, the only opening I've ever done where I don't have to make a speech. Just pull a lever or something apparently. Good to see you, Mac, Laurence. Keep up the good work.'

As he strode off into the crowd with his minders trailing, Mac and Sir Laurence watched thoughtfully, respectfully, determined to indeed keep up the good work, whatever that might be. Finally, Mac turned to his chairman. 'Laurence, I have to thank you. You've absolutely excelled yourself. I've never seen anything like this. I don't think anyone in Sydney has. It'll be talked about for years. How did you do it?'

Sir Laurence was beaming, although low beam was the height of his illumination. 'Thank you, Mac. I'm delighted you're enjoying it, but I assure you there's a great deal more to come. I, of course, am merely the facilitator. I'll introduce you to the woman who organised most of it later. I think you might have met her once before.'

Sir Laurence wandered away as Mac was claimed by more admirers and there, champagne flute in hand, eyes glassed over (but not, tonight, by the champagne, more by the wonder of what she'd created), was the very woman he'd been referring to.

'Popsie, my dear woman, what a triumph. You'll be famous once it leaks out, as these things inevitably do, that you had a hand in organising this.'

There was no chance of it leaking out that she had 'had a hand' in organising the party as Popsie Trudeaux knew very well, since she'd already informed everyone that she'd talked to, which was a great number of people, some of whom had turned out to be waiters, and one of whom was obviously the Prime Minister's security man since he was wearing an earpiece and couldn't hear her, although she was talking very loudly into his other ear, that she was the sole driving force behind every single facet of this mind-blowing, once-in-a-lifetime event.

'I'm just so grateful to you, Laurence, for asking me to do it. I mean, I've only ever done my own parties, and not one of those for a while, so you were very brave to give me the job. I knew I could blow them all away, but how did you know?'

The thin mouth curled delicately. 'You just trust people. Pick the right person and trust them.'

'I don't know how I can ever repay you. It's been such an exciting experience.'

'Dear lady, you don't have to repay me. And besides, I think your experience is just starting. Everyone's going to want you and only you to do their parties after this. You could build a real business. If you want to, of course. I realise money isn't relevant, but I can see you might enjoy the challenge.'

Popsie thought she might. She was almost certain she would. Archie Speyne had already offered her a contract for all the museum's functions, and one of the Prime Minister's people, not the one with the earpiece, had asked for her card. Laurence was right, they'd all want her. Oh, to be wanted, and to be paid for it.

'I'm terribly grateful, Laurence. I promise I won't forget it.'

'Please, my dear, we all help one another where we can. Now I'm sure you have more surprises in store for us all, so I shall just drift away.'

And drift away he did. Popsie followed his path, wondering. Why had he taken a risk on her? He'd always been distant with her before, polite but distant. And then this solid gold gift. Who cared? She'd made it her own and now she could fuck the whole town anytime she wanted.

Maroubra peered nervously through the shrubbery at the Botanic Gardens. He didn't like gardens, their neatness, their artificiality, their suggestion of rules, of places to walk and places not. He liked the bush, where tracks appeared because animals had found a path to water or because the ground fell evenly for padded feet. The only cut grass should be on ovals where rugby or cricket were played, where rules were necessary so crafty people could break them with a cuff to the ear or an elbow on the stomach. But no eye gouging or biting. And definitely no fingers in orifices where they didn't belong, like that disgusting rugby league oaf had done a few years ago. Many disgusting oafs played rugby league, whereas gentlemen, like Maroubra and his son Gordie and various other men of character, only played rugby union. Somehow he felt the eyes on the back of his neck and he turned with a start to find the Pope a metre away.

'I fucking told you none of that Mafioso crap with your fucking lowlife mates. I told you everything had to be clean, kosher. Again and again. How many fucking times do I have to tell you?'

The Pope threw a newspaper down on the park bench, but Maroubra didn't look at it. He'd never heard the Pope swear before. He always spoke directly, definitely, and never with a vocabulary that was anything but specific and spare.

'It wasn't us, I swear to God. I heard it on the radio just before I got your text. None of my people were in it. No way.'

The Pope remained in attack mode. 'Coincidences aren't my thing. Here we are searching around for stuff on Mac Biddulph, very specific stuff that's not in the average file drawer, here you have a brief from me to get it, then someone breaks into the Biddulph home while he's at the party of the year and it's not you?' Maroubra returned the angry stare in kind. 'Okay. I'll accept you didn't order it, but obviously one of your people got overzealous. Who the hell are they all, anyway?'

'You don't want to know. And no one got excited. I checked the lot on the way here. We're not involved. One hundred per cent.'

The Pope searched his face, nodded slowly and held out his hand. 'I'm sorry. Shouldn't have doubted you, but—Christ, what does it mean?'

Maroubra shook the hand. 'No problem, mate. When I heard it this morning, I thought the same thing—someone's jumped the fence.'

They sat together and read through the newspaper story. On the front page was a large photo of Mac and the Prime Minister accompanied by a gushing story on the party that had run in all the editions—only this late edition had a small box on the break-in. According to the scant details, nothing appeared to have been taken.

'That's why I thought it was you.' The Pope folded the paper. 'When it said there was no real burglary.'

'There was; they took a computer and a printer, but left the more valuable stuff lying around everywhere.'

'How do you know that?'

'Friends. You don't want to know. But it definitely wasn't anything other than pros looking for the same sort of stuff we'd be after.'

They stared out at the harbour for a while.

'But we're supposed to be the only ones looking. We're running the game. Mac's our target. Who the hell else is out there?'

Maroubra shrugged. 'How can I know? You tell me the parts you want to tell me. I don't know where they fit in the jigsaw and I don't want to.'

The Pope closed his eyes, tried to see the patterns in the red-black. He was a chess player, he could see patterns before they formed. He could see where the pieces would rest before they arrived at their destinations, the positions people would take before they realised themselves. It was the skill of his life—not just of his business success, but his whole life. When he was a young boy, nine or ten, the chessboard had become a defining world of challenge, of fascination, of intellectual stimulation and, not unimportantly, of conquest. He learned from his grandfather. They would work together in the terraced vegetable garden that sustained the old man in his declining years, not with vitamins and minerals, but with the nourishment of usefulness. His grandfather would weed and prune and mound the soil, and he would follow with a hessian bag full of dead leaves and cuttings and the flat cane basket for the picked crop. When the basket was full and they were sitting together with ginger beer gazing contentedly at the neatly balanced pile of carrots and leeks and crisp pea pods, the gnarled old hand would hug his shoulder and the voice he loved would say, 'Keep the wolf from the door, hey?'

It was only three years before he could win the chess contest some times and then most times, and then, because he could see the patterns of life, not just those on the board, deliberately lose enough to sustain the other's dignity. Someday, maybe, his grandson would humour him this way, or some other and he wouldn't know, the brain cells or the synapses or whatever wouldn't register the subtler tones of life anymore.

But not now, surely. And yet there was no emerging pattern in this dilemma. What unseen hand was at work in the puppet show of which he was the supposed master? A break-in at Mac Biddulph's, a stolen computer? There was another predator in the hunt, a grey shadow running fence lines, skirting waterholes, hiding in hollows and rock piles, taking small prey, waiting for something more. He had to flush it out. Apply pressure, beat the bush. He opened his eyes and was surprised to see Maroubra still sitting quietly beside him.

'It's not all bad news. I've got something for you.' Maroubra handed him a fat envelope. 'I don't know exactly what it means but there's a lot in there on the Beira Company and a flow of transactions to a Swiss bank. No doubt you'll work it all out.'

The Pope took the envelope. 'Thanks. But I'm not sure I will. I think it's time we got some fresh minds on this. I don't like the feeling I'm about to lose a game before it's started.'

chapter ten

They sat in a panelled room with paintings jumbled onto the walls in the Victorian fashion. A landscape of dubious origin was resting askew above a self-portrait by one of Australia's leading artists, which was in turn dwarfed by a nautical scene of two ships of the line, apparently about to open fire—whether on the landscape or the portrait was unclear. In all, the small dark room was generously adorned with over twenty pictures arranged, if that was the appropriate word, from eye level to ceiling with disdain for the neat and orderly ways of art galleries and, some would say, for the artists.

In truth, the committee of the Colonial Club had disdain for the ways of a great many people, mainly those who were not members of the Colonial Club. It was likely that they would have evidenced these feelings for all but one of this group gathered in the members' reading room, had they known of their presence, but the room was booked in the name of one of the most respected of their number. Nothing more was required, except appropriate dress. And, of course, appropriate sex—females, however attired, were not permitted on the third floor.

There were only four figures huddled in the gloom, leaning forward intently as their leader, nearly invisible in a charcoal suit, only the extreme whiteness of the shirt directing the sparse light onto a shadowed face, addressed them in hushed tones. The other three had been amazed when the venue for the meeting was nominated. The last place any of them expected the Pope to be familiar with, let alone a member of, was the Colonial Club. But the aforementioned committee was well aware that the name Normile had been entered in its books for three generations and that present member Clinton had served the club in many distinguished, if not publicly recognised, ways. A great deal more than the members' reading room was available on his request.

'So there you have it. We're chasing down alleys trying to pin Mac Biddulph's colours to the wall and someone else is there before us. I can't make sense of it, so I'm hoping better brains can see the angles.'

Murray Ingham spoke in his brusque manner. 'We're going to need more. It's a puzzle where you can't see the pieces so there's no chance to fit them together. No facts, no story.'

The Pope nodded. 'Fair enough. You ask me the questions and I'll answer them as best I can. Maroubra can also fill in a few gaps.'

Tom Smiley's voice seemed to boom out into the quiet room as he drew his chair forward and loosened his tie. 'Are you allowed to take your jacket off in this mausoleum or do they behead you at dawn with a cavalry sabre?' Tom dropped his suit jacket onto the floor as he spoke. 'Let me put a few questions on two issues: first, the information we've gathered thus far that might implicate Mac Biddulph in wrongdoing, and second, on the facts of the robbery itself—yes?'

The Pope gestured assent and the relentless questioning of Thomas Smiley QC commenced its seemingly meandering, purposeless course, like a river twisting through deep gorges, shallow turns, silent valleys, until it straightened its line.

'So. It seems we have a clutch of theories supported by minimal documentation. The theories fall into three broad categories. First, Mac Biddulph is draining off HOA funds to pay for personal expenses through a company called Beira Proprietary Limited which, you surmise, but cannot yet prove, is controlled by the said Mr Biddulph. Second, and more damning if proven, it is suggested that the accounts of HOA are being falsified or manipulated by the use of financial reinsurance contracts with no actual transfer of risk in order to artificially boost profits. Third, it is suggested that other directors and executives may be complicit in these alleged activities. Is that a fair summary?'

Again the Pope nodded.

'May I ask if some legal mind other than my own is applying itself to the analysis of whatever you have gathered.'

The Pope responded quickly. 'There is someone, but I'd rather not say who, if you don't mind.'

Tom Smiley held his gaze. 'I do mind. When people start breaking into houses, a line is crossed. Our friend the Judge has already excused himself from any further involvement in this matter and I'm giving serious thought to similar action. We'd all like to help Jack Beaumont, but I want to know who's running this show and how it's being run.'

The Pope looked down at the dark oak table and then up again at Tom Smiley. 'Hedley Stimson.'

There was an intake of breath from the lawyer. 'Well. And well again. How in God's name did you bring him out of retirement? Is he planning to appear in court, if it comes to that?'

Murray Ingham broke in. 'For those of us who don't spend their waking hours immersed in legal gossip, a little background would help. Who is this new character in the saga?'

The Pope gestured to Tom Smiley to respond.

'Let me put it this way: if I was representing a client in court tomorrow, the only barrister I wouldn't want to see acting for the other side would be Hedley Stimson. If that remark is ever repeated, I'll deny it.' He paused. 'At least we know any improper behaviour hasn't been intentional.' He turned to Maroubra. 'But has it been accidental?'

Maroubra shook his head. 'No. We've been using our sources, but all above board. We had absolutely no involvement in the break-in at Mac Biddulph's house.'

Tom Smiley nodded. 'Okay. I'm greatly reassured by both those responses. And that brings us to the break-in. Nothing was taken, I gather.'

Maroubra responded. 'A computer and a printer.'

Murray Ingham's gruff voice cut in again. 'That's not what the papers said.'

Maroubra smiled. 'The papers are wrong. A computer and a printer.'

Murray persisted. 'How do you know that?'

It was the Pope who answered. 'I think this is an area where we just have to accept the information we're given as accurate without identifying sources. I do.'

There was a brief silence before Tom Smiley continued. 'Has there ever been a break-in at these premises before?' He was now directing the questions at Maroubra.

'No.'

'How was entry effected?'

'A window was unlocked.'

'So no force was required?'

'No.'

'Surely the premises were electronically secured?'

'Switched off. Never used. I guess they figured there'd be no problem with insurance.'

'Servants?'

'There's only one live-in. The others come in daily. She was given the night off. Mac and his wife were at the museum party.'

'Ah, yes. The party. So the thief presumably picked this night because of the publicity surrounding the party?'

'Probably. Although I think most of the publicity came afterwards.'

'And I assume there were many more valuables lying about for the taking?'

'Everything you can imagine and a lot of things you can't. Jewellery by the handful, huge amounts of cash, every electronic gadget known to man, artworks—you name it.'

'So, hence our dilemma. Someone is searching for the same information we are.'

The Pope spoke. 'Exactly. If we can figure out who that is, who the thief is, I believe we'd fit in a crucial piece of this puzzle.'

'Nonsense.' It was Murray Ingham. 'You don't read enough novels, that's the problem with all you logical analysts. Follow the story. Watch the characters. There is no thief. There is no coincidence. Party, no one at home, no alarm, unlocked window. The one person who couldn't have stolen the stuff because everyone in the world knew where he was—at the party of the year—was Mac Biddulph. And he's the one person who did. If anyone comes asking for records—regulators, lawyers, courts—he doesn't have them. Gone. Stolen. Disappeared in a puff of wind through an open window. Neat as you like, on the record, certified by the police, incident number, and so on. And he probably makes a claim for a new computer. But you won't find much on that, other than golf games and a letter to his dead mother.'

They all stared at Murray. Finally Maroubra spoke. 'It makes sense. Those documents I handed over, he knows someone made a copy of them. There was no way we could avoid that and obtain them legitimately. So he decides to clear the decks. I buy it.'

Tom Smiley shook his head. 'I'm not so sure. It's all sounding too cloak and dagger for me. Surely someone with Mac Biddulph's resources would come up with a more sophisticated plan than a fake burglary if he wanted to destroy documents.'

'People don't.' Murray's thick brows appeared to be pushed up onto his head like an unwanted pair of spectacles. 'People don't do "sophisticated" things in these situations. They look for simple, quick solutions. When we're threatened, we panic. Doesn't matter who we are. The panic is the autonomic nervous system dealing with the threat, pumping some adrenalin, letting the animal take over from the logical. Mac Biddulph junked the computer. Forget about the spectre of other people ghosting our man. They're just that—ghosts.'

The Pope pushed his chair back from the table. 'He's right. I don't know why I couldn't see it. Must be losing my touch. God that's a relief. This matter is complicated enough without another hunter in the forest.'

They poured coffee from the silver urn on the ornate sideboard and munched thoughtfully, and with some difficulty, on the club's famous Anzac biscuits. Exactly why these rock-like discs were famous was unclear, but one member had been known to comment: 'Few survived the battle, none will survive the biscuits.'

Tom Smiley drew the Pope to one side. 'What does

Hedley Stimson say about the evidence you've gathered thus far? Where are we heading?'

'I don't know. I don't speak to him; only Jack does, and never at his office.'

Tom rubbed his chin. 'This is as odd a situation as I've ever been in. I can't see that we're breaching any ethical codes at the moment, so I'll hang in there for the time being. Let's just say I'll keep a watching brief.'

'I understand. It's complex and dangerous—mainly for Jack, I think. His whole life's at risk and I'm not sure he understands that yet.'

They departed one by one with thoughtful faces and aching jaws, leaving the Pope alone in the panelled tomb. He sat at a small games table by the only window and began to arrange the chess pieces. He remained staring at the board for a long time, moving nothing, and then rose quickly and strode from the room.

It was black as a mine shaft when Jack gingerly picked his way through the gate from the leafy cavern of the liquidambers. The few street lights that hadn't been pinged into darkness by the accurate stone throwing of private schoolboys in straw boaters were shrouded in dense foliage, and the moon had given up and gone home.

He never left the old lawyer's house on a Sunday night without conflicting emotions. This time the evening had started with a lecture on the wizardry of the foot pedal that operated the lathe so that both massive hands were available to nurse the wood as the shavings flew and shapes were revealed. It was explained to him, in more detail than he needed to know, that, of course, commercial models of this nature were available for those who had neither the wit nor application to invent their own, but they were crass and insensitive devices that no true artist would consider. Hence the extraordinary contraption that lay like some primeval growth beneath the workbench, constructed, he was told, with pride from old locomotive parts from the Everleigh railway yards. He was made to sit on the tall stool, a product of this very workshop, and operate the pedal in order to experience the hair-trigger nature of the beast. It was true, the lightest touch with his foot caused the high-pitched scream of the lathe to burst forth, but for Jack, the result was more frightening than impressive.

They'd met a dozen times now, and gradually the crusty surface of old Hedley had cracked like crisp pastry and Jack had glimpsed more and more of the complex mixture beneath.

Hedley stood at the workbench like 'an old stone savage armed', as Robert Frost described the neighbour in the only poem Jack could ever quote from memory. He looked like the picture of Robert Frost on the dust cover of Jack's copy of *Collected Poems*, and seemed to Jack to speak with the voice of a prophet, not a lawyer.

'Anyone can work a machine, son, anyone can follow a pattern, but only the chosen can see the shapes in the wood before they're revealed and release them into life. Would you like to try now? I can set this piece for you; it's beautiful mahogany but only an offcut, you can't do any harm. Sit here. Take the master's chair.' He felt the strong hands holding his shoulders and guiding him onto the stool. As much as he hated the machine, he wanted to try for the man.

Later, when they sat with tea and documents, only the sounds of the pages turning and the scratch of the thick pencil interrupting the Sunday peace, Jack waited for the leonine head to lift and the judgement to be delivered.

After some weeks of his material being dismissed as inadequate, he was hoping for approval.

'Hmm. This is good stuff. We nearly have him on breach of director's duties and related party transactions. We can't prove he controls Beira, but the authorities, even with their limited intelligence, could track that down relatively easily. But on the big one, falsification of accounts, we're still lost in the jungle. I'm going to write a list of questions for you, and you need to put them to that chief financial officer, Renton Healey—in person and without warning. Just turn up in his office when you know he's there, put the questions to him and demand the relevant documents on the spot. Don't leave without them. And take a witness, someone you can trust.'

Jack nodded doubtfully. 'He's as slippery as they come. He'll try to put me off, say he doesn't have them—anything. And who's this witness? There isn't anyone inside the company I can trust, and he'll clam up completely if I turn up with an outsider.'

The old lawyer shrugged. 'You figure it out, son. You're the genius running the biggest insurance company in the universe. Get on with it. The document I want has to be there. It's an addendum, a side letter, an email, something attached to this reinsurance contract that effectively removes any transfer of risk. So it makes it just a piece of financial manipulation, in order to artificially boost the profits. And no doubt the share price. Find it and I'll nail these bastards.'

They talked of other things for a while—sport and books and what made men great and what diminished them. Finally Jack said, 'How can these people live with themselves when they do these things? It can't just be about the money. Mac's a wealthy man, Renton Healey is paid a fortune. How can they look at themselves and know they're stealing people's money and breaking the law?'

'They never think that. People like this never break the law—in their minds. It's a stupid law, or it doesn't apply to them or there's another reading of it—or any other rationalisation you can think of. Everyone does this sort of thing, it's not just me. It's like insider trading in the share market. We all do it, all of us big businessmen. We built the companies, we're entitled to the spoils. All those poor dumb shareholders sitting at home shrouded in cardigans and ignorance can pick up the crumbs we leave, if they're lucky. If they want to play with the big boys, they can't cry foul if they get hammered.'

He rose and walked to the workbench and took the piece of wood from the lathe. 'They remove themselves from reality. They look down on the world from the sixtieth floor of an office building or some hotel where a two-hundred-dollar meal has just been delivered and maybe the thousand-dollar hooker will arrive in an hour, and all the suckers in the street below look like prey that's there for the taking. It's not immorality, it's amorality, which is much more dangerous because there's no gate into the garden. No opening where you can say, "That's the wrong path, this is the way through the trees into the paddock." They lose touch with families, with kids, with old people falling down and struggling with their memories, with splitting logs, lighting fires, cleaning shoes, with cooking their own food or cleaning up for the one who did, with dogs or horses or whatever pets they had when they were kids, with life. Their world is all slick and shiny and easy, it's deals and limousines and boats called ships, and whatever is good for them is good.'

Hedley paused. 'You hadn't expected this, had you, son? Someone taught you we're all fine citizens in the end?' The younger man nodded. 'Who was that?'

'I'm not sure. Strangely, probably my mother—and certainly my wife.'

'Ah, yes. The women who see beyond the competition.' They sat together quietly, while the leaves of the birches rustled on the windows above the workbench. 'It's going to get difficult very soon, I'm afraid. You need to know that, son. We're almost at the point where we have to take our material to the authorities. Some would say we're there already. Certainly if we find that side letter, you'll have to inform the Australian Securities and Investments Commission. Then all hell breaks loose. Are you ready for it?'

Jack stood and held out his hand, smiling, and then walked into the night. As he was heading out the gate he tripped and almost fell on a dead branch, and was shaking and collecting himself when the soft voice came and a hand touched his arm. He turned with a start and nearly tripped again, on the gutter. He could barely make out the figure in the dark, but it was a woman's voice and shape.

'I'm so sorry to startle you, Mr Beaumont.' The use of his name and the softness of the voice was reassuring, but he was nonetheless unsettled by being recognised in a lonely street while leaving a supposedly clandestine meeting.

'I'm Marjorie, Hedley's wife. He's never wanted us to meet, and I'm not supposed to know you come to the house. But I'm not entirely lost to the world of bowls and books. I need to speak to you. Is that all right?'

Jack could see her more clearly now as a shaft of light filtered through the canopy and struck her head. It was a lined, sad face capped with a halo of dense hair, permed in a way he remembered from his youth. But behind her glasses, sharp, intelligent eyes were anxiously awaiting his response. 'Of course. I wasn't expecting anyone out here and you used my name. Perhaps we should talk in the car, it's just around the corner.'

He led her gently to the car, opened the door for her, and held her arm as she lowered herself, painfully it seemed, into the soft leather. Somehow he immediately felt protective of her. She even smelled like his mother in the intimate interior of the sports car.

'What a lovely car.' She laughed nervously at her own remark. 'What a stupid thing to say. You don't want to hear me talk about your car at this time of night. Or any time, I suppose.' She looked around wistfully. 'It is lovely, though.' Her hand stroked the leather and then pulled away quickly as if she might damage it. 'I shouldn't be here at all. He'd be furious if he knew. But even he needs looking after. And I'm the only one. Everybody else just wants something from him, even though they pretend otherwise.' She looked at Jack. 'But he likes you, really likes you. I know, even though I'm not supposed to know anything.'

Jack reached across the gearstick and held her wrist gently for a second or two before drawing his hand away. 'Please tell me why you want to talk to me.' Then he added, 'I really like him, too. He's a great man.'

Her half-stifled, nervous laugh came again. 'Yes. He is. Most people don't realise that. They think he's clever and knowledgeable, but they don't see the breadth and the depth.' She paused. 'But he's also frail. Very frail. That's another thing you can't see. He looks and talks strength and power, but it's all show. He's a weak, frail old man and this thing he's doing for you is going to kill him. You mustn't let him go back into the courtroom.

He's planning to, I know he is. It's all running through his body again like it used to. The doctors said it would kill him if he continued, and they're right for once.'

The words had been rushing out as if she wanted to be rid of them, to expel them before they contaminated her body, but now she stopped for a moment and looked straight at Jack, almost challenging him. 'I wanted you to know.'

Jack saw her mouth quiver as the words struck him and he reached out to hold her hand firmly, and to keep holding it. 'I'm not sure I understand, Mrs Stimson. Is he ill? I thought he gave up appearing in court because he was bored with it.'

She withdrew her hand and sat, drawn inwards now, with arms folded tightly as if to warm herself. 'That's what everyone's meant to think. But it's his heart. They say it's hereditary, or that diet or exercise or fish oil or some such will fix it. But it can't be mended. It's split in half by something that happened a long time ago. Instead of healing, the split's just widening.'

Jack felt he was struggling for air in the enclosed space and he lowered his window a crack. 'He told me about your son.'

He could see she was shocked as her head jerked up from the floor and she grasped the door handle. 'Did he? He never talks about it to anyone, not even me. I sit with my quilts, he sits with his wood. We lie awake in the night, but we don't talk. It's not how we started. He's very funny, you know, when he wants to be; he could always make me laugh. But he doesn't want to anymore.'

They sat, not talking, looking straight ahead as the mist of their breath gradually cleared from the windscreen. Finally Jack spoke. 'I'm not sure what you want of me. He seems completely wrapped up in pursuing these matters.

I think he's more committed to nailing the hides of any wrongdoers on the courthouse door than I am. I don't know if I could stop him, even if I wanted to.' And then he turned to her. 'To be honest, I'm not sure I want to.'

She smiled resignedly, a smile of knowing defeat, a practised smile. 'I know. It's stupid of me. I'm a silly old woman. I shouldn't have spoken.' But then she added determinedly, 'If someone else could handle the court work. He gets very emotional in court. No one knows. It's all inside—and that's where the damage is.'

She opened the car door and Jack hurried around to help her out. 'I'll take you back to the house.'

She shook her head. 'No, I'm fine. I'll just say I went for a walk. I do that often. Thank you.' She had already turned to go when she spoke again, softly. 'You must be a fine man, Mr Beaumont. Good luck.'

He watched as she disappeared into the shadows. She seemed incredibly brave to him, as if to venture into a suburban street outside her own home on a quiet Sunday night required courage. Yet he knew that surviving the life she was reduced to required endurance he mightn't have.

He waited until she must have reached the house and then drove slowly past. There were no lights in the studio and only one lighted, curtained window in the main house. Were they talking as they prepared for bed? Was he already lying there, reading? Did he ask, politely, 'Did you have a pleasant walk?' Did she reply, politely, 'Yes, thank you.' Would they lie awake, not speaking, in the dark, each listening to the breathing of the other?

chapter eleven

The *Honey Bear* lay at anchor where no boat was supposed to be anchored. Immediately off the bow was the impressive sweep of the Woolloomooloo Wharf, the world's longest wharf building, once a great wooden structure where the trade ships disgorged their cargo, now a great wooden structure where tourists and arrivistes engorged themselves. Above the restaurants lining the quay, apartment dwellers peered out at the diners below or at the aging remnants of the Royal Australian Navy on the east side. At the harbour end of the old building, a lump of concrete had been moulded into the approximate profile of the wharf and here, in apartments large enough for the *Honey Bear* to undergo its annual refit, celebrities of one kind or another—namely, persons who had spent the large part of their lives endeavouring to be known—crouched behind elaborate security measures pretending they wished to be known no longer.

It was the presence of both these elements, the Australian Navy and the celebrities, that rendered the proximity of the *Honey Bear* illegal. Boats were not permitted to anchor within view of either. For the navy, security was said to be the issue. However unlikely it might seem that the *Honey Bear* would launch a broadside of any projectile other than champagne corks, the navy was taking no chances. As for the celebrities, while they sympathised with, and indeed encouraged, the propulsion of champagne corks, they preferred to gaze out at nothing, rather than other people's boats—particularly not other people's boats that were larger and costlier than their own. It was sufficient embarrassment that it was rumoured, while unproven, that one of their number owned no boat at all. The navy had already despatched a tender to order the intruder to retreat and had been informed that, as soon as repairs were made to an engine malfunction—something which should take no longer than a couple of hours—the boat would be on its way. The sailors so informed were well on their way to enjoying the fruits of a most friendly and profitable visit. And the celebrities were mildly pleased to see activity of any kind. It made a stimulating change from watching videos of old game shows in which they, and others they had known but risen above, once featured.

Mac sprawled on a teak lounge on the stern with a bloody mary on one side of his mainly bare torso and the great heaving mass of Harold Wilde on the other. As he watched the senator shovel handfuls of almond kernels into his gaping maw, he thought, 'He doesn't just represent all Australians, he eats for them.' But the words that eased forth from the mouth tingling with the spicy beverage were more appropriate.

'You love a bloody mary, Harold, don't you?'

'I do, Mac. I love a good bloody mary, and this is a great one.' Hardly one, thought Mac. It was the third towering glass to disappear into the cavern. One crunch of the celery stick, three swallows, a nod to the waiter watching from the door, and the fourth would be on the way before the ice had shed two degrees. Mac caught the waiter's eye and gestured with his head for him to absent himself. He had business to conduct before Harold slipped into a stupor, although he suspected a crate of vodka might be required to achieve that end.

'And you love a good feed, Harold, don't you? I like a bloke who loves a good feed.'

Harold Wilde gazed at Mac appreciatively. He couldn't see the waiter any longer, which was disturbing, but he was on the *Honey Bear*, where everything was available at all times, so he was relatively relaxed. Waiters needed to know their business, which was to bring sustenance to honest, hard-working citizens and then clean up afterwards, just as he tried to help people in his capacity. And indeed, sometimes, to clean up afterwards. But to have a host like Mac, who understood the basic needs of man, who was more than a hard-working citizen, a veritable towering colossus of business, and the arts apparently (something Harold hadn't known before), and a friend of the Prime Minister apparently (something Harold couldn't forgive himself for not having known)—well to have a man like this still able to appreciate the small things, like food and drink—it was a blessing for society.

'And Harold, I happen to know one of your favourite restaurants is right on that wharf in front of us. Am I right?'

A greedy smile crept over the flabby folds around the senator's various chins. 'Oh, it's true, Mac. I can't deny it. I do love the Capricorn. They are so welcoming to me and their food is so beautiful. And a wonderful cellar.'

It was true also that the owners of the Capricorn Ristorante were never so pleased as when Harold Wilde lowered his vast posterior into one of their leather chairs. It was certain that, over the next four hours, those dishes and wines that all restaurateurs pray will be ordered would be so ordered. Not that Harold ever paid a bill, at the Capricorn or anywhere else. A senator's pay was meagre and he had a family to feed. Not that he ate often with his family, affairs of state prevented it, but, metaphorically, the responsibility was onerous.

'So here's the menu, Harold. What'll you have?' The plasticine-like consistency of the skin enveloping most of Harold's features did not allow a great number of subtle expressions to shine forth, but surprise overcame these impediments. 'Are we going ashore, Mac? I thought we were dining aboard. Please don't incur any trouble on my account.'

Mac smiled. 'No trouble ever, Harold, to plan a pleasant evening for friends. We are dining aboard. The Capricorn awaits our order, our tender will be at the wharf as soon as we ring it through, it will be on board in three minutes and served by one of their own waiters. Take your time checking the specials while I get Bonny and the others into gear.'

When Mac returned from the saloon—where Bonny and friends, along with Maxwell Newsome and Shane O'Connell, were playing charades—he noticed an out-sized glass of white wine by Harold's side. Either the whale was capable of raising itself under its own power, which he doubted, or it had somehow sent a telepathic message to the waiter.

'So many delicacies, Mac. They have the truffles again. Marvellous, pungent little things, the Tasmanian ones. Some say not as good as the French. I say give me both and I'll let you know, hey?' A laugh of sorts shook the jelly mould under the white garment covering Harold's upper body. 'But they also have the local mussels. I love mussels. And mud crabs are in season. Oh, I love mud crabs.'

Mac interrupted before the entire menu was broadcast in a symphony of love. 'Yes, it's all great. But they're not quite ready for us to order.' Harold's face managed an attempt at crestfallen. 'Don't worry, it won't be long. There's something I want you to do for me.'

Reluctantly, Harold placed the menu where a lap would normally be and took up the wineglass, but its trajectory was interrupted.

'I want you to ask a question in parliament for me.' Asking questions in parliament was exactly what Harold Wilde did not do. Ever. They were bound to offend someone, even if it was only members of the Opposition, and intelligent senators were not in the business of offending. They were there to serve, even if it was only members of the Opposition.

'Of course, Mac. How can I be of assistance?' It was excellent wine; French, he thought. Perhaps a chablis. Very dry anyway. Lovely.

'It's a simple inquiry, Harold. I just want you to ask how the government's review of the application of Australian Prudential Standards to foreign insurance companies is progressing and how quickly the new rules will be introduced.'

Harold's small eyes narrowed, which meant they virtually disappeared into the folds of skin surrounding them. 'Is there such a review?'

'There is indeed.'

'I've not heard of it before.'

'Exactly. That's the point. We want people to know. People should know it's underway.'

Harold shifted again, but it was a half-hearted effort. 'Yes, of course. And will anyone be surprised to learn of it? I mean, is it known in the higher circles of government?'

'As high as you can go. Everyone wants it known before it gets too far down the track. But the government doesn't need to make a big deal of it and frighten off foreign investment. You see the point?'

Harold wasn't sure he did see the point, but nor could he see any means of escape which would still enable him to enjoy the comforts of the *Honey Bear*, the loss of which was too painful to contemplate. Particularly with the menu resting comfortably below. 'You don't think someone more distinguished than myself, Mac? I'm really not all that familiar with these matters.'

Mac beckoned the waiter to refill the glass. 'You're the man, Harold. I wouldn't trust anyone else. I'll send the exact wording to your office on Monday, and I'd like you to do it first up when the Senate resumes on Tuesday. Now let's get that order in.'

When the guests had been despatched, or slurped in Harold's case, into a fleet of chauffeured cars, and the *Honey Bear* had slipped away to the quiet bay off Clifton Gardens on the harbour's north shore, Mac lay beside the perfect contours and mounds of a fragrant Bonny, listening to the even, relaxed breathing of a fit, young body full of grilled vegetables and peach juice. His body was full of a very different brew of gnocchi with four cheeses and spatchcock with bacon and a chocolate slab that seemed to be made of pure cocoa and was now swimming for its life in a sea of chablis and shiraz. Topped with a little cognac. He felt terrible. Inside and out. That was the disturbing part. He wasn't exercising anymore. There was no punching at Bonny or skipping in the park—or anything much. Ever since she hadn't been invited to the party of the year, privileges had been withdrawn. It was the old 'power of the pussy' trick. Well it wasn't going to work on him. He'd ride it out until she relented. Still, he wasn't riding at all at the moment and no one was coming anytime soon. And he was developing those handfuls of flab at the extremities of the waist that ordinary mortals of his age carried around. It was distressing. He wasn't an ordinary mortal.

The real problem was, however, the banks didn't seem to understand that. Ever since the HOA share price had tumbled, now an unpleasant memory long in the past, they'd been asking impertinent questions. Just because it had seemed for a while that a margin call might require speedy liquidation of a few of Mac's assets, they were now poking around trying to get a fix on precisely what those assets were, and where they were. It was unprecedented, unnecessary, impertinent. They'd virtually thrown the money at him in the first place, fallen all over themselves to grab the biggest slice of debt, never asked for any security except the HOA shares, lunched and massaged and arse-licked their greasy noses into the Big Mac pie, and now they wanted to cover themselves. It had been the presidents and the chairmen and the CEOs who'd been swanning around in the selling stage. Now, suddenly, he'd been called to a meeting of the syndicate—they'd formed a fucking syndicate, for Christ's sake—and he'd had to sit in some nondescript building in a crappy little room with no view and one window and answer questions asked by a bunch of schoolboys. Fucking children they were, asking him, Mac Biddulph, Big Mac, what he owned and owed. And the coffee, if you could call it that, was served in a paper cup. A paper fucking cup, for Christ's sake.

Still. The problem was that even though none of them had reached puberty, or if they had their voices were never going to break because their tiny balls had disappeared up their tiny arses, despite this and their synthetic shirts and cheap ties with fake symbols, the questions were very specific. The questions were grown-up. Someone else had obviously written the questions and handed these little shits a list of instructions. But they were quite good at improvising. And they seemed unimpressed by bluster and evasion and bullying. Some of them didn't even seem to know who Mac was. There was one slant-eyed little prick from a bank in Hong Kong who didn't even appear to know what HOA was. He'd kept saying inane things like, 'It's our shareholders' funds we seek to protect. We must have adequate security or return of the funds.' And the others had followed his lead. Next time the yellow turd arrived at Sydney Airport, he'd be told to hop it back home for a bowl of noodles, Mac would see to that.

Still. The problem was, Mac couldn't answer the questions. He had the assets, of course he had the assets. But proving he owned them, that was another issue. They were tied up in companies whose whole frameworks had been established to prove he didn't own or control them. For obvious reasons. But not reasons that could be made obvious, not reasons that could be stated on the record, without the tax commissioner and the securities regulator and a raft of other busybodies burying their noses in the middle of it all. And the boy scouts wanted it all on the record. They took notes of everything he said in black, spiral-bound notebooks. Even when he'd made an ironic joke, they'd written it down. When he tried to explain he'd meant the opposite of what he'd said, the slant-eye wrote that down, too.

Now they were on to cash flow and that was a step too far. How did he fund the properties and the boats and all the other paraphernalia from just director's fees and dividends? The cash flow was there, of course it was there, but the source? Well, they wouldn't understand the nature of the ever-running spring. How could they?

They were insignificant little pricks, one step up from bank tellers, who'd never make more than a living wage and would run home to their mothers wetting their pants with excitement any time they were given a month's bonus. The vision, the guts, the effort it took to create a business was beyond their limited comprehension, and so was the right to be justly rewarded for it.

Still. It was a problem. They'd presented a folder with a set of forms to be filled out—assets and liabilities, income and outgoings, cash flow by month, God knows what. He couldn't do it, he didn't know. That was the frightening thing, the really gut-wrenching thing—he didn't know. Everyone assumed he was a disciplined businessman with an immaculate set of files documenting every aspect of his vast holdings. But it wasn't like that. It was a patchwork of ragged pieces held together with a stitch here and a pin there. If he needed cash, he took some cash. If he needed to borrow, he borrowed. His accountant was supposed to work it all out some time, or his tax lawyer, or some other hanger-on who copped a huge fee. But they were all running for cover, saying they just did their bit and no one knew the whole picture. Except Mac. Except he didn't.

He'd have to pay back some money, that's all there was to it. He hated that. What was the point of borrowing if you had to pay it back? It was something he'd never done before as a matter of principle, and it was wrong to break principles. Still, HOA shares, a lot of them, most of them, would have to go. It depended how high the price went. It would certainly rise once it was known the government was considering further regulation on foreign competitors, but how much? He had to commit to giving the banks the money before he knew the price. It was dangerous. But not too dangerous. The question would be asked in parliament, the share price would rise, the sale would be made before anyone knew if the regulations were actually being implemented and he'd be back in the saddle.

He looked across at Bonny, and sighed.

They were both sweating as they picked their way cautiously through the boulders, with the mountain stream gurgling about their feet and splashing its slipperiness onto rounded surfaces. The sun was filtered through a high canopy and the tree ferns grew thickly on the banks and arched their fronds over the water, but the combination of humidity and sustained effort was draining. They'd been walking for over two hours and even though the climb down the cliff face next to Wentworth Falls was an almost vertical descent down a narrow staircase cut into the rock, it required concentration to avoid injury. Now they had made it as far as the Valley of the Waters, both were feeling the tension in calf and thigh muscles and a need for rehydration. Water was no issue, it was everywhere; the mountain stream seemed merely the most visible evidence of a world living through water. It oozed up from the ground, dripped from ferns and branches, was pressed from moss and lichen with even the lightest pressure, provided music and movement and dancing light as waterfalls and rivulets fell from the cliffs above. They stopped to fill the water bottle and sat on a flat rock ledge above the stream with some relief.

However, Jack's concern was not just related to the protests emanating from muscles he hadn't used in years. He was lost. There were two aspects of this fact that were disturbing. First, the embarrassment, followed by the heckling, followed by the anger this would produce from Louise, was galling to contemplate. He was the intrepid leader of this expedition, following the paths of the great explorers of the Blue Mountains, or at least of the park rangers who'd built the steps and railings and other tourists aids. He was equipped with a special watch containing a compass—and a variety of dials and bezels that, if manipulated in a particular way which he'd now forgotten, were able to determine the speed of a passing cloud—as well as a bone-handled folding knife of unusual dimension and a heart-rate monitor he'd thrown in the small backpack for good measure. Yet none of these, including the compass, appeared to be of any use in alleviating the second disturbing aspect of his predicament—that he was lost.

He was considering the most adroit manner in which to broach this unpalatable and unexpected dilemma with Louise, when she spoke first.

'Darling boy, mighty leader, conqueror of all injustice, sex god, I need to talk to you quietly for a moment. There's something I want to tell you and I don't want you to get angry about it. You've brought me to this magical place—where better to speak the truth and be gentle with one another?'

Jack looked at her with surprise. Despite the mocking words, her tone and attitude were serious and concerned. She reached out one hand to hold the back of his neck and pull him closer.

'What? Yes, of course, we always talk, about anything. We don't need rocks and streams. What is it?'

She shook her head. 'No we don't. We don't always reveal ourselves. You hide things from me, and I've been hiding a few things from you.'

He waited. How lost was he about to be?

'Just stay calm. You promise me?' He nodded uncertainly. 'It's about the kids. They've been hassled a few times over all the rubbish in the press about you and it's upset them. I didn't want you to be worried.'

Instant relief, from what he wasn't sure, was followed by a surge of blood to his face. 'What? What mean little bastards have been doing this? I'll speak to the parents, I'm not having this sort of bullying. It's disgraceful. Who was it?'

She took him gently by both shoulders. 'You promised—no anger. And in Sarah's case, it was the parents.' He held back the words, but she could see the rage flare in his eyes. 'You know that boy she's been going out with—John Alderton? Bruce's son. She went to dinner there a couple of weeks ago and that bitch Leigh started in on her. "How is your father, it must be so distressing for him, and particularly for your poor mother, do give them our best." You know the deal. And then the boy's birthday party was to be a black-tie dinner at the Colonial Club and I bought Sarah a lovely dress—and she wasn't invited. It's all over. I don't think she really liked the little prick anyway, but she's angry, for you and me, and confused about it all.'

She saw the flushed cheeks and the red line around his neck and even his ears, and waited for the explosion. But he spoke very softly.

'What about Shane?' She let her hand slide down his arms and locked their fingers together. 'Not so bad. Sledging at rugby. Where do young boys learn words like that? He's okay, he can look after himself. So can I. We'll get the real perpetrators. Forget about the gossip-mongers, they're just pawns. I'm proud to be with the man who won't back off.'

He turned away, peering into the soft green light, trying to control his breathing, trying not to imagine the pain of his fist crashing into jawbone. The sweat on his back was cold now and he shivered as a light breeze arrived with the setting sun. Louise wrapped her arms around him, not for warmth. 'Don't worry about it. We're fine. Just get us back to the fire before nightfall and I promise ecstasy will overcome anger.'

'I'm lost.'

'I know, darling. I was so bloody mad when I first heard about it, I could have killed someone. But we move on.'

'No, I'm really lost. I forget how we get up from here. There's no track markers through the stream. There used to be an arrow cut into a tree on the other bank, but I can't find it. It's years since I was down here.'

She pulled back from him. 'You've heard of the agony and the ecstasy? The former is appearing more likely by the minute. Gird your loins, part the bubbling waters, get us to the fire. The alternatives lie starkly before you.'

When they finally climbed wearily from the taxi, the only taxi in the Blue Mountains it seemed, there was a fire alight in their cabin at the resort to ward off the unseasonal chill. Finding the track had been the least of their challenges. The climb out of the valley had been much longer and harder than Jack remembered and they were less than halfway before the light failed. The track was indistinct, rocky, treacherous. It grabbed at their ankles, tried to twist them into hollows and ditches, threw up tree roots to up-end them, left patches of loose shale where a firm foothold was needed. By the time they reached the car park above the valley, they hated the track and swore at it as if it was a live and vicious animal.

But the next problem redirected Louise's venom immediately. This was not the car park from which they had set off, where their car conveniently awaited. It was three kilometres to the nearest main road and a long wait for the elusive taxi before a bath and wine eased the tension. They'd barely spoken on the trek out, more from tiredness than from any rift between them, and thoughts of sexual activity other than a cuddle by the fire had disappeared on a lonely road under an avenue of eucalypts rustling in the chill night air.

When they were finally sprawled together on cushions by the fire, too tired to bother with eating, Jack spoke. 'I can't do it any longer. I'm not going to have my family subjected to this harassment. Particularly the kids. I don't care anymore what these people have done or haven't done. I'm out. I'll tell Hedley Stimson on Sunday and that's the end of it.'

She pushed away his comforting arm and turned on him like a female lion snarling at an intruder. 'The hell you will. You mean I go through the humiliation of all the snide rumours about you and other women, the kids have to put up with stuff they barely understand, but they wear it because they love their father, and it's all for nothing? It's too hard for you to bear? How is it too hard for you? You've forgotten about us, have you? You've forgotten about all the little people who are getting ripped off by these greasy pirates lining their own pockets. It's all difficult now so Jack's picking up his crayons and running off to draw nice pictures where it's quiet and easy. That's the idea, is it? The hell it is. You'll fight this thing to the end, whatever end it may be, if I have to drag you through the courtroom door.'

He hated it when she was like this, even while admiring the fierce spirit. He hated it being directed at him. He knew she'd defend him with the same courage and passion, take the bullet if she had to, but when she attacked him, she diminished him in some way. He'd always looked for her approbation, always placed the plans under her eyes for praise, always checked to see if she was watching from across the room at a party, without wanting to know she was focused on him. He knew she would forgive him many things, but never weakness of spirit.

'I'm not concerned for me—I've put all that aside a long time ago. But I can't put our whole family life at risk on some unproven matter of principle, can I?'

She stood over him. 'Really? And do we have any say in this? You decide to enter the battle, you decide to abandon it. We just stand around and provide sustenance for the great warrior when he needs it. You think that's the deal? Who am I then, Maid Marion? Bullshit. I'm a fucking Amazon and I ride in front. We fight together or we're not together.'

She saw the shock and fear on his face and waited a moment before she knelt and held his head in both hands, looking straight into his eyes. 'You're my man. I'm your woman. Nothing can change that, nothing can hurt us, or our family, unless we damage ourselves. We can't lose against these people. Whatever happens, we win because we fight. You see?'

chapter twelve

Laurence Treadmore sat, at dawn, in the study of his apartment and watched the sun rise over the palm groves of the Botanic Gardens. He normally rose promptly at eight o'clock and the romance of early morning light was entirely lost on him. Indeed he stood and closed both the louvres and the thick curtains over the casement windows. The dark room was now lit only by a desk lamp. Sir Laurence reached behind him to one of the twenty-two filing cabinets and withdrew a thin white folder. He'd already taken two phone calls, one from London, one from Geneva, and although these had been the purpose of his early rising, now that he was up there was no point in wasting these unwanted hours.

He looked at the name on the folder with some distaste. It was one of the burdens of his life that he had to deal with, even to promote, people of such undistinguished character. Sometimes it was necessary in order to resolve—or create—an intricate dilemma, but one hoped that one could redress the balance at a later time. How any person with a name like Popsie could expect to be taken seriously was beyond him. Of course, as the file demonstrated, she appeared not to have any desire to be taken seriously—just to be taken. She was an opportunist with money problems, some of which he'd helped to alleviate, briefly. It wasn't a recipe for admiration, but it was for usefulness.

He read the document carefully, then wrote a name and a phone number on a notepad. He replaced the folder, opened the second drawer and removed a similar, but much thicker, file. As he slowly leafed through the file, a steady stream of entries flowed into the notepad. Nearly two hours had passed by the time he'd read and re-read the document and then distilled his note-taking onto one page. It was eight o'clock and Mavis would be bathing downstairs. She'd be surprised if he didn't emerge shortly from his quarters, showered and dressed, and he never liked to surprise Mavis. He was unaware that he had done so many times in their early years, but not for a long time now. He rang his office number in order to leave a message for Mrs Bonython to make separate appointments for the two people he'd just been reading about. He would see them later in the morning. And he had no doubt they'd be there, even the second one. Proud, and a stiff neck he might have, but he'd be there. But first Sir Laurence would breakfast at the club. Eggs, he felt like scrambled eggs. The croissant on his desk could sit there or Mrs Bonython could have it for her dinner. On a day like this, Sir Laurence Treadmore would eat eggs in the main dining room at the Colonial Club, cholesterol be damned.

He arrived at his office only five minutes before the first of the two appointments. Mrs Bonython became flustered when told to remove the newspapers from the desk and take the croissant home. Sir Laurence was a man of strict habits and any interruption to his rituals was unusual and disturbing. As was the appearance of the woman who arrived promptly at ten o'clock. She was not the sort of person who usually entered these austere and sombre rooms, dressed expensively but showily in a frock more suited to a romantic picnic than a business meeting with a Knight of the Realm. It was also unknown for Sir Laurence not to keep a visitor waiting, but there he was at the door to his office calling, 'Come in, dear lady, do come in,' before Mrs Bonython could reach for the intercom. If it had been any other employer she might have thought Sir Laurence was engaged in a liaison of dubious nature, but some things were not possible.

'What a delightful office, Laurence,' said Popsie Trudeaux as she looked around with distaste at the bland interior. No colour. Popsie liked colour, loved colour, what was life without colour? Her present attire was ample evidence of this passion and Sir Laurence recoiled from it surreptitiously. It was still early in the day, and it was upsetting an excellent breakfast.

'And how is your new business progressing? I only hear most impressive reports.' Sir Laurence was seated behind the exceptionally wide desk and had pushed his chair back towards the window as if to situate himself as far as possible from both the violent kaleidoscope of contrasting hues and the sizeable bosoms encased in it.

'Thanks to you, Laurence, it's a triumph. I've been showered with work by everyone. I really can't handle it all.'

Or any of it, thought Sir Laurence grimly. It was true the work was pouring in, his sources confirmed that, but Popsie's ability to administrate and control costs appeared to be in inverse proportion to her ability to conjure up bizarre concepts.

'Indeed, how wonderful. I'm so glad to have been of minor assistance. And I hear you're bidding for some of the Grand Prix work. Now that would be a major project and a tremendous coup. The chairman of the committee happens to be a personal friend of mine. Should I mention it to him or would that be indiscreet?'

Discretion was not a consideration that had weighed heavily in any previous concern of Popsie's. It was certainly not a factor she wished to play a part in deterring Sir Laurence from mentioning her favourably to the chairman of the Grand Prix Committee. The chairman of this committee could save her life. She'd never met him, whoever he was, but he could have it all, on a plate, if he'd just give her this contract. She couldn't believe it had come to this. It had never occurred to her you could lose money running a successful business. The money poured in one end, a veritable tropical thunderstorm of dollars thundering into the bank accounts, but then it seemed to wash away down some stormwater drain and she was left with unpaid bills and an overdraft. At first she thought her accountant must be stealing it. After all, he was also her husband's accountant, and now that she had pretty much told Angus to fuck off—because why would a successful, creative businesswoman need a dull lawyer husband with a limp dick hanging around?—well maybe the accountant was siphoning funds off to Angus. So she'd hired another accountant and he'd said the same thing—cost control was not one of her skills. He'd also said if she didn't hire a professional manager and win a big contract instead of just parties and weddings, she'd be begging Angus to represent her on reduced fees in a bankruptcy court.

As these thoughts were tumbling through her mind, she examined Sir Laurence in minute detail. Was he gay? He looked gay. Neat as a hotel bed, all those pink shirts and flowers in the buttonhole. He was married, but that meant nothing. How many married men's jockey shorts had she run her hand into only to find out they were pillow biters? Besides, no one ever saw his wife. Perhaps she didn't exist. And yet the old prune didn't seem to have any juice running through him at all. She was sure he was asexual, just not interested. Which made it more mysterious. What did he want with her?

'I'll take your silence as tacit approval to have a word with Ron Strutter. No reason he shouldn't know of the talent on offer.'

Sir Laurence removed a sheet of paper from a drawer and placed it carefully on the bare desk. The leather surface was slippery from its morning polish and the paper slid gently towards Popsie.

'I've another small matter that may interest you. From time to time clients and associates ask me to find trustworthy persons to act as directors of their private companies. I serve in this capacity myself for a few friends where the companies aren't particularly active. But I don't have the time for too many. There's one on foot at present with a small private concern—a subsidiary of a company in Bermuda needs a local director, largely inactive, perhaps a little share trading or banking from time to time. They don't pay a great deal, only fifty thousand dollars per annum in this case, but it all adds to business experience and some people find a little extra cash flow helpful. I realise money isn't a consideration for you, but I thought you might enjoy expanding your corporate knowledge base.' Sir Laurence smiled broadly, as he thought, and gestured to the paper on the desk. 'This is a "Consent to Act" form, and really signing that and a few other documents from time to time, plus a rather nice lunch once or twice a year, is all there is to it.' He paused. 'And, of course, the annual visit to Bermuda. If you have the time.'

Popsie thought she would have the time. She also thought 'extra cash flow' was a term she could come to respect quickly. She was also aware she was being set up as a stooge for someone or something. Even Sir Laurence couldn't think she was a complete idiot. But who cared? He wasn't a crook, he was a highly respected doyen of Australian business. If some friend of his wanted a tame director to sign a few documents for fifty grand a year, ring Popsie. That's what she thought.

'How kind of you to think of me, Laurence. You really are the most generous of men. I would love to learn more about corporate life. Naturally, I'd need to read all the relevant documents and so on. Company rules and—all those documents.'

Sir Laurence waved a dismissive hand. 'Of course, dear lady, the company's articles, balance sheet, all of that will be provided immediately.' He waited a few moments, feigning thought. 'Would you prefer to receive those first, or are you happy to sign this document now? Mrs Bonython could witness for you.'

The next visitor sat quietly in the waiting room for ten minutes before the phone buzzed on Mrs Bonython's desk. Her cubicle was only partly screened from this room, containing one hard-backed chair and no reading material, but she made it a practice not to chat to Sir Laurence's supplicants. She would be bound to say the wrong thing and, somehow, he would know she'd said it. She emerged to conduct him to the office door. 'Sir Laurence will see you now, Mr Normile.'

It had been three years since Clinton John Normile had sat opposite this man he hated as much as any he'd ever met. No, that was wrong. He'd never hated any person before, except in the abstract. But this was a visceral, gut-wrenching emotion that caused him to recoil when he had to say the name or shake the hand. The fact that he was required, forced, to do both only added to the turmoil in his stomach and spleen, and his bowels, in the lungs that couldn't seem to catch enough air, in the throat that wouldn't swallow. He tried to remain still, arms folded, the unaccustomed collar and tie half-strangling his shallow breathing, eyes looking through the figure in front of him to the light beyond.

'There's little point in wasting time on pleasantries. You agree? Good. And how is your son?'

The Pope turned in on himself. He wasn't in this room, there was no light blinding him behind the seated figure, he would hear no words if they were spoken, feel no pain if it was administered. He was in a very different room where he could hear too much, see too much, feel the pain of others, and especially, sickeningly, of his son. Yet, was this his son? This wasted, filthy, ragged, shivering bundle. Could this be the boy who stood erect, shining, leather straps polished, leather boots blackened, brass glinting in an afternoon sun, receiving the Winston Churchill Award as the Senior Army Cadet of New South Wales? Or the boy, man perhaps, who placed the steadying hand on his father's arm when they stood together at a sister's, a daughter's, funeral?

He would save his son. It was simple. He would analyse the problem logically and solve it. That's what he did, solved other people's problems. There were three issues:the medical issue, the question of criminality— ridiculous as it may be to suggest these tragic, wasted waifs were criminals, but it had to be dealt with—and whatever was the underlying cause. He would deal with all three. His son would shine again.

How long had it taken him to understand some problems have no solution? It was the most jarring realisation of his life. He heard a voice far off in another world and jerked back to attention. 'I'm sorry, what did you say?'

'I merely stated that no bad comment has reached me about his behaviour, which is, in its way, good. I'm sure you agree?'

The Pope looked directly at Laurence Treadmore for the first time. Why did he hate this man? He'd no reason to do so. On the contrary, gratitude would have been a more reasonable emotion. He would be visiting a jail every Saturday instead of a halfway house if not for Sir Laurence's intervention. But he hated being beholden to someone who literally made his skin crawl—an expression he'd never understood before he shook the limp hand. The fact that this aloof, cold mannequin even knew of his son's predicament seemed peculiar, abnormal, to carry a portent of evil and corruption. There had been no publicity, they had no mutual friends, they nodded to one another at the club but nothing more. It was years since there'd been a passing connection in the insurance industry. Yet help of the most valuable, most essential kind had been proffered. And later, it was he, not Sir Laurence, who had vented unreasonable rage at eminently reasonable questions. If either had cause for animosity towards the other, it was the wraith he could barely see behind the desk in the glaring light.

'He's holding the line. He's taken up sculpture. He's very good at it. He started with pottery, but has since moved on to working wood and stone. It helps a great deal, but it's not everything.'

Sir Laurence nodded thoughtfully and drew another paper from the desk drawer. 'No, I suppose not. I confess I'm not greatly familiar with these matters.' He paused. 'I've come across something that may be of further assistance. An acquaintance of mine has directed my attention to a foundation that helps with problems of this kind. They've established a retreat in the Southern Highlands, away from any temptation, where long-term residency is available and where, if I recall correctly, one of the major activities is art, in particular sculpture. They're searching for a new chairman, someone who would take a close and personal interest. I thought of you. And your son.'

There it was again. Where he should have felt gratitude and relief, only anger and suspicion reared up. The man had known about the sculpture before he mentioned it, he must have done. Why was he watching them, why was he helping? And yet it was exactly what Gary needed. Maybe it was exactly what he needed himself.

'It's very considerate of you, Laurence, to spend time on this. I don't know how to thank you. I never have thanked you properly and I deeply regret the comments I made. It was a time of great stress.'

Sir Laurence waved away the words with the dust mites. 'We all say things we don't mean from time to time. Here's a background paper on the foundation. They need to move quickly, so let me know before the end of the week.'

The Pope reached forward to take the document. 'Thank you again, Laurence.' He waited a few seconds. 'Is there anything I can do for you?'

Sir Laurence stood immediately and walked from behind the desk to the door. 'Not at all, not at all. We help where we can. I'm sure you do the same.'

The hand was extended as the door opened and the Pope, reluctantly but gratefully, shook it and walked unsteadily to the lift.

Renton Healey strolled, some might say waddled, back to his office in a comforting haze of cabernet sauvignon and garlic fumes. Life was pleasant, very pleasant indeed. He earned a great deal of money, was ferociously intelligent to the point where he could confuse directors, regulators and his wife with a few convoluted sentences, he was no longer made fun of because of his appearance, because he made a great deal of money (some women, an increasing number of women, were prepared to overlook his appearance—yes probably for the same reason but who cared), and he was comfortably full of the aforementioned cabernet sauvignon.

His secretary, Janet, who was not yet one of his women but who, he felt reasonably certain, soon would be, was not in her position outside his office when he reached it. He would scold her for that, gently. If she wanted to eat, and it was probably better that she didn't, she could have someone bring her a salad of bean sprouts at the desk. He was about to lower himself into the high-backed chair, and nearly toppled forward with surprise when he noticed Jack Beaumont and a woman seated on the sofa behind the door.

'Afternoon, Renton. Hope you don't mind us waiting for you? I thought you might have been back a little earlier.'

Renton Healey was outraged; this was his sanctum sanctorum. People weren't permitted to enter it unannounced, without a reservation as it were. Janet would never eat again. 'Not at all, Jack. Sorry to keep you. The meeting went longer than I expected. Still, we got what we wanted.' He attempted a wry laugh. 'Negotiation's all about hanging in there, isn't it?'

Jack nodded. 'Certainly. And were you meeting with Global Re? Renewing the reinsurance contracts? I know they're coming up soon.'

Renton was now more than furious at the violation of his corporate space, he was at security warning level five. All his antennae were rotating to pick up danger signals. Jack Beaumont wasn't supposed to know about Global Re, the renegotiation of contracts, or anything else of note. Jack Beaumont was an insurance neophyte, an intellectually inferior used car salesman who was sent out to sell a message to the market and the media whenever Renton, and Mac, with the blessing of Sir Laurence, decided there was a message that needed selling. Nevertheless, he was, nominally, the CEO and he was, unfortunately, here. With someone.

'No we're not at that point yet. Still crunching numbers. Actuarial football—you know the game.' He gestured to the woman on the sofa. 'But I don't think we've met, or am I mistaken?'

'This is Louise; Louise, Renton Healey. Louise is one of my assistants. But I'd like to talk about Global Re for a moment. Reinsurance seems to have quite an impact on our P&L. By my calculations, we would have made a loss of fifty-four million last year rather than a profit of seventy-eight million if we hadn't had the benefit of that Global Re contract. Am I right? I don't quite have my head around it yet, but I want to understand it a lot better.'

Renton controlled his breathing as he eased down into the leather. So the man knew nothing. He wanted to understand things better. He would understand them better. 'Of course, delighted to lead you through the labyrinth. Horribly complicated stuff, I'm afraid, but we'll do our best. Let me get the file together and we'll set up an appointment. Early next week okay for you?'

Jack shook his head. 'No. I'd like to do it now. I already have the file.'

He watched Renton's face with deep satisfaction as, finally, the smug veneer was stripped away and fear spread over the squashed pumpkin. 'Is that my file? Where did you get that? This is quite improper, taking people's files.'

Jack raised his eyebrows. 'Really? But it's not your file, Renton, it's the company's. And as CEO, I can view any document I want whenever I want, wouldn't you say?'

Renton appeared dazed as he looked around the room for help. He noticed Louise taking notes. Why was she taking notes? Red wine was no longer a factor in his addled brain. His ability to brush aside alcohol was legendary. He just needed to fix on a point, as if gaining balance on a rolling deck, and then outwit the lesser intellect.

'Yes, of course, but I can't have people removing files at will.

I'm responsible to APRA for the integrity of these documents and if you wanted something you should have come to me, through Janet.'

'Janet gave me the file. And I assure you it's completely safe. I've already copied it, so you can have the original back.' Jack placed a thick folder on the desk. 'But let's move on, Renton. I want to ask you a few questions about some of this material.'

Renton Healey stared at the papers in Jack's hands. They were covered with highlighter colours and post-it notes, signs of extensive, diligent reading. These two must have arrived the minute he left the building. There was a great deal of complex material in that file. Just how complex, Renton couldn't remember. Was the side letter in there or in a separate file? He needed Janet. He would deal with her indiscretions another day.

'I'd like to help, Jack, but I think I'm pretty booked up this afternoon.' He commenced the standing-up process. 'I'll just check with Janet and see how soon I can give you the time this deserves.'

'Janet won't be back for a while. She's helping me out with an urgent project, hope you don't mind. I asked her to clear your diary for this afternoon, so we're in good shape. Let's get going, shall we?'

When they were together later that night, the times were old, but new also. They were all knitted together again. They'd made love as soon as the kids were asleep and they were now propped up in bed with papers strewn about and wine on the bedside table.

'How did we do, lover boy?' Jack was bemused. She never asked questions like that. 'Very beautiful, my love, as always.'

She snorted. 'Not the sex, you idiot. I'm talking about the old team, on the job. Did we get the goods or not?'

He laughed and picked up her notebook, filled with pages of immaculate script. 'I doubt Hedley Stimson has ever seen a court reporter produce as accurate a record. It was wonderful watching Renton's face as you took all that down. Now and again he was so caught off guard by some of my questions he had to take his eyes away, but most of the time they were fixed on your flying pen. How many times did he ask for your surname? Was it two or three?'

'Only two, I think, but no doubt he's scouring the records of every Louise among your thousands of employees as we speak. I wonder how many there are.'

He looked at her with deep affection. There would have been no meeting without her, he knew that. He would have been planning another picnic or figuring out how to fit three spa baths and a sauna into one apartment. Had he only taken the job in the first place to impress her? Maybe. Louise and a few friends. Now he needed to impress himself.

'Did we do the business, lover boy? Will they all hang by the neck until dead, that's what I want to know? They'll need a strong rope for Mr Healey, that's for sure.'

Jack selected a page from the litter on the bed. 'I think this is it. The smoking gun. It's just a one-page letter written in completely obtuse language, but I reckon it's the one. Renton nearly threw up his lunch when I referred to it and he'd hate to part with that. What was his response again?'

She took the notebook and flipped to another page. '"I don't recall seeing that letter before. It's not addressed to me. The addressee is no longer with the company. Its meaning is not immediately clear. Its terms may not have been implemented." He handled it like a poisonous spider.'

'Exactly. Only Hedley Stimson can confirm if it's the missing piece, but I think we've got them.'

She wrapped herself around him and buried her hands deep into his hair. 'You were unrelenting and ruthless in your pursuit. I didn't know you understood all that complex jargon. Very sexy in an odd way. The thinking warrior is quite a turn-on.' She scratched his scalp and his eyes closed as they always did. 'What will you do when they're all pinned on the wall? Will you try to clean up the whole company or go back to property and lead a quiet life? Or just make love to me and live off our fat?'

He smiled and shook his head. 'I don't know. I actually like the insurance business and I want to make sure our policy-holders don't suffer. The shareholders will, for a while anyway, because the share price will take a big hit when all this comes out. So I'd have to stay and hold the company together for some time. But let's not count our chickens.'

She bounced up and down on the bed like a child. 'I want to count them. Can't you go and see old Hedley tomorrow? I want to come.'

He laughed and put a hand on her shoulder to stop the bouncing. 'I'll go on Sunday, as we agreed, and I'll go alone. I'd love for you to meet him one day when it's all out in the open.

I don't think it'll be long. But we'll wait till Sunday.'

chapter thirteen

The knocking started Mac on a long journey. He was floating over the rocky outcrops of the Kimberley, drifting above the lapis lazuli of coral reefs, darkened here and there by the black shapes of Spanish mackerel or queen fish or barramundi closer to the shore, and then, suddenly, was staring down at the white sails of the Opera House, a train snaking its way over the Harbour Bridge, a massive container vessel squeezing beneath the span. His was the deep sleep of physical contentment and mental peace. Knocking, whatever its origin, couldn't disturb it. Besides, there could be no such knocking here. The only way to reach Bonny's penthouse on the twenty-fifth floor was via the concierge, who would buzz. And he wouldn't buzz, ever, before seven-thirty. Mac pulled himself back to consciousness and looked at the bedside clock through half-closed lids. Six a.m.

What the hell was going on? He eased quietly out of bed and reached for his kimono, cherry blossoms winding their way through the patterned silk. It was a present from Bonny. At first he'd thought it too feminine and pretty, but now he loved the slippery softness on his bare skin. Pushing his knobbly feet into a pair of kangaroo-skin slippers he headed for the door. There must be some problem with the security system, but why they couldn't leave it till later was beyond him. If that concierge expected a big tip at Christmas, he'd better plan on buying his own cherries.

When he opened the door, expecting the obsequious, smiling face of James in the blue uniform, his mouth fell slightly open. There were three figures confronting him, all in drab grey, none of whom appeared obsequious or anything near it, none of whom were smiling. One stepped forward and spoke, holding something in an outstretched hand.

'Mr Biddulph, we represent the Australian Securities and Investments Commission. We hold a duly executed warrant to search these premises. We also wish to ask you questions pertaining to a current investigation. We will now enter the premises.'

As he spoke the other two moved from behind him, past Mac, into the apartment's foyer. Mac was still staring at the document in the man's hand without seeing it, partly because he was stunned, partly because his glasses were on the bedside table. He was suddenly aware that he must present a slightly ridiculous, even pathetic, figure—an old man with a face creased by rumpled sheets, swaddled in a Japanese prostitute's gown, standing with legs apart and mouth open, not quite dribbling but damn close to it. He struggled to regain composure and control.

'Hang on. Get those two out of there. No one is searching anything until my lawyer is here and probably not then either.' The man with the document ignored him and followed the other two into the foyer. 'Now listen here, you've got no right. Get yourselves out of here and back down to the concierge's desk. When my lawyer comes he'll sort it out with you.'

The spokesman nodded to the other two and they moved off into separate rooms. 'On the contrary, Mr Biddulph, we have every right. You may call your lawyer, of course, but in the meantime we will commence our search. Once you've made that call, we'll require all forms of communication from these premises to be suspended during the course of our search and questioning.'

Mac heard a scream from Bonny. Obviously one of them had found the bedroom. 'What the hell is this all about? What investigation? I have no knowledge of anything like that. Surely you have to notify me if you want some information. What does it relate to?'

The man remained motionless, unsmiling, watching Mac carefully, hands now by his side. 'We're not required to give you notice of a search or of the commencement of an investigation or the nature of any such investigation. We have the right, by law, to remove any documents, files, whether paper or electronic, computers, phone records, notes, recordings or any other material we consider relevant, and will do so. It's an offence for you to interfere with or impede this process in any way.'

Suddenly Mac exploded. 'You fucking little prick.' His right hand, which had been clutching the kimono because he hadn't bothered to tie the sash, jerked out to grab a collar. The man stepped neatly back and seemed more perturbed by the revelation before him than by the threat of violence. 'I'll fucking throw you out of the place, you little cunt.' As he spat out the last word Bonny emerged from the bedroom in a matching, but tightly sashed, garment.

Bonny paused in front of the spokesman. 'Charming. The whole lovely morning. Utterly delightful to be woken by a pack of nerds with bad breath and cheap suits.' The spokesman appeared to blanch slightly at this.

Mac glared at her until he noticed her eyes were also drawn to the widespread kimono drifting softly in the air-conditioning currents. He hastily drew the folds together and double sashed. 'I'm trying to get rid of the bastards, but it doesn't help to have you moaning about it. Here's Gerry Lacy's number. Tell him what's going on and get him over here fast.'

She took the cell phone and turned to the other man. 'Would you mind asking your colleagues to leave my bedroom till last? I promise I won't burn the sheets, but I would quite like to get dressed.' She gave him a coquettish smile. 'And if you're very nice, I'll give you a pair of my knickers to keep all for yourself.'

They both watched her bounce away down the hall.

Four hours later, whatever dream started Mac's day had developed way beyond a nightmare. And not because of bad breath and cheap suits. Bonny had departed as Gerry Lacy arrived. Waving a breezy goodbye, she tucked something into the ASIC man's pocket with a whisper: 'Don't forget to hide them before your wife takes the suit to the drycleaners—which, incidentally, should be quite soon.'

And then the Mexican stand-off had begun. It was surreal, Mac felt, watching his lawyer, tanned and relaxed in a cashmere sweater, chinos and loafers, discussing him with the ASIC nerd as if he were a prize heifer. The nerd was like the bankers, writing everything down, even though he had a tape recorder running on the coffee table. The nerd insisted questions would be put now, the lawyer insisted his client wouldn't answer them in the course of the search. The nerd replied they would wait until the search was concluded. The lawyer responded that his client would reserve his rights. Mac was instructed, 'instructed' for Christ's sake, not to speak at all in the 'interim period'. The interim period had proved to be four hours. It wasn't that big an apartment. They must have been stripping the wallpaper from the walls to be taking this long. Even though he'd gouged a discount out of Jack Beaumont, he'd probably still paid too much for the place. Jack Beaumont. The name clanged in his head like the ringer on a bell. Did he have anything to do with this disgraceful shambles? Before he knew it the question had voiced itself.

'Did Jack fucking Beaumont put you up to this? Is that what this is all about? Some crap about corporate governance or something? I'll kill the little prick if—'

Gerry Lacy was on his feet, hands forward in a stop sign. 'Do not speak. You will say nothing, Mac. My client has nothing to say, you will erase that comment from your records. It is improper to put questions in the process of a search as you well know.'

The nerd barely looked up from his notebook. 'I didn't put a question. The comment was offered and is duly recorded.'

'This is unlawful. This entire search is unlawful. Any material you may acquire in the course of it will not be admissible.'

Gerry Lacy was more equipped for objecting to a line call in tennis than confronting hardened government investigators. He hardly ever called 'fore' at golf. His forte was the civilised conference. He never appeared in court and regarded the barristers he briefed to do so as reminiscent of bullies he'd known at school. The word 'golf' jagged a thought into the mix. It was Tuesday, his golf afternoon. He always played in the Tuesday comp, he'd even won it last week. Seventeen drives in the fairway. Never achieved such accuracy before. It was the new driver, had to be. Wonderful club, enormous head. But he was keeping the left arm straighter, that was the key. It wasn't just equipment, you had to have skills. Suddenly he realised Mac was speaking again. He'd told him not to do that.

'Please don't speak, Mac. I cannot stress sufficiently the damage you may cause to your case in the course of any subsequent proceedings should charges be laid. You do understand this?'

Mac stood. 'The only proceeding I was speaking about was a visit to the toilet. Is that okay or do I need a note from Mummy?' He nearly tripped on the edge of the kimono as he flounced off, bumping into one of the nerds who was emerging with Bonny's notebook computer—fat lot of good that would do him, unless he wanted to learn how to tighten his buttocks and stomach muscles simultaneously.

Gerry Lacy checked his watch. He loved to have an excuse to check the time because he adored his watch. All watches were fascinating, but his watch was an artwork. He could never understand people who lavished large sums of money on great hunks of ugly gold just so people would know they were rich. This watch was a Patek Philippe Mondiconum in platinum with day date. To an ignoramus, like the appalling individual seated in front of him taking notes, who appeared to be wearing a plastic Swatch, it might be mistaken for an average, stainless-steel time-piece. The afficionados would recognise it as one of the rarest, and most expensive, chronometers on the planet. Even though Gerry received the customary thrill from his prolonged glance at the Mondiconum, he was also distressed to see the time was nearly eleven o'clock. His tee-off time was midday. Decisive action was required.

Mac was returning, wiping his hands on the kimono, leaving dark patches in the scarlet silk. Both the searching nerds were now packing notebooks and diaries into archive cartons. Mac laughed at them. 'Oh yeah, you'll love reading that lot. Appointments for waxing jobs and recipes for mung bean salads, you fucking idiots.'

Gerry was between Mac and the nerds in a flash. 'My client has nothing more to say. Your search is clearly at an end and so is this conference, if it can be called that. You'll leave these premises, as will we. My client does not reside here. He has cooperated with you in the process of your search, unlawful as it may have been, but will now attend to his business affairs. If you have questions you wish to put to him, issue the proper notice and he will respond. Not otherwise. Now, in a word, out.'

Somewhat to Gerry Lacy's surprise, ten minutes later they were all in the street and the archive boxes were being loaded into a van. As it drove off, Mac turned to the lawyer. 'I must say you came through there, Gerry. Never seen you so forceful. Thanks, mate, I needed those bastards out of there. I was starting to lose it, I don't mind admitting.'

Gerry placed a hand on his shoulder. 'Not at all, Mac. Glad to help. We must discuss this fully tomorrow, but I have to dash now. Important conference.'

Mac was startled. 'What? Shouldn't we talk about it now? Get some of your people, have a brains trust session?'

Gerry shook his head vigorously. 'No, no. They're all at the conference. Tuesday partners' meeting. Much better to sleep on it, anyway. I'll call you first thing tomorrow morning.'

Mac stood on the footpath, dazed and dishevelled. He'd swapped the kimono for a pair of jeans and a spare shirt he kept in Bonny's wardrobe, but he was unshaven, unshowered, un-kempt. He thought he could smell himself. He hadn't even used deodorant. He sniffed the air. At least there'd be the musky smell of sex mixed into the potion. First time in a while. Probably last time in a while, too, at least with Bonny. He glanced down at the cell phone in his hand as it began to bleep an endless stream of messages.

Tuesday. Had Gerry said Tuesday? Christ. He looked at his watch. The question would have been asked in the Senate by now. First up, he'd told Harold Wilde. Max Newsome would be starting to market the shares, which should be soaring. And he'd been locked up with a group of orang-outangs. He almost ran to his car, parked in the fucking street—car park door wouldn't open, fucking technology—and was out of breath when Maxwell Newsome answered the call.

'Mac, thank goodness you've rung. I've been desperately trying to contact you all morning. Are you all right?'

He held the steering wheel with both hands for support. His mouth was dry, he hadn't even had coffee, and his odour was strong in the enclosed space. He seemed to be breathing with more difficulty than he should be just from a dash to the car. He saw his chest heaving under the shirt and he was afraid, for no reason.

'Don't worry about that now. What's happened with the HOA price? What are we going to get for the shares?'

There was a long pause. 'They're gone, Mac. All sold. They went as soon as we put them on the market. I've been trying to call you.'

'God. Just like that? The lot? I can't believe it. What did we get?'

He heard breathing like his own on the other end of the line. 'It's this ASIC thing, Mac. And I couldn't reach you. But you said to put them all on the market this morning. You said just get the best price I could on Tuesday. I wrote it down, Mac, it's all written down. I asked you for a bottom price, but you said sell them on Tuesday.'

Mac was desperate for air. He jabbed at the window button but it wouldn't respond. He fumbled for the key but couldn't find it. He swung the door open and a passing cyclist swore at him as it nearly crashed into the bicycle frame. The roar of the traffic reverberated into the car's interior and he shouted into the cell phone. 'What are you talking about, Max? What ASIC thing? How do you know there's an ASIC thing? They've only just left. Did Gerry call? Why would he call you?' He pulled the door shut again to hear the response.

'It's on the front page of every paper, Mac—surely you've seen it. It was on the screens before the market opened. The press have been outside your house all morning. Where are you?'

Where was he? God knew. His mind was tumbling over itself, trying to sift information into logical order and failing. He opened the door again, climbed almost drunkenly out of the cavernous interior and leaned against the bonnet. He hated this car. Pretentious piece of crap Rolls-Royces were, but it had become a sort of trademark. People waved at him as he drove around, and he liked to be waved at. Usually they spat at Rollers, but not at Mac, because they knew he was just one of them who'd made it. There was no silver spoon anywhere near his mouth. His head swivelled as if searching for clues to his whereabouts.

'I'm at Bonny's in Potts Point.' What did it matter where he was? That wasn't the question he was searching for. What was it? How had the press known about the raid before it happened? How could so many shares have been sold so quickly? Why was Max talking about writing things down? No, none of that. Only one thing mattered. The price. The fucking price.

'What did we get? What's the price?'

'You know the market, Mac. Anything that creates uncertainty, anything that smacks of wrongdoing, or false accounts, not that there is anything yet, or at all I'm sure, but this sort of thing spooks the market, you know it does. It'll come back, I'm sure it will, in time, but well—you said to sell, I wrote it down.'

'What's the fucking price?' He could barely get the words out and the response hit him with the impact of a bullet.

'Four fifty, average. We sold a few closer to five dollars, but average four fifty.'

Mac slumped. It wasn't possible. The shares had been at seven dollars. With the revelation that the government was considering restrictions on foreign insurance companies, eight was an easy mark. Of course he'd told this idiot to sell the shares immediately. He couldn't explain he knew the question would be asked in the Senate, and that he'd promised the banks they'd have the money by the end of the week. He certainly couldn't explain to them where it was coming from before it arrived. That would have killed the share price in a minute. But it had been cut off at the knees anyway. By what? By nerds in grey suits? No, not by that. By someone knowing the nerds were coming before they came.

'You sold them all? How could that large a parcel move so fast?' Gradually his brain was picking through the debris of the bomb blast.

'I don't know. They went in three lumps virtually the minute we put them out. I mean you wanted them sold quickly, Mac, those were your instructions.'

Mac slammed the phone onto the bonnet. It made a slight dent but didn't penetrate the eight layers of enamel. Maxwell Newsome's voice could be heard squeaking from it briefly as it lay in the sun and then all was quiet, except for the roar of passing traffic.

Equations were swirling in front of Mac's closed eyes.

Numbers and multiplication signs jostled with plus and minus symbols on the red surface of his inner eye. Dollars swam through the sea of black dots. A thundering headache was gripping his cranium in a vice, squeezing all the redness together until he felt it would burst out from his ears and nose and eyes. He never got headaches; he gave them. There was no humour in the thought now. He clutched at his temples to ease the pain and it was then he heard his name called.

As he opened his eyes he heard the whirr of cameras and that was the picture on page one. An old man, in pain, dishevelled, slumped on a ridiculous car, stripped of dignity and reputation, never to be restored no matter what the facts might prove.

• • •

The press had been outside Jack's house when he returned from the park with one hand on the dog lead and the other holding the small plastic bag. They hadn't been there when he left, but at that hour the light was only just starting to creep over the electricity cables, to illuminate the garbage bins strewn about the normally tidy street. Alice Street was anally neat, every edge clipped, every lawn shaved, except on Tuesday mornings when the garbage collectors delighted in showing these rich wankers who was really the boss. A little yelling at five a.m., a little throwing of bins and lids, off to the pub for a wake-up call or two.

Jack had walked past the hockey fields on the reservoir at the top of Centennial Park and down into the pine forest, where he set Joe free to run and snuffle in the fallen cones. As he stood listening to the light breeze sigh in the needles above, he noticed a soft crackling noise from high in the trees, and when he looked up, a flock of sulphur-crested cockatoos was contentedly grazing on the remaining cones. He heard the kookaburras calling across the valley and the barking of other dogs from the exercise area below.

He called to Joe, a border collie of superior intelligence and wit, and they sloped off together towards the ponds and the paperbark forest, past the pelicans and other waterbirds, and through to the unkempt, dank section of the park, away from the cyclists and the pony track. Jack half knelt to undo the lead again and found himself looking into the dog's eyes. He took the lead in both hands and scratched behind the ears and rubbed gently up and down both sides of its neck. He could hear himself mumbling without really knowing what he was saying and Joe stared back at him as if he did.

He felt tension he hadn't realised was stored inside him uncoil and run down through his fingers into the hair and the warm body. Then he stretched and reached his arms up over his head towards the sun. They were so close now. He would see the old lawyer on Sunday, and hand him the folder with the smoking gun. They would pass the whole stinking mess to the authorities to unravel, and he, Louise and the kids could go back to real life.

The photographers hadn't seen him approaching in tracksuit and sneakers, cap pulled down against the angled sun, and probably wouldn't have recognised him anyway at this distance, even though he was often recognised now, just by people in the street. It was part of the job he secretly liked—being known for something. And he quite liked the press, and felt they liked him too, his easy candour. He'd nothing to hide and the venomous pieces had been written by gossip columnists, not the serious business journalists he mixed with. He thought about turning away, buying a newspaper from the corner shop just to check before he met them, because his home-delivered one would still be in its wrapper, but then he tugged the dog forward and they walked together into the fray.

chapter fourteen

Sir Laurence sat with arms folded tightly against his chest and a grimace of extreme distaste across his face. He disliked folding his arms at any time, certainly not tightly. It creased the lapels of an expensive suit and, unless one was particularly careful, risked crushing the petals of his boutonnière. He glanced at the clock on the boardroom wall again, well aware that it would show eleven minutes past the hour. It was one minute since he'd last checked it. When the door swung open and Jack entered, he tried unsuccessfully to alter his expression, but only succeeded in unfolding his arms.

'Sorry I'm late, Laurence. Had to run the gauntlet of the press before I could get here. No doubt you've been doing the same.'

Sir Laurence had been doing nothing of the kind. He did not run gauntlets. He was a non-executive chairman. Chief executives and others of their ilk were paid a great deal of money to run gauntlets. Besides, the press, if properly handled, if fed and watered regularly, if left tasty morsels on their doorsteps, didn't do their droppings on yours. 'I've rather a busy day, so let us get on. You agree? This business with Mac is most distressing. I'm sure there's nothing in it, but it's distressing nonetheless. To the board, to the shareholders. You agree? But before we discuss that, I am concerned to know the findings of the committee I asked you to establish to investigate any issues or irregularities on matters concerning our reinsurance contracts, balance sheet, and profit and loss account. I'm surprised, disappointed I may say, to have received no report from you.'

They stared at one another across the curved table. Jack ran his hand over the polished mahogany. He was trying to remain calm in a storm where the wind blew from all directions at once. He needed to sit quietly in the workshop with the old lawyer and listen to a logical analysis of events he couldn't piece together, of documents he couldn't match, of people who wouldn't remain in the roles they had been cast for. Why was ASIC investigating Mac when Hedley Stimson hadn't yet passed the case to them and the Global Re side letter was still in the safe at Jack's home? Why was Sir Laurence questioning him on matters he was assumed to want to avoid? What had Jack done about a committee, if anything? He couldn't remember. The shock of seeing that front page with the headline about Mac, of seeing it for the first time in a journalist's hand with photographers clicking away at him—well, he was still in shock.

'Ah, I really can't recall, Laurence. About the committee, I mean. Did I agree to set it up? I'm not sure I did.'

Sir Laurence's face was a picture, but more a Breughel than a Rembrandt. 'You can't recall? Is that what you said? Am I to understand no such committee has been formed? No progress made? No documentation is to be forthcoming on these important maters? I specifically instructed you to report directly to me on this. You agree?'

Jack loosened his tie and unbuttoned his collar. Why he was wearing a tie today when he hated them he wasn't sure. Somehow he felt it was important to face the world, his staff, the business community looking every inch the chief executive. The founder of the company, its biggest shareholder, was under attack from the authorities—for what, nobody knew—and it was up to the leader to lead. But where? The share price was tumbling, there were rumours of a takeover, and the chairman was asking him about a committee. Suddenly Jack saw the issues in perspective.

'I'm sorry, Laurence, I really don't have time to waste on this today. Frankly I don't think you do either. We can talk about committees some other time but our shareholders and the press are expecting us to make a statement about what's occurred and I want to concentrate on that.'

Laurence Treadmore's face became the colour of his shirt. 'Waste? Did you say waste? A waste of time to consider serious questions concerning matters that could profoundly affect the interests of shareholders? Questions you were instructed to examine by the duly elected and appointed chairman of a public company?' He paused, took up a crystal glass from the tray on the boardroom table and sipped delicately. The water seemed to give him strength. 'And the reason you don't have time for this is that you wish to rush to the press to discuss—what? Issues of which you know nothing. That Mac is being investigated, but you don't know why. I'm sure your prepared statement will be penetrating in its wisdom and of great comfort to all.'

Jack's resolve was shaken by the outburst. There was some force in what had been said. What could he say to the press? That he supported Mac? Hardly. That he didn't? That he had no knowledge of the issues, that the company was in great shape? That it mightn't be in great shape if he could ever understand the balance sheet? He settled back into the chair and examined Sir Laurence with more respect. Why did he feel he was the one on trial here when he suspected the chairman was as mixed up in all of this as anyone?

'Appearances. They seem to be your main concern, not matters of substance.' Sir Laurence drew a sheet of paper from his breast pocket, where he preferred to store nothing, not even a wallet, lest it disturb the line of the fabric, and slid it across the table. 'There is no statement the company can or should make other than this.'

Jack read the wording. 'The board of directors of HOA has no knowledge of any matters under investigation by ASIC concerning the company. Nor does it have any knowledge of the reason for or nature of this morning's search of premises reported to be owned by one of its directors, Mr Macquarie James Biddulph. The company will cooperate fully with ASIC in any investigation related to its business if asked to do so.'

Jack rubbed his chin. 'Yes, on reflection I think you're right, Laurence. We really can't say more than that. I'll have it released right away.'

Sir Laurence reached out a hand for the return of the paper. 'It was issued at nine this morning, under my signature. While you were running gauntlets, I contacted the other directors. It is a matter for the board not the executives. Mac is one of our number.'

Again Jack felt he was somehow at fault, when he should have felt righteous. He'd wanted to appear before a press conference and make reassuring noises. He was good at that. He wanted to stroll the factory floor and embrace the workers. He was good at that. Suddenly he was cut off at the knees by a man he'd assumed was a weak second fiddle playing Mac's tune. How was he going to spend his day now?

The prim voice interrupted his reverie. 'I've called a board meeting for ten o'clock today. Your notice of this is on your desk. Most directors are able to attend, although I've been unable to contact Mac. Since the meeting will commence shortly, we may continue this discussion in the meanwhile. I should inform you that the subject of my instruction to you to investigate the matters referred to earlier, and your response, is a major item on the agenda. I trust your response to the board will be more forthcoming and detailed than the one provided to me.'

Finally Jack heard danger ringing in the forest of words.

A board meeting called suddenly? A discussion of his failure to follow up on instructions? How was he to answer any specific questions on material he'd obtained about reinsurance contracts, Mac's private company or any related matter without revealing their whole case—just when he thought they'd finally nailed it? He desperately needed to speak to Hedley Stimson; waiting till Sunday night was no longer an option.

He looked up from the table at Laurence Treadmore. 'I'm sorry, Laurence, I can't continue the discussion at the moment. I have to make a call.'

He stood and started to walk to the door but the waspish voice stung him. 'You will not leave this room.' Sir Laurence's legendary self-control was close to cracking as the words were spat out. 'I instruct you, as your chairman, to resume your seat and answer my questions.' Jack remained standing. 'If you ignore an instruction from me, legally given, as chairman, relating to serious matters concerning your responsibilities as CEO, you will be in breach of your contract. Do you understand?'

Jack smiled. Now it was starting. Now the phoney war was over and the bombs would fall where they may. God help the innocent.

'The contract I never wanted? Yes, I understand, Laurence.' He opened the door. 'I'll see you at ten o'clock.'

He listened to the ringing tone repeat itself as he gazed out at the squared-off shapes of the buildings surrounding his office. It was a view of angular, heavy lines; of drones, like him, sitting in boxes staring across alleys at other drones sitting in boxes. It was no view at all. He placed the phone back in the cradle as the voice came on the answering machine: 'Hedley Stimson is unavailable. Please leave a message.' This was the number he'd been told never to call, but the churning in his gut told him it was now or never. And not even a clerk or a secretary answered at the old lawyer's chambers—just his own gruff voice. Jack heard a noise and swung round in his chair to see his secretary standing in the doorway. 'Is there someone I can call for you, Mr Beaumont? Are there any other calls you'd like to make?'

This was just what he needed, this busybody inserting her pedantic presence where it wasn't needed. Why he hadn't insisted on bringing his own PA from his old business instead of listening to Sir Laurence carry on about corporate governance, he'd never know. 'Thank you, no, Beryl, I make my own calls, as I think I've told you more than once.'

She smoothed her already immaculate skirt. 'Of course, Mr Beaumont, I do know that. But you seem extremely busy this morning and with the board meeting in a few minutes, I thought I might be of assistance.'

Jack breathed deeply. 'Yes, I'm sorry, but I do have to make a call now. Would you mind shutting the door?'

He pushed up Hedley Stimson's number on his cell phone screen and was about to dial it on the desk handset, when a chill fell around him, as if the air-conditioning had suddenly dropped a gust of cold air on the desk. He replaced the handset and pushed the dial on the cell phone instead, about to make another call that he had been told never to make.

This time it was a real voice, not a recorded one, but a soft, nervous voice. 'Yes?' No hello, just that one, almost frightened word.

'Is that Mrs Stimson? It's Jack Beaumont. I'm terribly sorry to call you at home.'

She sounded almost relieved. 'Yes, it's me. It's all right, Mr Beaumont.'

There was pain in the voice, that was it, not fear. Somehow he wished he was alongside her again, in his car, on a lounge perhaps, where he could reach out and hold her arm. 'Is Hedley there? May I speak to him?'

There was no answer, but he could hear her breathing. 'He's here, but he won't speak to anyone. He's more angry than I've ever seen him.'

'Could you give him a message for me? Or should I try his office later?'

'He won't be back at his office. Just come tonight, Mr Beaumont. To the workshop. I'll tell him you're coming.' There was a long silence. 'We all read the newspapers, Jack, even silly old ladies like me can read.'

She hung up before he could tell her she was— something else. And the door to his office opened with the words, 'It's ten o'clock, Mr Beaumont.'

They were all seated in their customary places when Jack entered the boardroom, except for one empty chair;

the chair that was always Mac's, vacant or occupied. No one spoke as Jack took his place alongside Sir Laurence, who didn't turn to acknowledge his arrival. The horseshoe table was completely bare, denuded of the usual clutter of board papers, notepads and coffee cups. The speakerphone from which Mac's voice had so often echoed was also eerily absent. Only a thin white file lay in front of the chairman's place. As Jack glanced down, he could see his own name on the cover.

Finally, the voice came. 'It is well past the hour. As the CEO is now present, I believe we can commence. Thank you all for coming at short notice. We have, of course, no papers for this meeting. There are only two items, related items, on the agenda. The first is the alleged ASIC investigation of one of our directors, possibly relating to this company. We've no direct knowledge of this and, as far as I am aware, the company has received no written or verbal advice from ASIC. Perhaps the CEO can advise the board if that is correct?'

Jack was stunned. Of course, it was the first thing he should have checked, but he'd been making other calls. 'No report has reached me of any contact from ASIC, Chairman.'

Sir Laurence sighed, very softly. 'No report has reached you? The question was more what inquiries you have made to ascertain whether any communication has been received from ASIC, or indeed from the insurance regulator, regarding these matters. A response to that specific question would be appreciated by the board.'

Jack tried to catch the eye of each of the directors around the table, but all eyes were down. He barely knew these people, he realised. He'd made little or no effort to become close to or understand any of them, just regarded them as appendages of Sir Laurence, or captives of Mac. 'I'm afraid I haven't had time to check directly, this morning, Chairman. I'll follow up on it right after the meeting.'

Sir Laurence eased his chair away from the table slightly.

His eyes appeared to shift almost imperceptibly to the ceiling before they settled again on the file resting on the table. 'Don't bother. I have contacted your secretary. Your office has received no communication. The company secretary has received no communication, nor has the chief financial officer or the chief actuary. And as chairman, neither have I.' He paused. 'I believe, however, the board would appreciate a reordering of your priorities as CEO and placing this matter at the top of the list. You agree?'

There were murmurs of assent from around the table and Jack nodded. All the eyes were on him now. He felt like a rabbit caught in a dozen spotlights. And as the interrogation continued and unrelenting, specific, reasonable questions flowed from the white file, an appalling realisation fell on him. He wasn't up to this job. Maybe all these people were neglecting their responsibilities, maybe they were complicit, directly or tacitly, in the machinations of Mac and Renton Healey—and Laurence Treadmore, if he was involved—but what about his own efforts? By his own admission he couldn't understand the complexities of the balance sheet. Then what was he doing running the business? He had no sound relationship with any member of the board, or the chairman, or the largest shareholder. Why? Because he assumed he was right and they were all mixed up in the same muck. But other than Mac, what evidence did he have for that assumption? Maybe Laurence Treadmore was genuine in his quest for answers.

'Do you intend to answer my question?' Jack snapped back into the room. 'I'm sorry, Chairman, would you mind repeating the question?'

Sir Laurence sighed again. 'You obviously have other issues on your mind. I think it's fair to say, however, that the board requires you to address these matters. You agree? Yes. The question I put was specific and direct. I trust the answer will be equally so. Did you remove a document from Renton Healey's files relating to reinsurance contracts?'

Jack was a butterfly pinned to a corkboard. 'Yes.'

'Why did you remove this document and what relevance does it have to the inquiries that you were asked to make by me?'

There was a long pause. 'I couldn't say at the moment, Laurence. I've not had time to have it properly analysed.'

Sir Laurence steepled the fingers of both hands together very gently. 'Analysed? By whom? Have you engaged people outside the company to examine confidential documents? If so, by what authority?'

Jack reached for the water jug and spilled freely on the table as he filled the glass. He drank it off in one long gulp, as much for the pause as the moisture. 'I prefer not to say at this time. And I believe as CEO I have the right to engage whatever consultants I think fit within approved budgets, without the approval of the board.'

The two combatants glared at one another, but there was a hint of a thin smile on Sir Laurence's face. 'In the general course of business, perhaps. Not in matters concerning corporate governance, and particularly not when you've been directly instructed to report to the chairman. I require you, on behalf of the board, to answer.'

Jack looked around the table. 'I'm sorry, but I can't do so right now. I don't want to hold anything back from the board, but I want to report in an orderly fashion and I don't have a complete picture as yet.'

Again, the lips curled slightly. 'Have you engaged a lawyer named Hedley Stimson to consult on these matters? If so, what is his brief?'

Jack's face was ablaze. Blood was rushing around his body in a whirlpool and he had to stand, to move, to allow it to circulate before it burst some vessel. There was no way to answer this question. Yes. No. Both were impossible. 'There is no brief from HOA to any such lawyer.'

'No brief from HOA? Are we to understand from the phrasing of this response that you are briefing lawyers regarding company matters on your own account?'

'I prefer not to answer that question.' The silence in the room was filled with the hum of machines.

The air-conditioning could be heard grinding away, there was a faint buzz from the speakers in the roof, the electronic gear that ran the sliding screen and the computer graphics was humming softly in its cage. Jack resumed his seat.

'I need a day or two, Chairman, before I can report properly.' Sir Laurence closed the white file. 'If I may summarise for the board. A series of relevant, specific questions has been put to the CEO regarding significant matters, some of which may relate to an ASIC inquiry. The CEO has either been evasive or refused outright to respond to the board. You agree?' He paused, but not for agreement. 'I suggest the board needs a few days to consider the critical question of whether it can continue to place its trust in the CEO. Do you agree?'

There were murmurs of assent from around the table.

'The board will meet again at ten o'clock on Monday. The presence of the CEO will not be required. Thank you.'

Jack wandered about the car park in a daze. Where had he left the car? He couldn't remember. He'd abolished the old system of allocated places with names and titles as part of his egalitarian push. He'd been good at all of that, hadn't he? He knew the staff loved it, loved Jack appearing in their workspace without warning just to chat, eating with them in the canteen, even pissing with them. No more executive toilets. They even seemed to love the snide articles in the press about him. But where was the car? He clicked the key remote and was relieved to see a distant flash of tail-lights. It was too early to drive to the old lawyer's house. His wife had told him to wait till this evening. He didn't want to go home to Louise, but he needed to talk to someone. He rang the Pope.

As he sat with a brown paper bag on the bench by the canna lilies, the terse nature of the response came back to him. Perhaps it was unreasonable to expect a meeting at short notice, but surely the headlines would excuse it. The lean figure was beside him on the seat before he was aware of its arrival.

'Pass the sandwiches. I don't have much time.' It was an uneasy conversation, or monologue, that ensued.

Jack sketched out the lines of the board meeting in broad strokes but, even to his own eye, the portrait was of a guilty suspect stuttering under the harsh light of interrogation. He described his confrontation with the press outside his house and again he could see himself as a weak reed. Why was he the victim when he should have been the aggressor? He put the question to the Pope in a variety of ways, but elicited only a series of grunts.

Finally the Pope screwed the brown paper bag into a tight ball and threw it in one clean arc into a rubbish bin.

'This is difficult. Very difficult. But I may not be able to help you anymore.'

Jack was stunned. The day was a series of sharp blows to the stomach. 'Christ. Why? Have I done something? Or not done something?'

The Pope shook his head. 'It's nothing to do with you, Jack, I give you my word. It might be okay, I'm not sure. But the group did say from the start that if any of us had conflicts, we might have to walk away. I'm just warning you.'

Jack held the rough wood on the weathered bench with both hands and felt a splinter pierce his thumb. What was happening? The world was closing in on him without remorse. 'I need you around. If you can. I really need you now.'

The Pope stood. 'I know. I'll do what I can, but I may have to go.'

He walked away a few paces and then turned back and held out his hand. 'Good luck.'

chapter fifteen

When he drove past the house, the workshop was a brooding shadow in the birch groves. He was too early. They never met before eight, but he had nowhere else to go. He parked outside the gate. What did it matter who saw him now?

The street was alive tonight. Executive cars were ferrying executive persons back to the safety of their leafy driveways and the welcome of their patient wives. Buses were disgorging schoolboys weighed down with backpacks full of football gear and *Catcher in the Rye*. Young women in tailored skirts and blazers were returning from law firms and accountants' offices insisting to their mothers that they wouldn't be waiting by panelled doors with peep holes for the return of the master. Dogs were leaping for joy at the gathering of the pack and the smell of lamb roasting in the oven. All was safe, placid, pleasant in the realm of suburbia.

Jack waited for an hour, watching. It reminded him of the life he'd grown up with and the relaxed easiness of it all came back to him in a drift of nostalgia. He remembered riding his bike down streets like this, arms in the air, just balancing with the sway of his body, not a care in the world. His cell phone rang and rang out. He switched it off. The street was quiet now. Dinner was being served. Homework books were being discovered under unwashed tracksuits next to half-eaten apples.

Television was siphoning off minds into unreality. The lights went on in the workshop.

Still he lingered. He was reluctant to go in. He placed both hands on the steering wheel, expecting them to be shaking with the irregular rhythm of his breathing, but they rested calmly on the yellowy leather. It was time.

He eased open the door then closed it gently behind him, as if it were important to be quiet. Clandestine meetings that everyone knew about still required respect for the conventions. He trod carefully on the soft covering of leaf litter. There was no wind to rustle the birches tonight, no moon to silver the trunks. A possum hissed and leapt in the branches above. He hesitated on the stone path when he could see the lighted window above the workbench, and listened to the whirring of the lathe. Sometimes it screamed and yowled as it tore at the wood, but tonight it was a steady, mechanical whirr. He knocked on the heavy, ribbed door.

There was no response. The lathe whirred, the birches stood guard. He rapped with a closed fist and the door rattled against the jamb. Nothing. Normally, all sounds would cease at his first knocking and then he would hear only the soft pad of slippers on the wide boards. He reached for the forged hasp, its manufacture previously described to him in loving detail, and the door swung open. He could see the dense bulk of the old lawyer hunched over the workbench, intent on the machine before him. He called out a greeting, but there was no response. And then he knew.

He was frozen. He couldn't approach the workbench. He had to move, but his systems wouldn't obey. He gulped great lungfuls of air. And then, in a rush, he was at the bench and his hands were on the shoulders and the body fell forward, face down on the rough wood.

He cried out as the lathe continued its scream, dangerously close to the gnarled face. Why was it still operating? The foot pedal. He sank to his knees and grasped the ankle in the thick wool sock and pushed, hard, but the foot wouldn't shift off the ugly contraption. It was wedged somehow, the weight of the body twisted onto it. He tried to lift the leg, to free the man from the machine, to stop the appalling noise that was now screaming into his brain. If only he could stop the noise everything would be all right.

He knelt higher, sweating under the bench, frantic, panicked, grasping at the legs and the trunk to shift the weight. He lifted and pushed simultaneously and suddenly the foot was free and the scream was stifled. He fell back in relief and sat, panting like an exhausted hound.

And then, before he could prevent it, the body began to slide, crashing to the floor in a swirl of sawdust and shavings. Now it wasn't a body anymore, but a man. The face was compressed into a grimace by the neck forcing it onto the floorboards, but it was the face he'd come to trust, to admire, maybe more.

He crawled to the man and held the face in his hands and wiped the shavings away. Should he be forcing the mouth open, breathing his breath into these lungs, pounding this old heart, running, ringing, someone, somewhere? But he knew he was holding only the body, not the life. He gently turned the face away from the floor and straightened the bent legs and flayed arms. The old lawyer was sleeping now, at peace in the detritus of his life's work, ready for the rituals of the world he'd left behind.

Jack slumped into the chair by the stove. He was shaking, shivering, still gulping air to no purpose and then, without warning or knowledge, he began to howl.

The long, haunting wail rose into the beams and rang off the iron roof and seemed never to stop.

That was how she found him, in her husband's chair, keening over his body. She'd lost a son, and part of a husband, long ago; she knew the living had more need of her. She knelt before the chair and wrapped his head in her and gradually the howling subsided into sobbing until finally his whole body relaxed into her, and it was over.

It was late, Louise would be worried. He'd rung no one. He felt he'd never switch on the phone again. They would retreat somewhere, the four of them, cocoon themselves in a safe haven. Run away, start anew. Tasmania, perhaps. Yes, Tasmania, Louise loved it there; the great forests, the wild rivers, the cleanest air on earth, the cleanest water. That was what they needed—to be washed clean of the grime of falsity and fakery.

It was finished now. There was only the old lawyer's funeral to come. The rest of it was buried already. He could leave any time he liked. He owed no one anything. He'd tried; it was more than most people bothered with. It was good enough.

But then there was Louise. Would she let go now? She'd have to see there was no chance without the old lawyer, have to realise their hopes lay in the sawdust on that concrete floor. She didn't have to know about his own failure. She could keep believing he was a hero defeated by circumstance. The truth wasn't always a necessity.

The house was ablaze with light when he drove up Alice Street. She was standing in the doorway, waiting, and ran to meet him on the path. She enveloped him and almost carried him into the house, and he was sobbing again before they reached the door.

'How did you know?'

'She rang. His wife. She said you needed looking after. What a remarkable woman.'

Sarah and Shane were waiting inside and the four of them held one another, wrapped together in a knot of limbs, not speaking. Finally, exhausted, they all found bed, if not sleep. He wanted to talk now, to tell her everything, even the failure, even the frailty, even his guilt. He'd killed an old man with his arrogance. He'd been warned, asked to stop, begged for compassion. But no, he'd known what was right, what was wrong, what was black and what was white. Well what did he know now? The sour taste of bile in the mouth, the rank odour of defeat and death.

She was patient with him, but pragmatic. Over-dramatisation was dismissed, though gently. She would have nothing of the guilt, nothing of the failure, but when he said he wanted to walk away, she didn't oppose it.

'We'll see. You've all your other friends helping you. The Pope or whatever his name is, and the others in the group. Talk to them. Seek their advice. That document is still in the safe, don't forget that. Yes, it's a tragedy this man has died. I think you loved him in some way. But be sorry for him, and his wife, not for yourself. And maybe we can make his death worth something. And if it doesn't all resolve itself, a stone cottage by a river in Tasmania with lupins in the paddocks and salmon in the oven sounds fine to me.'

When sleep came, it was the deep, still sleep of spent emotion from which waking is the only dream.

He was being shaken, he could feel it, but he was still in the half-dream. And then the voice, the soft voice of his daughter who had never woken before him in sixteen years. 'Dad. Dad! There are men downstairs. They want you. You have to come.'

He almost fell from the bed, but gestured for her to be silent as he saw the deep breathing of his wife under a sheet pulled half over her face. He was in the foyer before he knew it, with a robe pulled across a pair of striped boxer shorts and his feet bare on the stone floor. There were three of them, already in the house, waiting, in business suits. He looked at his watch. It was six a.m.

'Mr Beaumont, we represent the Australian Securities and Investments Commission. We hold a duly executed warrant to search these premises. We also wish to ask you questions pertaining to a current investigation. We will now commence the search.'

He didn't protest; what was there to protest about? He turned to Sarah and said, 'Go back to bed, darling. It's all right. It's just a business thing, just routine. Don't worry.'

But she came to him, clung to him. 'What's happening, Dad? Why is all this happening? I want everything to be like it used to be.'

'I know, darling. It will be. I just have to help these people and then we can go back to our old life. I promise.'

Still she held him and he could feel the shaking.

'They're not after me. I haven't done anything wrong. I'm trying to help them. You don't have to worry.' Finally she released him and he pushed her gently away down the corridor, though he could see her glancing back doubtfully as she turned the corner to her bedroom.

He sat in the breakfast room with coffee. He'd offered the remaining ASIC man a cup, but the offer had been politely refused. The man just sat there, not speaking—waiting, he supposed, to ensure no calls were made. That had been the instruction. He didn't need an instruction. He couldn't think of anyone to call.

The sun fell into the room in patterns on the floor just the way he'd designed it to fall. He'd stood on this site, with the model in his hand and watched the light strike the roofline and lifted the roof to imagine the shafts falling through the skylights. And now here they were, here he was, here was the ASIC man.

One of the others entered the room. 'There's a safe in a room out here, Brian.'

The seated man turned to Jack. 'Would you come and open the safe please, Mr Beaumont?'

He followed tamely and dialled the combination. He sat in a deep chair and tried not to see the body fall again, tried not to see the puff of sawdust as it hit the floor, tried not to hear the dull thud.

'What is this, Mr Beaumont?' He looked up. There was a pile of Louise's jewellery boxes on the table and the man was holding a paper. 'I'm sorry, what? I didn't hear you.'

The man handed him the paper. It was the Global Re side letter, the smoking gun, which might never fire now.

'Why is this company document in your private safe?' Exhaustion overcame him again. Sleep had restored no energy or, if it had, it had dissipated with his daughter's hand. 'It's a long story. It's the story you're searching for, I think, but I'd like to tell it some other time.'

'We'd like to hear it now, Mr Beaumont. In fact, we insist.' They both pulled chairs towards him and the spokesman placed a small tape recorder on the arm of one. How could he explain the saga? Where to start? Was there a finish? 'It's very complicated. We were about to turn over a whole pile of documents to you, a whole case really. This is one of them.'

'Who is we? Mr Beaumont?'

Jack pressed one hand to the top of his head, pressed down hard as if to prevent pain from spreading, dug his fingers into the scalp. 'Can't we do this some other time?

I'm trying to help you people. I'm the one who started all this, started digging into all this dirt. But I need a little time to put my thoughts in order.'

The man sat impassively and removed a small notebook from his breast pocket. 'What "dirt" are you referring to?'

Jack sighed. 'Look, I don't want to have to call lawyers and all that nonsense. I'm on your side. Just give me some time. It's been a rough period.'

'You referred to "we" in your previous comments. Who is we?' And so it began. He tried to outline the process, his initial concerns, his meeting with Hedley Stimson, their peculiar arrangement, his search for documents. As he sketched the lines, it sounded complex, even to him. The chief executive of a major company ferrying documents to a retired lawyer buried in the suburbs. He left out the group's involvement; that was too hard to explain.

'And we were nearly there. We felt we'd just about pieced it all together.'

The man stared at him. 'I see. That's what we normally do, Mr Beaumont, piece it all together. That's what the Australian Government has charged us with doing. It's not normally, or ever, the role of private citizens. Whoever they may be.' He turned a page in the notebook. 'Please give me the phone number and address of Mr Stimson.'

Jack hunched his shoulders up into the base of his neck and arched his head back. The tension in his skull was unbearable. He wanted to be out of this room, away from these people, running with his dog, riding bikes with his kids, away.

'He's dead.'

The pen remained poised over the notebook. 'I'm sorry, your meaning is unclear. Who is dead?'

'Hedley Stimson. The lawyer. He died last night.' Still the pen didn't move. 'But you've told us you were going to speak to him yesterday. That you were taking this document to him.'

'That's right. But when I got there he was dead.' He was starting to shake now. He could feel the tremors coursing through him. The body was falling again, slowly, so slowly. Why hadn't he stopped it, caught it before it hit the floor? He should've moved, should've held it to him, taken the weight and lowered it gently, with love. It was a shameful thing, the worst failure, to allow that fall, to hear that thud.

'So you replaced the document in the safe?' He was shivering uncontrollably. The sun was on him and he was as cold as he'd ever been. 'I killed him. I killed him with all this.'

'That's enough.' It was Louise's voice, calm, in control. 'He's not answering any more questions without a lawyer. We're prepared to cooperate with you, but in a proper environment with lawyers present.' She came down the stairs and stood behind Jack with both hands on his neck. 'I can confirm everything he says and am happy to give evidence, but in due course. Not in an atmosphere of tension and intimidation, and I repeat, not without our lawyer.'

The ASIC man switched off the tape. 'We have the right to ask questions wherever we wish, and in any manner we wish, Mrs Beaumont. It is Mrs Beaumont, I take it?'

She didn't flinch. 'It is. And we have the right to refuse. And we do so.'

'You have no such rights, Mrs Beaumont. But your refusal is noted.'

The floor was terrazzo, the walls panelled in dark wood, the tables clothed in white linen covered by paper, the waiters in long aprons. She might have been back in Rome, where she'd lived for a year after university, scratching a living as a part-time research assistant for an American professor, except the atmosphere was Sydney cool, not Italian buzz. She'd arrived early, nervous, still shattered by the events of the previous days and the effort of holding Jack, and the children, together. The day her father had left the house forever kept flashing into her mind. Her mother had run after him into the garden, into the street, clutching at him, trying to draw him back, when only minutes before she'd seemed set on driving him away. She'd always felt her mother was wrong. She should've forgiven him whatever the fault. What did it matter? They could have been together with forgiveness, they could have been a family. Instead there were all those years of a mother and a daughter pretending they preferred life alone.

'I'm sorry I'm late, Louise. I hope you haven't been waiting long.'

He slid into the chair opposite her and she found she was unreasonably glad to see him. 'You're not late. I was early. Remind me, it is John I use on Thursdays, isn't it?'

The Pope smiled. 'Yes, it is.' He waved a waiter to the table. 'Will you eat, or just coffee? A glass of wine?'

'I'd love something. I haven't eaten today. The pattern of life is a little confused at the moment.'

She watched him order, take charge, and relaxed back into the chair. That was what she wanted—for someone to take charge. Everyone assumed that inside she was as strong as the shield she wore externally. But to have someone else command, take over, what a relief to be able to cast off the burden of care.

'How is Jack?' He saw the disappointment on her face. 'More to the point, how are you? It must be very hard.'

She began to speak, but the tears came before the words. It was impossible, to be crying in a public place, with a man she barely knew, but it was impossible to stop. He slipped around into the chair alongside and took her hand, not speaking, just a strong hand holding hers. The waiter placed the food and water on the table and glanced at her as he did so, but still she cried. Finally the hand was withdrawn.

'The pasta will be cold and the wine will be warm.' He passed her a white handkerchief from his pocket and she took it gratefully. It smelled of sun and she could see his initials in blue in one corner.

'It's a beautiful handkerchief. Thank you.' He laughed. 'Please keep it, although you'd better unpick the initials or your husband might get jealous.'

'I don't think he'd have any case on that score, do you?' He glanced at her quizzically. They ate in silence for a while. 'We need help. It's too much. Hedley Stimson's death, ASIC, Jack's suspension. You heard about that?'

'Yes, it was on the screens this morning. Along with a beautifully crafted press release from Sir Laurence. "The company makes no presumption of guilt regarding the investigation of the actions of its CEO, but believes the suspension of his duties pending the outcome of such investigation is in the interest of shareholders."'

She let her fork fall into the remains of the pasta. 'I notice they didn't suspend Mac Biddulph.'

'You can't suspend a director of a public company. The shareholders can vote him out in a general meeting, but the board has no power to oust a director.'

She folded her napkin and placed it beside the bowl. 'Can you help us? I mean, can you help us more? I know you've already contributed a great deal, but now we need a new direction, a new lawyer—I don't know. This is all beyond my experience.' She leaned forward, trying to hold him with her eyes. 'I feel we'll never recover from this if we don't fight. Jack's reputation may never recover anyway. Mud sticks, doesn't it, even though you wash it clean. It sticks in people's dirty minds.'

He watched her carefully as she spoke and saw the turmoil beneath her struggle for composure. 'There are enough people who know Jack's real character to outweigh the others, if he holds on.'

'You really believe that?'

'Yes.'

'So will you help us?' He took the bowls and stacked them with the side plates and gestured for the waiter to clear the table. Her heart sank as she watched him. 'I can't help you any longer. I'm deeply sorry.'

Somehow this seemed the worst blow of all. He'd been her secret hope, the mysterious, powerful boundary rider who would make it all come right.

'I'm ashamed to say this to you, but I must say it.' He reached for her hand again, but she drew it away. He nodded resignedly. 'It's difficult to explain, I—'

She cut in. 'Don't bother. You can't help. Let's not confuse matters with unnecessary explanation.' She took up her handbag from the spare chair, but this time he grasped her arm before she could withdraw.

'Please. Don't go. It's not like that. I'm not a fair-weather friend.' He held her to the chair. 'Will you answer one question for me? If you could save a child of yours or a friend of yours, but not both, which would you choose?'

She looked into his eyes and saw the pain and knew it was real. 'I don't understand.'

'And I can't explain.' He stood and placed money on the saucer with the bill. 'Go to the group. Go to Jack's friends. I'm not a member anymore, but they'll help you.' He held out his hand. 'One day, I hope you'll forgive me and want to see me again. I'll always want to see you.'

When she stumbled out into the glaring sun, she was blinded and confused. She crossed the busy road with cars hooting at her. She wandered into Hyde Park without reason or purpose. She felt old and unattractive and lost. She was a woman in an expensive suit with eyes red from crying, stripped bare of artifice or mask. She came upon a giant chess board cut into a corner of the park, with a group of men moving the pieces about the squares. She sat on a stone parapet nearby, to watch, without seeing. An old man smiled at her, but it was a smile of pity.

She walked back to the street and past a newsstand. The poster had the letters HOA and a picture of Jack with some other word, and she hurried away from it. She tried to hail a taxi but none stopped, so she just stood there, for how long she wasn't sure, watching the traffic roar by. And then she heard the voice and focused on the taxi with the driver calling to her through the open window.

She was going home.

chapter sixteen

Mac was already seated in the wicker armchair on the verandah when the dawn chorus greeted the promise of first light. First came the raucous laughter of the blue-winged kookaburras—a satirical parody of the bigger laughing kookaburra he was used to hearing in Sydney. Then the single-note contact calls and territorial screeches of the galahs, followed by the loud yodelling of the secretive black butcherbirds. He'd never seen one of these birds despite years of trudging through creek beds with binoculars at the ready. He wondered if they sometimes impaled their prey on a thorn before devouring it, like their cousins, the grey butcherbirds. But then there were so many conflicting calls ringing out through the eucalypts and bouncing off the rocky outcrops that he couldn't distinguish one from another.

He sat very still in the chair. He loved this time of day in this place. He loved being alone here. He smiled inwardly at the thought. Most people wouldn't believe Mac Biddulph was a nature lover, but of all the things he stood to lose, the loss of Bellaranga would hurt the most. Fishing in the rivers for barramundi, hunting for rock art in the helicopter, riding into palm-filled valleys surrounded by red rock cliffs, the dawn chorus. And the people. There was no pretence in these people; they were straightforward, blunt, as tough as the landscape. They were his sort of people—honest and hardworking.

Well, who would ever see him as honest again? All they had to do was charge you with something and your reputation was shredded forever. Not that they'd charged him with anything yet. But they would.

What would happen to his people here? Who would look after them if he lost this place? When he lost it. It was when, not if. He had to be realistic. Even if the banks didn't take it, even if they couldn't navigate their way through the reefs of dummy companies and legal atolls littered in their course, he couldn't pay the bills anymore. Simple as that. Now the cash tap was turned off it was frightening how quickly the pipes blocked up. So who would look after his people?

In the half-light he saw a shadowy figure making its way slowly to the windmill. He was always first up, old Frank. Too old to ride, too old for mustering or even cutting out. Reduced to gardening, but still one of his people. There were no Aborigines working the cattle anymore, all that magic horsemanship lost to welfare cheques and booze, but old Frank stayed and worked and rose at first light everyday. He was going blind now, but he could see enough.

Mac called to his dog and hurried across the lawn to catch the old man before he disappeared. Frank could disappear in a desert.

'Morning, boss. You're up early, eh? Not sleeping well, eh?'

'I'm sleeping fine, Frank. I just didn't want to miss the dawn. When you're our age you don't know how many you've got left.'

The old man cackled. 'You've got a few on me, eh?'

'I wouldn't be too sure. You look pretty fit, Frank. But how are the eyes? Any worse?'

The furrowed black face was almost obscured by a large pair of spectacles smattered with grime and dust. 'Not so good, boss.'

'Maybe you need to give the specs a wash now and again.' The cackling laugh escaped once more. 'Tried that, boss. Didn't do any good. Gave it up. Save the water, eh?'

Mac gestured for him to sit down on the edge of the trough. 'Tell you what, Frank, they're pretty good with eyes now. They can probably fix you up in a real hospital, no problem.'

'No hospitals out here, boss. Too far for me to go, now. Just a bit too far.'

Mac stroked his chin. 'What about this, old fellow. The helicopter will fly you up to the Mitchell Plateau and then we'll get a plane to take you down to Perth. We can find a good man down there—fix you up in no time. What do you reckon?'

The shoulders slumped a little and the face looked down at the dirt. 'Don't know, boss. Don't know any blackfellers ever been in one of them. Plane maybe, not helicopter. Bit too old, eh?'

Mac clapped him on the back. 'Bulldust. We're gonna do it. I'm going to fix it right now. Soon as one of those lazy bastards is up and about I'll be onto the doctor. We'll fix it up, Frank. What do you reckon?'

The eyes looked up at him cautiously from under the brim of a battered hat. 'Don't know.'

Mac laughed and jumped to his feet. He was alive and full of action now. 'But I do, Frank. I know. That's what you've got me for, to know what to do. You'll be bringing down roos at two hundred metres before you know it.'

They walked together for a while, discussing which trees to plant before the wet, which fruit would set in the harsh environment of the Kimberley. Frank was the only one who stayed on the property in the wet season, when roads were impassable, mosquitoes and mould were ubiquitous, and life was unbearable. Mac wondered if he'd ever be back after the wet. Probably not. This was probably his last good season before the rains came and his own troubles with them.

He could hear the helicopter by the time he'd reached the homestead and he thought to himself, 'Here they come now.'

Gerry Lacy had never been to Bellaranga before, or the Kimberley, or Western Australia, or anywhere much in his own country. He'd been to New York and Paris and London any number of times, of course. He'd been to Rome more times than he could remember. Well, three, actually. He'd been to Tuscany, and sailed from Elba to Corsica. (Not sailed with sails, but 'sailed' in the normal sense, with a motor.) He'd been all over France in a rented Porsche which, while it wasn't French, seemed entirely appropriate for driving along the Côte d'Azur. But he'd never been further than a hundred and fifty kilometres inland in Australia. What was there to see anyway except a huge rock? What would be the appropriate vehicle to drive? Some ugly Toyota with a sort of snorkel poking up from its bonnet. It was hardly a Porsche, was it? There'd be dust and flies instead of cheese and wine. And no golf.

But here he was in the Kimberley, flying around in a helicopter no bigger than a hornet, with a lawnmower motor and no doors. He shivered at the thought of no doors and cowered into the bucket seat.

He could see Mac Biddulph standing in the only patch of green as they came in to land. It was sad, very sad, what was happening to Mac. He was a client, after all. They were not really friends, socially, or anything near. Mac didn't mix with the right people really, wasn't a member of The Golf Club, for instance. They never named the golf club, the members—just called it that, 'The Golf Club'. You either knew or you didn't, and if you didn't, there was no help for you. Mac was rich, or had been rich, but that wasn't enough. An unpleasant thought disturbed Gerry's ruminations. 'Had been rich . . .' was unfortunate terminology. He'd have to ask the firm's accounts department to keep an eye on the payment of fees. No point in letting things drift too far; it would only add to Mac's problems.

Gerry looked around nervously as the helicopter landed in swirling dust clouds. It was his own fault he was here. He'd advised Mac all his phones would be tapped and his cell phone monitored. They knew about the *Honey Bear*—who didn't—and that would be under surveillance, along with his residences and Bonny's apartment. So here they were in this godforsaken place. Two days with Mac Biddulph on a cattle property wasn't Gerry's idea of fun—but think of the years of litigation to follow, think of the fees. If they were paid.

'What a remarkable place, Mac. So . . . so far from anywhere, so . . . rugged.'

Mac took the oversize golf bag from the pilot. 'Lucky you didn't crash with this thing on board. It must weigh a ton. Planning a couple of rounds in a dry river bed, are we, Gerry?'

'All part of the cover, Mac. Off on a golfing weekend. We don't want your ASIC friends snooping around, do we?'

'You're kidding? You don't really think they'd come up here?' They sat in the relative cool of the louvred verandah with tall glasses of iced tea. Gerry tried to explain the powers lined up against them. They never understood, these business types. They always assumed they were above the law, or that corporate crime was softer than shoplifting and the corporate regulators had the muscles of a midget.

'They can legally tap your phones, run twenty-four-hour surveillance on you, subpoena you to appear whenever they want, search you and your properties and, if they develop half a case against you, freeze your assets, take your passport—the lot. Their powers are much wider than those of the police and the sanctions are severe.'

Mac nodded. 'I know, Gerry. I do listen.' His anger seemed to have dissipated, Gerry thought. At least that was something. 'What are the sanctions? I mean if they ever charge me with anything, and convict me, what can I go for? Fines, that sort of thing?'

Gerry drank deeply from the iced tea, which was excellent. Just the right balance of sweet and sour. 'I think it's premature to discuss that sort of thing, Mac.'

'Sure. But let's just say they get something on me, some weird breach of some feeble law no one even knows about, what could I go for? Ban me as a director?'

This wasn't the perfect start to close confinement under a corrugated-iron roof, Gerry felt. There were certain words in any solicitor–client discussion that were better left unsaid. He felt one of them coming on now.

'I mean, there's no chance of jail, is there? For Christ's sake, they wouldn't be trying for that, would they? Just for a few bucks out of a company I built from nothing?'

Gerry held up his hand. 'Please, Mac, don't tell me anything I don't need to know. Just respond to the exact questions I put to you. And the same goes for the ASIC examination. Only answer the question put, preferably with a yes or no. Don't add anything, don't give anything away. That's the art of it.'

But the unanswered question hung between them and Mac looked at him with raised eyebrows.

'You have to understand, some potential charges are criminal offences. Certain breaches of the Corporations Act, if proven, do carry severe penalties. It depends where they go.' He replaced the glass carefully on the low table and took up a lined pad, but Mac persisted.

'And where could they go?' Gerry referred to the notepad. 'I was hoping to summarise that at the conclusion of our discussions, but if you insist.' Mac nodded. 'Very well. There's the recent sale of your shares. That raises a number of questions—insider trading, failure to report, breach of directors' duties . . .'

Mac cut in angrily. 'But I lost money on the fucking sale.'

'I'm afraid that makes no difference. Whether you profit by ten million dollars or one dollar or lose money isn't relevant. And yes, there are potential criminal charges.'

There was silence for a few moments. 'What else?' 'There are three main areas of concern. First, what we might term corporate governance matters.' He saw Mac wince. 'That is, matters related to the company's accounts, reinsurance arrangements and the like, and your role as a director. Second, possible misappropriation of the company's assets to your personal account. And third, flowing from these but not really a matter for ASIC, possible tax fraud.'

Mac rose and walked to the verandah steps. 'Well, thank you, Gerry. That really sets me up for the day. Why don't you get settled—Martha will show you to your room. Then we can start. I'm going for a ride.'

Gerry had to admit the fish was superb. Grilled barramundi with just a slice of lemon and a dab of macadamia pesto. He'd never had pesto made with macadamias before but it was surprisingly good. And the wine—the wine was incomparable. When the '94 Grange Hermitage arrived with the meat, he was in heaven.

'This is beyond expectations, Mac. You really live very well here.'

Mac glanced at him sourly; it had been a long day. Gerry Lacy might not be his choice as a life partner, but he was thorough, very thorough. Not that five hours of questioning had improved Mac's temper, or his confidence. It was worse than the banks—at least they couldn't put you in jail.

'What is this meat, Mac? It's delicious. And the relish? Some sort of chutney, is it?'

'Wouldn't have a clue about the relish. Ask Martha when she brings dessert. The meat's kangaroo, killed on the old place. They don't hang it long. Better to eat it when the blood's still fresh.'

Gerry felt he hadn't needed to know about the fresh blood. But the meat was tender and moist, and then there was the wine.

'Seems bloody ridiculous. Some goddamn game of rules where you don't know the rules.'

Gerry was startled. Somehow they'd leapt from blood to rules. 'I'm sorry, Mac. Rules?'

'These ASIC idiots. Running around saying I've broken some rule or other. What fucking rule? Where are they written down?'

Gerry took more than a sip of the wine, to fortify himself for a long debate. 'Well, strictly, they're written down, Mac, in laws.'

Mac pushed his plate away. 'Laws. Who can read laws except you bloody lawyers? No offence. How does the average citizen get on? How's the average bloke supposed to know when he's breaking the law?'

Gerry's gaze took in the relaxed grandeur of the homestead's main room, the enormous cowhide sofas, the table they were dining at which could comfortably seat twenty people, the sideboard struggling to support an astonishing array of fruit, decanters, bowls of nuts and a silver dish of what appeared to be gold bonbons. He couldn't for a moment bring to mind an appropriate response, so he sipped the wine again.

'I mean who makes the goddamn rules anyway?' Mac's face was now beginning to redden, either from anger or wine, or both.

'Well, I suppose parliament makes them, Mac.'

'Fucking parliament. Fucking politicians. Scumbags. Arseholes. Never done a day's work in their lives, any of them. Who are they anyway? Who do they represent?'

It was difficult for Gerry to avoid responding. There were only the two of them in this vast room. There was nowhere to hide. 'I suppose the people. I mean, they're elected after all. In a democracy. So they represent the people.'

Mac's fist crashed into the table and sent a shower of cutlery onto the floorboards. 'Don't lecture me. All goddamn day I'm being lectured. By who? By a fucking lawyer.'

He stomped to the verandah door, then turned and walked back to stand over the seated figure. Gerry Lacy flinched visibly at the unbridled belligerence on the face glaring down at him.

'That's why you like golf, isn't it, Gerry? Rules. All the fucking rules in the world. "The Golf Club". Pretentious place for pretenders like you. Lawyers and wankers and people with a map of their family tree on the living room wall. They blackballed me, you know? Did you know that? No, I can see by your face you didn't. Years ago, some snide prick, even though they say there's no blackballing. One word to the committee—that's all it takes. Probably thought I was a Jew. They don't like Jews at "The Golf Club", do they Gerry? But they can't say it; only in the locker room. Let the Jews have their own golf club. I probably am a Jew, for all I know. My dad drifted all over the world and washed up here. I never looked it up. Never gave a damn what I was, what anyone else was. Just what they did. And I don't give a fuck for your rules either.'

He slammed the screen door and then there was silence. Gerry sat quite still for a moment. He'd been afraid there might be a physical attack on his person. His appetite had almost departed with the fury that stormed out the door. Although it would be a shame to waste the wine. He sipped. Perhaps a taste of the meat to complement that rich back flavour. He wondered if there'd be cheese—much more appropriate than anything sweet with a wine of this quality.

As Mac stumbled onto the lawn, his dog ran from its kennel under the steps. It was a working dog, a kelpie–blue heeler cross, never allowed inside the house. It brushed Mac's leg gently with its tail and waited for instructions. He bent down and rubbed its head. 'G'day, you mongrel. Just a mongrel like me, aren't you, Bluey? Come on, mate, let's have a walk.'

They left the house lights washing onto the soft lawn and trod, morosely in Mac's case but joyfully in the dog's, into the blackness of the Kimberley night. Once they were a short distance from the homestead and all the artificial light had vanished, the stars were as bright on the horizon as they were directly above. But there was no moon and the ground was rocky and uneven.

He was surprised to fall. It seemed unfair to be lying on your own ground, on a track you'd walked a hundred times, with pain in your leg and a rock under your hip. He tried to roll to one side and then the pain screamed at him from his hip. He cried out at the intensity of it, but there was no one to hear except the dog. Where was the dog? Off chasing roos or rabbits. No, here it was, licking his face and then stepping back to watch him. Christ, the pain was awful.

'Jesus, Bluey, this is crook, old feller. Mac's not so good.' He tried to sit up and gain leverage to stand but fell back with another cry. 'No good, mate, no good at all.'

He lay there, panting, with the dog walking around him now, sniffing. It whined quietly when he didn't move and then snuffled and licked at his legs. It was cold lying on the ground and he began to shiver with the night air and the pain. The dog came to his face again and licked his head and neck, and he didn't brush it away. He moaned quietly as he tried to ease the hip. The dog walked away a few paces and watched him, its head on one side. It came back and nudged at his body with its snout. He didn't move. It sat alongside him, watching, listening.

He was very cold now, and frightened. The Kimberley temperatures could be like a desert. No one would come for him till morning. He often walked at night, although usually with a torch. Martha would leave, Gerry was useless. They'd be here all night.

He felt the dog sniffing him again and tried to reach out a hand to pull it near him, for its warmth. But as he did so, he felt the whole body step over him and lower itself gently onto his body, with its face below his chin.

Frank found them that way after dawn, one on the other.

There were four of them this time. The three who'd come to Bonny's apartment and a newcomer. He looked different, the new one. Not just because he wasn't in a grey suit; the navy blue jacket, white shirt and the black shoes weren't enough in themselves to make a difference. There was something else Mac couldn't pin down. He was polished at the edges somehow, someone to watch, someone to fear.

'Good morning, Mr Biddulph, Mr Lacy. My name is Todd Gamble. I'm assisting the Australian Securities and Investments Commission in this investigation.'

There it was—an American accent. Gerry Lacy leaned forward immediately. 'Assisting? What is this? Are you an employee of ASIC, a lawyer assisting—what is your status?'

The nerd who had been the leader in the search, the nerd who'd had Bonny's knickers nestling in his suit pocket, interrupted. 'Mr Gamble is a consultant who's been employed by ASIC under the terms of the Act. We have a right to seek expert advice from wherever we choose. Mr Gamble was formerly a senior investigator with the FBI.'

Mac felt a shiver run down his spine. Shivers actually ran down spines? He'd only read about that in books or heard about it in movies. But it happened. He'd heard plenty about FBI agents in movies. And now they'd sent one after him. Jesus.

'My client reserves the right to object to the admissibility of any evidence obtained in this examination. It seems quite improper to have outside persons, people from other jurisdictions, involved in an Australian process.'

The nerd just smiled. 'This isn't a court hearing, Mr Lacy. There's no judge to object to. Now can we get on?'

Gerry placed a sheet of notepaper in front of Mac with one word handwritten on it in black letters. In their briefings Gerry had said: 'We're claiming legal privilege for each answer you give, Mac. That positions us better in any subsequent court proceedings, but you have to claim it yourself before each answer. You have to say the word "privilege" before each and every answer, otherwise that particular answer doesn't have legal privilege attached to it. You understand?'

Gerry could see him nodding now at the word on the notepaper. 'My client will be claiming privilege for each of his answers. This is not an admission of any guilt but merely the result of legal advice.'

The nerd gestured to the ex-FBI man and switched on a tape recorder.

There was no way they'd make him sweat, not even for a minute; Mac had sworn that to himself. He'd been in training in the Kimberley for weeks after Gerry had left, leading a monastic life, in training to beat the bastards. At first he'd been embarrassed when there was only bruising from the fall, but then he'd risen with the dawn every day, ridden before breakfast, eaten well, drunk only water and coffee, lost three kilos. He was fit and alert. He was Mac Biddulph. He'd been playing in the big time when these bastards were still on the teat. There was no way they'd make him sweat.

But it was stifling in the interview room. There were no windows and the air-conditioning, if they had any, wasn't working. After the first hour, he was dry in the mouth, even though the questions had all been anticipated in his sessions with Gerry. He gulped more water from the paper cup and tried to focus on the FBI guy. He was asking something about Renton Healey.

'Did you instruct Renton Healey, the chief financial officer at HOA, to initiate discussion with Global Re regarding a new form of reinsurance contract?'

This wasn't something they'd covered in the briefings. How could they know about the Global Re contract? Well, of course they'd know about it, it'd be listed in the company's filings with APRA. But that's all they'd know. They couldn't know about the side letter and they certainly couldn't know what he had or hadn't said to Renton Healey.

'Privilege. No.' He smiled at the FBI man. It was a 'fuck you' smile.

'Did you discuss with Renton Healey the subject of a "hole" in the balance sheet that would have to be filled?'

'Privilege. No.'

'Did you suggest to Mr Healey that the profit and loss account for last year needed "short-term support"?'

'Privilege. No.'

'Did Laurence Treadmore inquire of you whether you had had such discussions with Renton Healey and did you give him assurances that the Global Re contract was "kosher"?'

'Privilege. No.' A wider smile spread across Mac's face. They had nothing. But the FBI man just stared blankly at him.

'Let me play you this recording, Mr Biddulph.' Gerry Lacy was on his feet in an instant. Gerry seemed to have been in training also, as if he sensed a second breath in his legal career. Maybe he could be a killer if he wanted to and, suddenly, he wanted to. 'Recording? What recording? I object most strenuously. Is this a recording made without Mr Biddulph's knowledge or consent? This is outrageous.'

'You're objecting to a recording you haven't heard, Mr Lacy. Why don't you listen?'

The FBI man pushed the button on the tape recorder. Laurence Treadmore's voice squeaked thinly from the machine followed, unmistakably, by Mac's. Gerry stepped forward and punched the stop button.

'We're not participating any further in this discussion until you explain the nature of this recording, the circumstances in which it was made, whether Mr Biddulph had knowledge that he was being recorded, and by what authority you are in possession of the tape.' He glared at the FBI man, but it was a faint glare.

Mac cut in. 'I never authorised anyone to tape me—not even you bastards.'

'Privilege, Mac. Privilege.'

Now it was the FBI man's turn to smile. 'This is a recording made in the boardroom of HOA of a meeting between Sir Laurence Treadmore and Macquarie James Biddulph on September eighteenth last year. It was made with your permission, Mr Biddulph.'

Mac rocked back in his chair and was about to respond but Gerry Lacy spoke first. 'Leave this to me, Mac. My client had no knowledge of any such recording being made. You're perfectly well aware you can't use material obtained in this way.' And then, as an added thrust, 'Even the FBI can't use illegally obtained recordings, can they, Mr Gamble?'

The FBI man resumed his expressionless mask and placed a document before Mac. 'Are you familiar with this document, Mr Biddulph?'

'What is this? What document? We object to the document—' but Mac cut him off.

'Shut up, Gerry. Let me look at the fucking document for Christ's sake.'

He reached for the paper. It was headed 'HOA. Corporate Governance Committee. Policy for Security and Integrity of Information.'

'I've never seen this before in my life.'

'Privilege, Mac.'

'Really, Mr Biddulph. Would you turn to the last page, please. Is that your signature?'

Gerry was poised over Mac's shoulder. 'We object, most strenuously. This meeting is at an end.'

'It's not a meeting, Mr Lacy. You're here in response to a legal notice to attend, and the examination is just beginning. Now, is that your signature, Mr Biddulph?'

'Don't answer, Mac, I instruct you not to answer.'

'Shut up, Gerry. Privilege. If it is my signature, I never read the document.'

'Do you sign many documents you don't read, Mr Biddulph?'

'Sometimes. Fucking privilege. Sometimes. When they're crap like this. What does it say, anyway?'

The FBI man recovered the document. 'It authorises recording of all discussions held in the HOA boardroom between directors or senior officers of the company, whether during the course of board meetings or otherwise. It further authorises the use of such recordings in any legally constituted investigation or court proceeding relating to the company's activities. It's been signed by all directors, including yourself.'

The sweat was dribbling down the Mac frame now, oozing from the neck under the shirt collar, trickling onto the Mac chest—hairy at the moment, no waxing in the Kimberley—pooling in his navel, soaking through his non-sweat shirt, Sea Island cotton, hand made, initials on the pocket, double cuffs, wide gap for the big Mac wrists, wide tuck to the shoulders. It was reaching the linen boxer shorts made from pure Irish linen by his man in Jermyn Street, to his own design, to let things breathe, to let the big Mac prick breathe and flex and have a life of its own.

There was nothing to say. He was skinned, skewered, hung out to dry.

He stood and walked out of the interview room, heedless of the gaggle of protests he left behind.

chapter seventeen

She arrived at the restaurant early and parked outside to wait.

It was the quintessential Sydney summer day. The Bondi surf was rolling in with a series of long, even lines of white foam breaking along the curved beach; a line of athletic bodies in singlets and running shorts puffing past her car window, so close she could smell the sweat and suntan oil; the fragrant aroma of spiced meat sizzling on a barbecue drifting up from the grassed area above the sand; the sweet, tangy smell of freshly cut grass; and the languorous feeling of wellbeing on the faces of the tourists and surfers and posers who flocked to claim a towel's width of territory on the white sand. She breathed it all in but, for once, it failed to move her. It was her place, where she'd grown up, had her first almost everything, met Jack, breathed free. But she couldn't enjoy it today.

She waited for them to go in. But after half an hour, only two men had entered the restaurant and it was well past the appointed time. She pushed open the door and approached the pair seated at the long table. One came forward. 'Mrs Beaumont? Louise? I'm Murray Ingham.' She shook his hand and tried to avoid staring at his eyebrows. 'This is Maroubra. Please sit down.'

It felt very lonely, to all three, to be huddled at one end of a table for twelve with nine empty chairs staring at them with vacant seats.

'Where are the others?' She felt it was a question no one wanted asked, so she put it on the table before the pleasantries. Murray Ingham shifted in his seat. 'The Pope said you were direct.'

'Did he?' She placed her hands flat on the table as if to steady herself. 'I'm hoping you'll be equally straightforward with me, Mr Ingham.'

Maroubra spoke for the first time. 'We're here to help, Louise. We've been trying to help already, and we're going to press on if we can.'

She nodded and gave him a weak smile. 'Where are the others?'

Murray Ingham leaned forward, perhaps to take one of her hands, but she drew back and folded her arms tightly across her chest. He spoke softly, almost in a whisper, in a room where there was no one to overhear. 'I'm afraid we're all there is. You have to understand, when we started it was agreed anyone could drop out if a conflict of interest arose.'

She waited for him to finish, but there was no more. Her eyes travelled over the empty chairs. 'And a great number of conflicts have arisen?'

'Yes.' She seemed to press her arms tighter against her body and to draw back as if to protect herself. 'The Pope said there was a lawyer in the group who would help us. Are either of you lawyers?'

'No.'

She sagged almost imperceptibly. 'I don't really know much about the group. Jack doesn't even know I'm here. Can I ask what the two of you do when you're not lunching?'

Maroubra answered. 'I'm a salvage operator. Murray is a writer—novelist, biographer, that sort of thing—as you probably know.'

She began to laugh, too hard. 'God help us. A salvage man and a storyteller. That's what we have left. We're dead, Jack, we're dead and buried.'

Now she was sobbing, and Murray Ingham rose and stood behind her, resting his hands on her shoulders. No one spoke. Gradually she regained control and her hands flew to her face. 'God, I'm so sorry. That was unforgivable. You're trying to help us and I was rude beyond reason. Please . . .'

Murray cut her off and held her before she could draw away.

'It's all right. You're entitled.' He waited until she looked up at him. 'You can call me a storyteller anytime. And Maroubra has been called more names than he can remember. The only insult you could throw his way would be "coward", and I don't think you'll find cause for that.' He smiled and released her hands. 'We may not be much, but we're here.'

When she finally began to talk, the words poured out, tumbling over one another in a disconnected series of scenes and snapshots: the death of the old lawyer, the ASIC raid, their meeting with Renton Healey, the document in the safe, the old lawyer's wife, Jack's determination, Jack's lack of determination, her commitment. All were jumbled in a kaleidoscope of shifting pieces, out of context, out of chronology, beyond order. But they let her run on, allowed the catharsis of the outpouring to take its course. Finally she staggered to a halt, almost breathless, and looked around dazedly.

'Is there water? Please, could I have water?'

Maroubra rose and disappeared through the kitchen door. Louise and Murray sat in silence until he returned with a glass. She drained it off. They waited.

'The lawyer from the group, what's his name? Why can't he be here?'

Maroubra answered. 'Tom Smiley.' He paused. 'He's accepted a brief as Mac Biddulph's barrister.'

'Oh, God.' Now her body slumped down. She shook her head. 'The whole world's against us, isn't it? He said it would happen this way, the old lawyer. It's just as he predicted. He told Jack everyone would run for cover once the bombs started falling, and they have, haven't they?'

'Not quite.' Murray Ingham drew a small black notebook from his breast pocket and snapped back the elastic strap from its cover. 'Why don't you tell us the story again? Sometimes stories are more powerful than you imagine. Let's see if we can weave a warm coat from what seems cold comfort.'

She shivered at the words, although the day was humid and the empty restaurant was airless and lifeless. 'Did you meet him, Hedley Stimson, the old lawyer?'

Murray shook his head. 'No.'

'Nor did I. But Jack put all his trust, all his hopes, in him and I came to also. And then, when he died, I turned to Clinton Normile.' She saw their vague expressions. 'The Pope. And he brushed me aside. Now this other lawyer abandons us for Mac Biddulph. Where am I to go?'

Maroubra spoke. 'Try us. We're not sloping off anywhere. I know a bit more about this than you might imagine. I had people working on it for the Pope. Tell Murray the story again. His brain works differently. You might be surprised.'

And so she began. The sun patterned the yellow floorboards as the pen moved relentlessly across the lined pages. On and on she went, only stopping to clarify in response to a question or to drink when Maroubra returned with more water. As she watched the notebook fill with her words, with their life, her hopes rose. Unreasonably, illogically, she began to believe there was a power in those pages that would save them. When she stepped out into the sun again, leaving the two men at the table as they had been when she'd entered three hours earlier, her spirits lifted with the roar of the surf and the smell of salt. She wanted to run down onto the sand, into the breakers, fully clothed—to feel the grip of the water, to wrestle with the waves. But she turned away, to the car, to Jack. What news did she have to bolster him with? Pages in a notebook. She'd make something of it.

Jack wasn't at home when Louise returned to Alice Street. He was deep in the paperbark forest in Centennial Park, staring blankly at the peeling sheets of white-pink bark, listening to Joe sloshing through the reedy swamp. The dog was where it shouldn't be, in the pungent mud of Lachlan Swamp, but then so was everything else where it shouldn't be. He walked slowly along the raised boardwalk, counting the slats as he went, for no reason. He had nothing else to do, no office to go to, no speeches to make, no conferences to attend, no meetings to take, no plans to draw, no colleagues to converse with, no accolades to accept, no reports to read, no orders to give—nothing. Just the trees and the swamp and a dog mired in rotting compost. He came to a clearing in the forest and leaned against the pulpy surface of an ancient trunk. The sheets of fibrous bark compressed under the weight of his body and he let his head fall back into the softness. The tree was alive in its skin, welcoming, comforting, giving. You could strip great sheets of its bark and make vessels or carrying bags or wrappings as the Aborigines had, or just hold the skin and let the life flow into you, as he was now. He spread his arms around the trunk, three trunks really, melded together in a fluted pillar. He closed his eyes and let the sun fall through the dense canopy onto his hair and face.

When he opened his eyes, both Joe and a small group of Japanese tourists were staring at him with some interest, obviously intrigued to see a genuine Australian tree-hugger in a native forest. He wondered if they'd taken pictures. He called to the dog and they emerged from the paperbarks, heading towards a wooden bridge.

As they did so, he noticed the figure of a man he remembered seeing earlier in their walk. He was wearing a dark tracksuit and a peculiar cap with an unusually long brim. Jack glanced at him quickly then strode off at a brisk pace towards the ponds. He didn't look back until they'd reached the kiosk where the bike-riders came to refuel on Saturday mornings. He couldn't see the man and was relieved. Somehow he'd felt he was being followed. Paranoia was creeping into his psyche. He had just clipped the malodorous dog back onto the lead, when he noticed a familiar shape near the queue at the kiosk. There was the peaked cap.

He tugged at Joe's lead and they almost ran between the two ponds and into a dense palm grove. Why he should be running from anyone he wasn't sure, but panic was upon him. The dog sensed the change in mood and whined and pulled at the lead. He released him now they were clear of the waterbirds and the animal darted in and out of the palms, chasing shadows and sunbeams, looking back now and again to check if his master was still intent on a mad dash through the fallen fronds. Jack couldn't see the dark tracksuit behind him, but he could hear someone crashing through the brush. He was sweating, panting, dry in the mouth and, he suddenly realised, a ridiculous figure. What was he running from? Who could be following him? What harm could they do him in a public place? Well, not so public here, in this lonely dark grove, but who would want to harm him anyway?

He stopped, breathing heavily, and stood behind one of the palms to wait for whatever was coming. The dog also halted its insane careering about and stood to one side, a gothic hound covered in a coat of drying mud and attached debris. Jack could hear his pursuer's laboured breathing now as he made heavy weather through the thick matted fronds. And then, suddenly, the familiar shape with the long peak over the face emerged only a few metres away. Jack stepped from behind the trunk.

'Who the hell are you? Why are you following me?' The figure let out a startled cry, looked up from the ground in surprise, and as it did so, tripped and crashed into the crackling brush. The dog, growling at this bizarre disturbance, rushed at the fallen figure, snarling over the face. A man's voice called out from the ground.

'Jesus Christ. Get it away, for Christ's sake. It's me, Jack. It's Mac. Call the dog off.'

Now it was Jack's turn to cry out in surprise, but he had the presence of mind to clip the lead onto Joe's collar and pull it away. 'He won't hurt you. He's only frightened.'

He leaned down to help the bulky mass regain its feet. The cap had disappeared somewhere into the broken fronds and he could see the face clearly. There was stubble on the chin and a vague, uncertain look in the eyes. 'What are you doing here? Why are you following me?'

Mac was brushing the sticks and leaves from his clothing, watching the dog warily. 'It's a long story. Can we sit somewhere quietly and talk? I've been trying to get you in a place where no one's about, no one's listening.'

Jack examined him doubtfully. 'We're not supposed to talk. The instructions from ASIC are we're not to talk to anyone else involved in their investigation, not to discuss the matter at all.'

Mac nodded. 'I know, believe me I know. But I need to talk to you. I'm trying to help you.'

Jack snorted. 'Sure. Who isn't? The trouble is your sort of help's likely to land me in jail. No thanks.'

Gradually Mac's breathing was returning to normal. He stood erect, drew air deep into his lungs and exhaled slowly. 'It's not like that. I'm not what you think I am. I don't hang people out to dry. I don't stab in the back. If I'm coming for you, you'll see me. Please, just talk for a while.'

They sat, all three, on the mound of a massive date palm. Jack couldn't stop himself from staring at the evidence of Mac's decline: the muddy tracksuit, the unkempt hair, the unshaven jowls. He checked the normally manicured nails—ragged and dirty. All this in only a couple of weeks? He could see himself here, see the kids inspecting him with pitying eyes, see Louise looking away in order to preserve some semblance of respect.

'I'm not a crook, you know.' Jack was startled to hear the silence broken. He'd already forgotten they were going to talk. Somehow it seemed more appropriate just to sit, to be quiet.

'I only took what was mine. Okay, maybe some law or regulation says it should have been done a different way, or I should pay some extra tax, or whatever. But it was mine. I made it, I had the right to take it. Maybe we dressed up the accounts a little, but so what? All the shareholders benefited, didn't they? Not just me. And now I've suffered more than anyone.'

Jack thought of the bronzed commander offering sweetmeats on the deck of the *Honey Bear*, the captain of industry in the dark cave of an office, the arts tsar at the opening of his gallery. Alongside him now was a grizzled old man, absentmindedly patting the head of a filthy dog, trying to justify himself to anyone, to no one.

'Is that why you wanted to talk? To explain yourself?'

Immediately there was a flash of anger from the spleen of the old Mac. 'Fuck you. I don't explain myself to anyone. I've come to offer help. If you want to bite the hand, fuck you, Jack.'

There seemed to be no other people in this impenetrable section of the park. They were in the heart of a city of five million people, but alone, lost in a secret grove. A breeze rustled the swaying fronds above; a spent pod fell to the ground causing the dog to leap to its feet. Otherwise there was silence.

'What is this help?' Jack's eyes drifted to the minutiae of the world around him.

A caterpillar was making its painful way across a dead frond, clambering laboriously up one leaf, down another, on and on—to where? A tiny lizard darted out into the light, stared at them briefly, darted back. Somewhere high above, a bird was crunching at a fruit on the palm, rejected fragments drifting down softly into the leaf litter. He could hear Mac's tired voice speaking, but was somehow indifferent to what was being said.

'I'm a tough old bastard. You don't have to worry about me. I'll get out of this somehow. But they're after you, too. They think you were in on the whole deal. You've been set up. Haven't we all?'

Jack turned to him reluctantly. 'What do you mean I've been set up?'

'I don't know exactly, although I've got a fair idea. But they've got tapes, documents, you name it.'

Jack stood and the dog rose with him. 'Why should I care? I haven't done anything I'm ashamed of.' He thought about that statement for a moment, then repeated, 'Why should I care?'

'That's what I'm trying to tell you. Look, this isn't just a PR issue for you. Make no mistake—they're going to charge you.'

Jack looked down at him. 'Why are you telling me this?' Now Mac stood also, facing him, shoulders back—almost the old stance. 'I don't knife people in the back. You've got kids. You wouldn't know how to fight, anyway.' He paused. 'Once they charge me, I won't be able to speak. Same for you. Sure they've told us to shut up already, but that's different to being in court. If breaking that order was all I was charged with, I'd be delighted. So.' He placed his hands together. 'I'm going to tell them you had nothing to do with any of this. But you need to make it public somehow. Put them on notice there's no easy case. And quickly. You've got to defend yourself.'

'And what do I do for you?' The face was turned away from him and the voice was quiet, but a hint of the old edge crept into the words. 'You give me that letter you took from Renton Healey's file.'

Jack managed a short, bitter laugh. 'How many copies would you like? The bell has rung, Mac, the game's over.' This time they were alone on a seat on the coastal walkway between Bondi and Tamarama. A heavy sea was thumping into the cliffs below and the rock fishermen were scurrying for safety, their cleated shoes scratching across the slippery surfaces. Louise was listening to Murray Ingham's gruff voice intently, straining to hear the words over the roar of the surf.

'Jack may have difficulty defending himself, but I think there's another way. We've a great deal of material to work with. All you've told us, plus a storehouse of documents Maroubra has squirrelled away. It makes a compelling story.'

Louise stared into the grey ocean and shivered. The nor'-easter was whipping the whitecaps into scurries of flying foam and her summer blouse was no defence against the unseasonal chill. 'Maybe. But he can't speak, and who would believe him at the moment, anyway?'

Murray nodded. 'You're right, but that's where I come in. I'm a storyteller, remember. This matter's now significant news. I was a journalist before I became a writer. I still write the occasional opinion piece and I still know all the editors that matter. But whether I did or not, they'd publish this story. It's got everything.'

She turned to face him. 'You mean you'd arrange the material and pass it onto a journalist?'

'No. I'd write it under my own name. I may not be a bestselling author, but I am at what they call the quality end of the market. The name will help.'

'How will you do it? Won't the authorities try to stop you? Can't they prosecute you, or the paper?'

'It'll be a two-part story. The first instalment will have most of the factual material so we get that on the record before anyone does try to stop us. The second will have more of the colour, not that there are any dull moments in this saga. Our hope would be that ASIC or some other authority does try to suppress part two. There's nothing a newspaper editor likes more than a good stoush. I'll defend my sources all the way to a jail cell and you'll bring me home-cooked meals. What do you say?'

This time she reached for his arm. 'I don't know what to say. I'm terribly grateful. You'll be putting your reputation on the line.'

He laughed. 'Not at all. I'll probably win a Walkley Award, and who knows, there may even be a book in it. Strangely, we storytellers always come out all right. No one ever returns to check on us if events prove we're wrong. The messenger hardly ever gets shot in real life.'

They stood and began to walk on to Tamarama, climbing to the low walled lookout between the two beaches, the wind loading the air with salt now, as a goshawk hovered above them, hunting the cliffs. They'd met only twice and yet somehow they were friends. Louise thought of all the 'friends' she thought she'd had who'd disappeared into the ether of her social ostracism. Murray stopped her as she was about to walk on. 'There may be a job for you later. What usually happens is the electronic media pick up on a story like this once it's run in the press. But they're looking for the people angles, not so much the facts. They might want to interview you if Jack's not available and we'll make sure he isn't. Could you handle that?'

'Would it help?' He nodded. 'A great deal. It helps to keep the story alive. And besides, you're an impressive voice, not just because you're Jack's wife. You know some of the facts, you've seen some documents, you know the background right from the start. But it wouldn't be easy.' He paused. 'They might ask you about personal matters.'

She sighed. 'Ah yes, "personal matters". You don't need to worry. If it will help, I'll be there. Let them ask any questions they want. I'll be there.'

chapter eighteen

A brass band was playing 'Anchors Aweigh' on the wharf, somewhat inappropriately since the *Honey Bear* was securely tied to a variety of bollards and the engines were silent. The boat was at rest outside the chic restaurants of Woolloomooloo Wharf, and a long queue of Sydney's A-list partygoers was lined up at the gangway in front of the band. The diners in the restaurants were ogling this unusual assemblage, while delicately winding saffron noodles around silver forks.

There were a number of peculiar aspects to the evening that attracted the attention of all but the most casual observer. First, there was no party on board. Waiters with drinks, women in seductive gowns, jewels glinting in the lights reflecting from the water, dancing music—all the usual festive accoutrements were absent, just the brass band playing a repertoire of vaguely nautical tunes and the A-listers in business attire, trying to appear businesslike.

The clue to the mystery lay in the outsized flags flying from the *Honey Bear*'s funnel and stern. Instead of the boat's traditional gold standard with its symbol of a bear plunging a mitt into a honey pot, the rather more sombre and elegant navy and white colours bearing the Sotheby name adorned the vessel. This august appellation was also emblazoned upon the canvas sides of the gangway, lest the guests be in any doubt as to their purpose here. Bring your chequebooks and your invitation was the unspoken message. And indeed there were many chequebooks nestling in silk-lined pockets, for the range of goods to be auctioned was startling in its diversity. You could buy a magnet or a Moore. The exact use for which the magnet was designed was unknown, but it came in a brass case with velvet interior and was estimated in the catalogue at only two to three hundred dollars. To own something from the Honey Bear, from Mac Biddulph's effects, just to be here, bidding—well, you couldn't miss it, could you? The boat was only permitted to hold four hundred people, although Sotheby's had squeezed in five hundred on the grounds that all their guests were slim. But the applications to attend this 'invitation only' auction had exceeded three thousand. Three thousand, for goodness sake. They'd had to turn away over two thousand potential bidders. It was stomach churning. Of course, a large number would have been gawkers, tyre-kickers, but the money would have been buried there somewhere. Particularly for a magnet in a brass case, if not for a Henry Moore maquette, estimate eighty to one hundred thousand dollars.

Everything that wasn't bolted down was to be sold, no reserves.

And everyone wanted a piece of this story. It reminded the Sotheby's vice-president, visiting from New York—because how many auctions were held on boats, anywhere, and because this story of corporate fraud had even found its way into the *New York Times*, causing him to book a flight at uncomfortably short notice, in the sense that only business-class seats were available—it reminded him of the Andy Warhol auction. There was a madness in the air, a wonderful sense of irrationality that would cause people to spend money they had no intention of spending. The intrinsic value of the goods would bear no relation to the prices paid. It was an auctioneer's dream. The vice-president shivered at the wonder of it all. It was vital to be here, no matter what the discomfort required.

The other eagerly awaited thrill for the lucky invitees was the vicarious, guilty pleasure of rifling through the personal belongings of a famous, or infamous, person while he was still alive. This was living history—or a peepshow. Either way, it was irresistible. Virtually everything but the underwear was for sale and there were surprises in every corner for those with an eye for detail, and there were many such eyes on hand.

In a small study off the main saloon, for instance, was displayed a vast array of books of unexpected variety. There was an extensive collection of poetry in signed first editions, ranging from Shelley to Keats, from the American poet Elizabeth Bishop to the famous Australian expatriate Peter Porter. It was the collection of a serious reader and, by the look of it, had been read. Surely it wasn't Mac Biddulph's? He was known as a connoisseur of more basic pleasures. So whose were the books? His wife's? But she was said to barely speak, let alone to read. It was most curious and intriguing. There was a fine collection of biographies of political leaders, adventurers, scientists and inventors, but none of business people.

And then there were the artworks. Of course the Moore had been expected, and the gem of a Matisse, but they were trophy pieces that were assumed to have been acquired through a consultant. Yet here was a wide variety of drawings and artefacts, small sculptures, paintings by lesser-known Australian artists, and a fine collection of Aboriginal works from Arnhem Land and Kalumburu and Ramingining. Many were not of great value, but all were of high quality, all had been selected with a discerning eye. Whose eye? The leading dealers were here; none had any knowledge of some expert buying for Mac Biddulph. A few recognised works they'd sold, but not to Mac; some they'd seen bid for by telephone at one auction or other. None of it seemed to fit with their knowledge of the man who'd owned all of this.

If, of course, he had owned any of it. Nowhere in the catalogue or the provenance of any of the works was the name Macquarie James Biddulph mentioned. The banking syndicate had insisted on its omission, apparently despite the strong objections of the Sotheby's claque, who'd suggested that its absence would depress sales. The bank seemed to have been right—there was no chance of anything depressing the irrepressible spirit of this auction.

It was rumoured that the doyenne of party organisers, Popsie Trudeaux, had supplied the guest list for the evening, although Sotheby's denied this. They said they had no need for anyone's list except their own. But other than the art dealers, the crowd was suspiciously similar to that in attendance at the party of all parties, the opening of the Biddulph Gallery.

And that was the other piece of delicious gossip tantalising the unnaturally pursed lips of every Botoxed woman in the saloon. Was it true, could it be true, that the museum trustees were plotting to remove the Biddulph name? Surely not? He had given the money, after all. Perhaps it wasn't his to give, but did that matter? If someone coughed up, surely they were entitled to expect what was promised. It was only decent behaviour; otherwise there was anarchy—you couldn't rely on anyone. The general consensus was that the name should stay. After all, there were many other institutions and university chairs and whatnot named after brigands and bounders and bankrupts, weren't there? Someone in the crowd began to draw up a list of such persons to present to the chairman of trustees, who was standing at the front of the room, but soon realised it was unwise. The list was long.

Naturally, the subject of all this speculation, this delicious lip-pursing chin-stroking gossip, the former master of this proud vessel, which was itself to be humbled in another auction the next day, a show auction admittedly since the buyer was already identified, this ghost who may have browsed through these poetry books, have rubbed these bronzes with loving hands, he was a presence by his absence. But everyone else was here.

And there was a party mood, despite the lack of alcohol, despite the lack of real music. This was a festive occasion. It was true one of their number had fallen. That was, in its way, sad. But there were two mitigating factors. First, he'd never really been one of them, not really. Second, they hadn't fallen.

Whether Popsie Trudeaux had provided the guest list or not, she was intent on providing as much of her ample bosom as possible, to anyone who wanted it. Particularly to the Sotheby's vice president from New York. He was travelling alone. She'd ascertained that in the first thirty seconds of their conversation. He was visibly under fifty and came from an old Boston family.

New York was apparently merely a useful place of commerce for him. Old Boston families were rich, at least in the books Popsie read, which admittedly were few. And, surprisingly, he appeared to be interested in women. Not necessarily in her yet, but the man needed to relax, to have the tensions of travel eased away. She would do what she could. He was in conversation with

Archie Speyne, who was said to be here to direct the museum's bidding on the Matisse, but she drew the vice president away to ask his advice on certain artworks, on which she had no intention of bidding. People melted when asked for their advice.

And they always gave more of it than you really needed.

There was one other notably absent figure. The distinguished presence of Sir Laurence Treadmore, a presence that was known to have graced these rooms in better times, was nowhere to be seen. The Sotheby's folk were bitterly disappointed. Desperate phone calls had been made to any number of his intimate acquaintants, of which he had none, in order to lure this bird into their bower, but to no avail. They hadn't desired Sir Laurence as a bidder—they were aware he was seldom that—but as a phenomenon of the moment, as someone who had transcended mere public recognition and risen into the social firmament. For Sir Laurence was the only member of the cast in the HOA tragedy who had been lionised in the press as a messiah, a possible saviour, a man of integrity who had tried to hold back the forces of fraud and manipulation and trickery that were threatening to engulf the company. He'd spoken out for the shareholders, all the shareholders—why he was even buying shares himself, as an expression of confidence in the future of the company. He'd committed to remaining as chairman and had temporarily taken over an executive role until a new chief executive could be found. What more could be asked of a busy man?

It was said there were recordings of Sir Laurence pleading with Jack Beaumont and Mac Biddulph to investigate possible wrongdoing, more than once it was rumoured, but nothing had been done. For obvious reasons, in Mac's case. The question of Jack Beaumont's behaviour was more complex. The recent articles in the press, one headlined 'A Corporate Gladiator', had thrown confusion over what had seemed another unfortunate, but oddly satisfying, fall. People rose, people fell. But they seldom rose again; the resurrection was not a popular social phenomenon. Yet a great deal of factual material, cogently argued, had been presented in those articles, the second of which the authorities had tried to ban. The paper had won a court battle in order to publish, which had apparently boosted its circulation considerably.

And then there was the wife. She'd appeared on '60 Minutes' and had been, well, majestic. Everyone said it. When the interviewer tried to badger her with intrusive, personal questions, unnecessary, irrelevant questions, she'd batted them away to the boundary. She'd just looked him straight in the eye and said, 'Is this a stone you're sure you want to throw? Would you like to tell your wife now, on camera, that you've never looked at another woman? Or would you rather ask me questions of substance? It's up to you.'

God, she was wonderful. Everyone knew Tony Playford was a pants man from way back, but to pin him like that, on television, it was riveting. And she'd only cried once, at the end, and not in self-pity. She was being asked about some lawyer who was helping them, who'd died, who she'd never met, and she cried when she was speaking of him, let the tears roll down her face, never tried to brush them away. That was the picture the papers ran the next day. And her final line, it was almost Shakespearean, as if someone had written it for her, and yet she'd delivered it from the gut. 'The world is not cloaked in grey, not stained with soot. There are still those who can distinguish black from white. My husband is one such man.' It ran as the caption under her picture. It was a triumph.

But also confusing. Were they now in or out? Prime-time television and front pages, flattering ones that is, were not to be sneezed at, but there was still a lingering odour. Better to wait and see. Anyway, they weren't here and hadn't been invited.

Popsie Trudeaux had been abandoned, temporarily she assumed, by her charming vice president and had scooped up Archie Speyne to fill in the time. 'You can tell me, Archie dear, what's really happening with the Biddulph Gallery. You know I'm always discreet.'

Archie knew something rather different, but then discretion was not a quality he admired in anyone. Where would he be with it, he always thought. However, the question of the naming of the gallery was causing him some concern. He'd argued for naming rights in perpetuity and the trustees had overridden him. Now it seemed they had been proven right. Besides, if the Biddulph name was removed, Mac would hardly be likely to sue. Maybe Archie could sell the rights again and keep the original donation as well. But there were other donors whose names were on galleries who were nervous, upset at any suggestion these could be summarily removed. What did they have to hide, Archie wondered.

But back to discretion. How much to let slip to Popsie, how much to hold back? Art was all very well in its place, namely in his museum, but these were the dilemmas that sent Archie's heart racing. 'You know I can't say anything, Popsie, but if the trustees did decide to make a change, to preserve the museum's integrity, not that I'm saying they will, but if they did, where would I find another philanthropist as generous as Mac Biddulph? Or whoever's money it was. You see what I mean?'

Popsie did see what he meant. She saw it very clearly. It was a sparkling diamond in a dull crowd, a jewel in a sandbox. How to sift it from the dross, set it in platinum and wear it for the world, that was the question.

'Yes, I imagine it'll be very difficult for you particularly, Archie, having brought Mac Biddulph in with such a fanfare. A great coup at the time, but things change, don't they?' She saw Archie blanch at these remarks and felt pity for the little fellow.

She should comfort him, help him. 'I've one or two thoughts on a suitable replacement. Perhaps not quite the same money up front, but then you've finished the gallery now, the roof is on so to speak. You don't really need the money anymore, do you? But to have an impeccable name, someone you can put forward to the trustees the minute they decide, if they decide. Don't you think that would be preferable?'

When they parted, Archie virtually skipped across the polished boards in search of a bar from which to order champagne, even though he'd promised himself he wouldn't sniff a bubble before the Matisse was on the block. But of course there was no bar, no bubbles. Sotheby's wanted everyone sober tonight.

The room hushed as the auctioneer stepped, or more accurately leapt, to the podium. He was so charming, so athletic, always immaculately dressed, so knowledgeable and likeable, a few had even invited him to their homes, and not only for valuations. He was the manager of Sotheby's in Sydney and, in an unusual arrangement, would handle the auction jointly with the striking blonde woman standing beside him. She had hair that fell to her wrists and eyes that, once they were locked onto yours in a bidding frenzy, reached deep into your pockets. She would handle the middle section of the vast list, but the manager was their favourite.

'Ladies and gentlemen, what a pleasure to enjoy your company on such a night.'

They applauded. They actually applauded the arrival of an auctioneer, as if he were a conductor. The stage was set. It was only a matter of how high the prices might soar. The answer was soon known. The first few items were modest paintings by mid-career artists. They were knocked down for more than double the estimates. The Aboriginal works brought three and four times the highest estimate and the sculptures likewise. The Henry Moore maquette, a small bronze no more than eight inches high, went for a hundred and eighty thousand dollars. Someone bought a marble desk set of vaguely Italian origin, estimated at six to eight hundred dollars, for nine and a half thousand dollars. An ashtray went for nine hundred dollars. By the time a short break was called for the changeover at the podium, the room was abuzz. Sydney had never seen anything like it. It was Jackie Onassis, it was Andy Warhol—it was Mac Biddulph. And he was alive.

Maxwell Newsome felt a hand on his arm and turned to see the Pope standing beside him. 'Hello, John. I didn't expect to see you here. This isn't your sort of scene normally, is it?'

'No. But I'm interested in some of the sculptures. For my son. He's a sculptor.'

'Is he indeed? Wonderful to have creative blood in the family. I'm afraid all we know how to do is make money.' Max laughed at his own witticism, but received no encouragement. 'Sad occasion, though, in many ways. Very sad. Distressing to me, obviously. Mac's an old friend.'

The Pope leaned towards him. 'Yes. I gather you traded for him a good deal?'

Max's body stiffened under the cashmere, but his facial expression changed not at all. 'Occasionally. Mac kept things pretty close to the chest.'

'I'm hearing, Max, that all those shares he sold might have been consolidated into one entity. That HOA might have a new significant shareholder. Have you heard anything to that effect?'

Max's smile remained as Madame Tussaud would have wished. 'Very unlikely, old chap. They'd have to file a notice if that was so. Nothing's come to light. Certainly not known to me.'

The Pope nodded. 'I just thought you might have heard a whisper.' He turned to leave but Max held him with a question.

'What's your interest, John? Are you into HOA?'

'No. I just like to keep in touch. Good luck for the rest of the evening.'

Seats were being resumed for the final session of the auction. It would commence with the Matisse. Even though Archie Speyne was about to spend someone else's money, even though he wasn't bidding himself, his legs were shaking, his stomach was hollow, and he was sweating under the light jacket with the ivory buttons—but he loved it. The thrill of the chase, the despair of losing, the fear of winning. It was all around the room. Adrenalin and testosterone, no ice, shaken not stirred.

But it soared, the Matisse, took flight into the outer reaches of Archie's budget in five bids, hands flying from the telephone bidders, cards flapping around the room. What would he do? They had to have it, the museum, it was theirs by rights. It should have been gifted, by Mac, by the banks, by someone. He looked to his chairman of trustees in the front row. One more bid? A nod of approval. The museum's stooge raised the bidder's card. A responding call from the telephone desk. It was gone.

He was sickened, gutted. It was indecent. Nouveau riche people throwing money at things they had no real knowledge of, no deep love for. It should have been his; he meant the museum's. He stumbled into the night in search of sustenance, physical or emotional.

But no one else left, even though the lesser items were now on the block, even though stomachs were rumbling and not even a hipflask had been sighted. How could you afford to leave? Who knew if something unexpected might spring from a lacquered box?

'Now, ladies and gentlemen, we come to a special item. A rare collection of poetry books. A connoisseur's item, this one. We have the perfect audience for it, I believe. All first editions. All signed by the authors. To be sold in one line, ladies and gentlemen. What shall we say for it? One hundred thousand to get started? Do I have eighty? Eighty then. Eighty to get on. Thank you, sir, eighty.

Ninety? Ninety it is then. One hundred? Thank you, madam. A hundred and ten? On the phone. A hundred and ten. Against you, madam. One twenty? New bidder. Thank you, sir, one twenty. It's one twenty in the centre here. Against you, madam. Against you, sir, at the front. Do I have one thirty? Are we all done? Any further from the phone? I'm going to sell then. At one twenty, one hundred and twenty thousand dollars, all done, all—'

'One fifty.' The voice rang through the panelled room, ricocheted off the domed roof, seemed to cut the strings of the jerking marionette on the podium so that its arms flopped, its mouth fell open. Every head turned to see where its eyes were fixed.

He stood as he'd always stood on the decks of this boat—as if he owned not just the vessel but the ocean it sailed on. The feet were planted wide apart, the face was tanned and healthy, the suit looked as if the tailor had fitted it that evening. There was not a person in the room who couldn't pick that voice just from a radio interview, there was no one in Sydney who didn't know Mac Biddulph's squared-off face.

The charm of the auctioneer was lying on the floor somewhere under the podium. This couldn't be happening. There was no way he could accept a bid from Mac Biddulph. He had no money. That was the whole point of the auction, wasn't it? So the banks could harvest whatever was left on the stalks. But this was an auction. A bid was a bid. He looked around the room, desperate for guidance. He caught the eye of the vice president from New York, who shrugged. He probably didn't even recognise Mac.

'One fifty then. At the back. Do I hear one sixty? One sixty anyone? Going once at one fifty, twice, I'm selling then, all done at one hundred and fifty thousand dollars, sold to . . . to you, sir.'

Not a foot shuffled on the boards, not a cough escaped, not a catalogue rustled. For a moment, there was absolute silence.

And then, slowly at first, but building quickly like a wave flowing around the room, applause rang out. They dropped what they were holding—pens, papers, hats, whatever—and clapped like a crowd possessed. Mac smiled, let his eyes travel slowly over the faces, waved, and walked from the *Honey Bear* for the last time.

chapter nineteen

They walked arm in arm, bodies rubbing gently, legs swinging in unison, unconsciously wrapped together. The ground was covered with an indigo haze of crushed jacaranda petals. The scent of jasmine and gardenias mingled in the humid air. The faintest brush of a light sun shower drifted about them and the kookaburras were already calling the end of the day.

They entered the forgotten park through a rusted gate, jammed forever open. No one came here. They'd stumbled on this lost tangle of exotic plants gone wild on one of their long rambles. It was their favourite release now, to wander together along the harbour foreshore, or through the lanes and alleys of Paddington, past the nineteenth-century terraces and the art galleries and bistros, or to discover one of the myriad public pathways or open spaces that led down to the water.

Their park—it was their park now—had the ruins of a stone building buried in its undergrowth, the huge hand-cut, roughly pecked blocks of the city's convict past. Sometimes they sat on these tumbled monoliths and ate sandwiches or drank tea. But this evening they made their way to a sandstone shelf jutting out over the cliff, with the harbour lapping virtually beneath, and Jack drew a bottle of white wine and a block of cheese from his small backpack. They sat in the melting dusk, the shadows of the eucalypts falling around them.

Green and yellow ferries scurried back and forth across the golden harbour. Soon their lights would form rippling columns in the black water, but as yet the sun held to a faint promise. The birds fell silent, even the kookaburras left the stage to the animals of the night. They sipped in the deep congeniality of lovers who no longer needed to fill silences. Suddenly Jack thought he could make out a moving shape in the water. It disappeared. He followed the path that might have been. A great head rose from the swell and then a rounded smaller shape alongside. He stifled a cry and pointed for Louise. The whale and its calf swam calmly beneath them, beneath the houses and apartments of the lawyers and merchant bankers and chief executives.

'I love this city, ' Jack said. 'They say whales won't swim where the water isn't clean, but here we are in a working port, surrounded by millions of people and still they come. Somehow it means we haven't wrecked the world quite yet.' He turned to her. 'I want to go back to making beautiful things. Someone else can rule the business world. I want to design houses for ordinary people, houses that don't cost millions but are simple and functional and elegant. This place has given me another chance and I want to take it.' He held her forearm. 'Well, you've given me the second chance. No one else. But I've learned there are more good people than otherwise and now I've met a lot of the good ones. People come up to me in the streets, shake my hand, even shopkeepers—it's humbling. And, of course, there are the others. But we don't care about them, do we?'

They walked along the track by the cliffs and peered into the dark water, but the whales had vanished. 'Will you work with me again? Just the two of us and a couple of young graduates, the way we used to be? Will you walk on with me?'

He couldn't see her face but he felt the arms wrap around him and the breath in his hair. 'What do you think, lover boy?'

It took them over an hour to walk back to Alice Street. It was a long while since they'd been so relaxed. They chatted occasionally about the good times to come, the black times past. The landscape had transformed before their eyes when the press articles ran and the other media picked up the story. It was as if a breeze had blown thick fog from the hills and suddenly it was clear the sun had always been warming the valley ahead. They'd heard nothing from ASIC or any other authority, although Mac had been charged, as had Renton Healey. Louise stopped him at one point and said, 'I told you the good guys always win.' Jack laughed and held her to him.

As they entered the small front garden through the wrought-iron gate, they didn't notice the man standing beneath one of the street trees until he spoke.

'Mr Beaumont? Mr Jack Beaumont?'

'Yes.'

'I have a subpoena for you, sir. And Mrs Beaumont, is it? One for you also, madam.' He disappeared into the night as quickly as he'd emerged and they were left staring blankly at the documents in the half-light.

The whales had left the bays and coves of the eastern harbour now and were swimming slowly outside the shipping lane towards the heads. The mother nudged the calf gently to one side if it strayed towards the marker buoys. They felt the currents of the incoming tide and pushed on into the open sea, turning to the north to join the migration to warmer waters. Just five hundred yards from the shore, but well outside the surf line, they made their way past Manly and Harbord, edged out to sea to clear Long Reef, resumed their line by Mona Vale and Bilgola and Whale Beach, and then swam through the punctuated flashes of the Barrenjoey Lighthouse, leaving Sydney and its sleeping citizens well behind.

Maroubra set the cruise control on the steering column and let his mind, too, slip on to autopilot as the heavy frame of the four-wheel drive ploughed into the air currents. The course was set for Bowral, more than an hour's drive south-west of Sydney, a place he'd never visited before or even considered for a wet weekend. He thought of it vaguely, if at all, as the retreat of those who rode horses early in the morning—or at least wore clothes that looked as if they rode horses—and then spent the remainder of the day in vast gardens cluttered with daffodils and other colourful objects that sprang unexpectedly from bare ground. Maroubra disliked horses, at least horses that were groomed and cosseted and pranced about in arenas, ridden by people in tight jackets and ridiculous helmets. If they were afraid of falling off, why did they get on? He felt he might appreciate wild horses if he saw a herd of brumbies thundering down a gorge, but this wasn't an experience that had passed his way.

Yet here he was in the land of leather-patched elbows, searching for a name on a gate. At least you couldn't miss the gates here. They were all enormous structures of stone and wood or wrought iron, with English names emblazoned on them that sounded as if the Duke of Barwick Feld had slipped away to the colonies for a short break and was taking tea, and a muscular serving wench, just up the garden path. He pushed the accelerator down hard as the engine struggled up the thousand-foot climb through the dense eucalypt forest on the slopes of Mount Gibraltar. The towns of Bowral and Mittagong lay below, but Maroubra's eyes were searching for the name BLACKBUTT LODGE on a fence or gatepost.

It had been a curious, disturbing call that had brought him here. Late at night, on his home phone, his wife asleep, him dozing, asleep but awake as he often was now, jerked into consciousness by the night call that always rang of disaster. He hadn't recognised the voice at first. He was attuned to voices, always knew if a friend was sick or troubled from the voice, or if a lie was sliding down the line, or a hand reaching into his pocket. And there were few words to decipher; just 'Come tomorrow. Bowral, on the mountain, look for Blackbutt Lodge. Be there at eleven.' But it was the Pope's voice, flat and strangled and lifeless, nothing like the steady, calm tone he'd heard for so many years—there was no mistaking the timbre underlining the half-whispered instructions.

He saw it now, the name, not on a pretentious assemblage of inappropriate grandeur, but on the cross-pole of a simple frame of undressed trunks. He drove slowly down the steep road of crushed granite and parked in a turning area. No buildings were visible but he could make out strange shapes hiding in the dense copses, organic shapes or twisted, contorted metallic-looking objects. The view through the clearing was a hundred kilometres or more across to a hazy mountain range with honey-coloured escarpments. He stopped to drink in the colours and shapes. Suddenly he realised he was looking through the Jamison Valley to the Blue Mountains, without a structure or a road or any sign of human presence, other than the ghosts lurking in the trees, to interrupt his view.

He didn't hear or see the spare figure step from behind the tree until the voice startled him. 'You can look a long time.

There's a lot to see.'

Maroubra turned at the familiar voice, stronger than it had been in the dark hours, and saw the lean face, lined with tension. 'Yes. It's a surprise after all the clipped grass and rose gardens.'

The Pope attempted a smile, but it was thin and unconvincing. He was dressed more warmly than seemed necessary, in a thick woollen jacket and knitted cap, although Maroubra realised the breeze carried a sharp chill here on the mountain. 'Let's walk. I'll show you some sculptures. We won't go to the lodge, if you don't mind. I'd rather we weren't seen together.'

He led the way through the tall, straight trunks, rising thirty feet before the first leaves kissed a branch. Maroubra could see the shapes more clearly now, decipher the forms of something he might expect in an art gallery, if he ever went to an art gallery. They stopped in front of a commanding piece, claiming its right in the centre of a wide clearing, a bronze mask atop a tall wooden totem staring out into the mists of the valley. The base was a roughly cut block of granite, but where the stone met the wood even Maroubra's untrained eye could discern the skill in the fitting together of the two. The Pope stood back, waiting for a response.

'It's a wonderful thing. I don't know anything about sculpture, but even I can feel its presence.' Maroubra reached down to rub the joining places with his bare hands. 'And this work, it's alive somehow, the way this is done.'

Now the Pope's face broke into a wide smile as he came forward. 'It's morticed, you see. The stone is cut almost like the joints in a fine drawer. And look here at the pinning. They're cast bronze, cast to fit exactly.' He also knelt to place his gloved hands on the cold stone. Maroubra raised his brows inquiringly. 'It's my son's. It's his best piece so far. And he'll do better things yet. He's in his stride now, works all day from before breakfast till the light's gone. He's mastered the technical skills, now it's all the images springing up, all the emotion emerging through the hands into the wood and the stone and the bronze.' He rose and turned to Maroubra. 'You're right. They're alive. And so is he.'

It was the longest speech Maroubra had ever heard from the Pope, almost feverish in its intensity. He felt there was nothing to say, so he rose quietly and they both stared at the sculpture. He could hear the wind in the high trees but there was no other sound, not even a bird call, as the two men stood, almost like carved figures themselves, on the sloping ground.

Finally the Pope shook himself, as if emerging from hibernation, and took a folded envelope from his coat pocket. 'Here. Take this. Use it for Jack and Louise.'

Maroubra opened the envelope. He could see it was the corporate filing for a company, listing its head-quarters, directors, assets and liabilities, but the name was unfamiliar to him. 'What is this?'

'Just take it. I saw they were charged.' Maroubra examined the document more closely. 'Your name is here as a director.' He read on and looked up at the Pope in surprise. 'And that Trudeaux woman. What in God's name would you be doing on a company board with her?'

The Pope held up one hand. 'No questions. You take that and you follow wherever it leads you. Whether you'll find the person you want in a way that will pin him to the wall, I don't know. It's the best I can do.'

Maroubra watched his face as he spoke and read the strain. 'And what will happen to you if I do pursue it to the end?'

The Pope shrugged. 'That doesn't matter now. Get on with it, and quickly.' He turned to go. 'I have to teach a class.'

Maroubra stopped him, shook his hand, then watched him walk away into the forest. He remained in the clearing, staring into the distant mountains. He knelt and ran his hands again over the joints in the stone and wood before stuffing the envelope into his trouser pocket and hurrying back to the car, shivering in the thin air.

Popsie Trudeaux was in heaven. At least she assumed heaven would largely resemble this haven of pink houses with white roofs; with suntanned, attractive people strutting about in excitingly cut shorts;with dark waiters carrying colourful drinks on glass trays; with bougainvillea cascading over white walls and oleanders hiding money behind high hedges. The whole place was pink and white and rich. The smell of money was stronger than the scent of the flowers.

She'd loved it from the minute she'd arrived at the cute little airport and been escorted through customs by a handsome, young, darkish man who told her he was there to look after her during her stay. How thoughtful of her host, whoever he was. She'd really no information about him other than a name and the name of a boat and a time to meet. She loved the idea that the board meeting would take place on a boat. She loved everything about this company Sir Laurence had introduced her to. They paid their directors fees in advance and all she had to do was sign a few documents, share transfers and bank drafts, and come to Bermuda. The hardships of corporate life were bearable. Obviously it was a cover for someone who wanted to stay hidden. Fine. She hoped he'd stay that way forever. Although, probably, he'd be on the boat tomorrow.

Her hotel suite was pink and white—oceans of pink and white. Although the ocean itself was, of course, blue. It was spread before her through the tall French windows and the sun jazzed from it when she lay on one of the pink and white striped lounges on her vast terrace. She looked down on people below who did not have such vast terraces, but did not feel sorry for them. Try harder was all you could say.

She barely needed to try at all anymore. What a delicious feeling of comfort and security to know you could do absolutely nothing for the rest of your life except eat chocolate and have massages. What a sense of accomplishment. The money poured in and now the bucket stayed full. She'd won the Grand Prix contract, hired the most wonderful manager who produced graphs and accounts and full buckets, and wasn't bad looking either—although she'd vowed never to fuck him. No distractions for that little moneymaker.

She, however, was very much distracted by all the waiters and houseboys wandering about in their crisp uniforms, white shorts on dark legs. They were all that sort of light chocolatey colour, not black at all. Absolutely edible.

The last few months had been the most exciting time of her life. She'd barely had a minute to speak to Angus, not that she would have had much to say if a spare minute arrived. Angus was irrelevant. She was a woman of complete independence now, with her own business, her own money, carefully sequestered away from any joint assets in her own accounts, beholden to no one. Although she was terribly grateful to Sir Laurence for the chance to arrange the Biddulph Gallery opening party. And the suggestion to start her business. And that help with the Grand Prix contract, not to mention being here in Bermuda. Yes, all in all, she owed a great deal to Laurence Treadmore. She would find an opportunity to repay him, she was sure. Indeed she was anxious to see Sir Laurence. Not least because he would have the inside story on the latest with the Mac Biddulph opera. It was an opera, with great arias and sweeping scenery and even some bad acting. All of Sydney was in its thrall. The auction had merely confirmed it as the number-one news story of the year. Popsie had drunk in every minute of the auction night, despite the absence of any beverages. She'd even bought a small Aboriginal painting she'd had no intention of buying and didn't much like. It had some sort of serpent twisting across a brown background covered with small yellow dots. Perhaps she'd hang it in a toilet.

When Mac Biddulph himself had bid on those books, well no opera, soap or otherwise, had ever produced such drama. All sorts of serious academics and do-gooders had analysed the contents of the poetry books he'd bought, or re-bought, and suggested this was a truly cultured man, a man of taste and sensibility, morals, ethics even; that no one who appreciated those exquisite tomes, who understood the sentiments within, could be the callous fraudster painted by the authorities. And to want to keep only these from among all the other grander possessions on offer, this was the final proof of his complex character. And then an editor of a computer magazine claimed he'd found the very same books offered for sale on eBay just ten days after the auction. A newspaper rushed to buy the books, hoping to expose Mac or the magazine editor or anyone else it could implicate, but the items were withdrawn from sale. No one could track the email address and the mystery remained unsolved.

Popsie needed to be able to speak with authority on issues of this kind, important social issues. It was part of her persona now, as a doyenne of Sydney society, a sort of duchess of the dinner table, a diva of the cocktail circuit, to know more than anyone else about people who mattered, or at least to be able to appear to know. A wink, a nod, a nudge—maybe two nudges. Why, they might even ask her about it on the boat tomorrow. It would be embarrassing not to have inside information at her first meeting with these generous fellow directors. She'd called Sir Laurence several times, her lovely Laurence as she thought of him now, but his secretary, who Popsie disliked intensely, said he was away for two weeks.

After a light lunch—well not so light, but healthy, surely, in that it contained some fish and a great deal of lobster—she decided she would make her way to Hamilton Harbour to check on the whereabouts of the boat she was to sail on the next day. In fact, she wanted to measure the boat, more than find its mooring. She believed, and was firm in this belief, that it paid to know the size of a person's boat before you met them.

The afternoon was blessed with a light zephyr to keep the temperature perfect as Popsie wandered along the dock admiring the phalanx of handsome craft and their equally well-equipped crew. No wonder people came here to avoid tax; although obviously one had to be prepared to travel to less pleasant parts for the same reason. But the combination was heady. Perhaps she should have a residence here herself. A cottage on a hill, pink and white of course, with a couple of chocolate houseboys, one firm, one soft. She giggled at her own wit and sashayed further past more and larger boats. They seemed to be arranged in some ascending order and clearly her boat, the *Butcherbird* (a curious name, she felt), would be at the apex of the boat hierarchy.

But what was this? There, nestled in a vast berth between two suitably enormous craft, was a mere pup of a boat—a whimpering, cowering, snivelling puppy amidst all these magnificent beasts. And disappointingly, horribly, the name on its tiny rear bore the word she was looking for: *Butcherbird*. Certainly it was a pretty little thing in its own way. But a navy hull and cream canvas and polished brass, no matter how attractively presented, couldn't make up for lack of substance. Length was what mattered in boats. Popsie resisted the obvious parallel thought—she was not a vulgar person.

She sighed. She normally preferred not to sigh because that could be seen as a vulgar habit also. People who sighed a great deal were expressing cynicism, or resignation, or disgust or some other negative sentiment. It was better to express energy and sex. Those were the two characteristics Popsie admired most. She'd been in readiness to express both in a devastating manner on the decks of the *Butcherbird* tomorrow, but she doubted if it could contain her performance. Oh, well. It would have to suffice. Perhaps the mysterious owner was indifferent to boats and flew his own 747 instead. That was a gripping thought. Just one long reception room, one cocoon of a bedroom and a huge spa bath off it—now that would make up for this disappointing sprat bobbing about in front of her. She wandered back along the marina consoled by this image. Next time she flew into that cute little airport she'd be fresh off Air Force One or whatever it was called, and feeling very relaxed.

When she returned to the hotel and lay on one of her four lounges, she found she was anything but relaxed.

The evening stretched before her in blank monotony. What was she to do? She knew no one in Bermuda and could think of no visible activity that interested her. People seemed to be either playing tennis or riding about on those little mopeds. Popsie disliked any activity that made you sweat, and the idea of puttering about on a motorbike to no great purpose was extremely unappealing. There appeared to be no places to visit on Bermuda; no art galleries, museums, theatres—no cultural life of any kind. Not that cultural life was all it was cracked up to be, but at least it was something. You couldn't lie about on lounges all your life.

She rang for a bottle of champagne. It arrived with a box of chocolates, so to speak. She thought about that while the cork was being twisted gently from its resting place. Why not?

'Do you massage?'

'You would like a massage, madam? I could ask the concierge to arrange it, of course.'

She sipped. How to phrase it delicately, so as not to offend. 'No. I don't like all those people with folding tables and smelly oils. I just want someone to relax me. Surely you can do that?'

And he could, and did. And when she woke in the morning she felt refreshed and ready for her board meeting. She dressed in a businesslike yet nautical fashion. Navy linen blazer, white slacks, no shirt. That was the point of difference—no shirt. The blazer covered most of her perfectly tanned breasts, but not quite all. And then the strand of South Sea pearls glistening above. Subtle, yet obvious. Disappointingly, there were no board papers to carry to the meeting. She rather fancied arriving with a sheaf of important-looking documents, but she was carrying a slim leather briefcase in any event, even though it was empty except for a spare handkerchief and a new BlackBerry which she hadn't yet learned to switch on.

She arrived at the dock exactly on time. Whoever these people were they would soon learn they weren't dealing with an amateur. Professionalism in all things was her new motto. She strolled confidently to the *Butcherbird* and waved to a crew member.

'Mrs Trudeaux? Good morning, madam, and welcome. Please come aboard.'

It really was a pretty little thing when you examined it closely, Popsie decided. What it lacked in length and breadth, it partly made up for in the beauty and luxury of its fittings. Everything was of the highest quality and in exquisite taste. No doubt the plane would be the same. She lifted her arms above her head to stretch her muscles, or where she assumed muscles should be, and sipped her freshly squeezed juice. The crew seemed to be readying the boat for a departure but so far she was the only one aboard. She called out to the nearest sailor, 'Are we meeting here at the wharf, or moving somewhere?'

'I'm sorry, madam?'

'Are we picking the others up somewhere else?'

'The others are already on board, madam.' This was very confusing. She looked around the saloon. The boat simply wasn't large enough to hide her fellow directors on the face of it. Perhaps there was another level below. But why wouldn't her host come to greet her? Was he going to spring from a secret panel or something? She hoped so. It was mysterious and exciting—particularly now that the boat had slipped its moorings and was winding its way slowly through the maze of other craft. And then, when it was clear of the marina, it seemed to almost leap into the air in a surge of power and plane away at impressive speed with a great plume of spray behind. Popsie could restrain herself no longer. Gauche it may be to ask too many questions, but gauche it would have to be.

'Excuse me, but we are to have the meeting on the *Butcherbird*, are we?'

'Yes, of course, madam. The meeting is on the boat, as arranged.' This was not illuminating. 'I see. And the others are on board?' 'Yes, madam.' There was no help for it. 'Where are they exactly?'

Now the young crewman, immaculate in his whites, appeared as puzzled as she was herself. 'I'm not sure, madam. On deck, I imagine.'

Popsie looked about. There was no deck they could possibly be on unless they were invisible. 'On this boat? On the *Butcherbird*?'

His wonderful brown face cracked at the seams and a mouthful of the whitest teeth were presented in a wide smile. 'Oh, this isn't the *Butcherbird*, madam. This is just the tender. The *Butcherbird* is out there.'

She followed the brown arm to the brown finger. There, on the horizon it seemed, was a wondrous sight. A casual glance might have suggested some ocean liner was anchored in the harbour, but Popsie's glance was anything but casual. The vessel her gaze was directed to was clearly the largest private motor yacht she, or anyone else, had ever seen. Why the *Honey Bear*, previously her gold standard for size (and she'd paced it herself from stem to prow on the night of the auction), would sit on the top deck of this fabulous monster.

And the closer they zoomed, and they were zooming, the bigger it looked. Forget the plane. Who cared if there was a plane? Probably there was a fleet of planes if he had a boat like this. But this was it. This was life. This was what mattered. Length and breadth and, probably, depth, for all she knew. This was what the game was all about. You could say it wasn't, if you weren't in the game. Or if you were a trier who hadn't made it. Or a Mac Biddulph who'd lost it.

But this was what everyone wanted, like it or not. To be the biggest, the richest, the most powerful. It was the law of the jungle. Popsie knew it, even if the losers didn't. She sighed despite herself, but it was a sigh of deep satisfaction. She was racing to her destiny with a triumphant shower of spray in her wake.

The tender, her charming tender, she'd grown to love the word, eased back into the water as it approached the shadow of the great ship in its path. Crew persons were scurrying back and forth over its innumerable decks and she could just make out a group of guests under a long canopy at the stern. She must be the last to arrive. Excellent. She loved making an entrance. She checked her clothing and stroked her pearls for luck. Somehow stepping on board this boat would take her into a new life. She could feel it. You'd sell your soul for this.

And then, as they pulled alongside, a familiar voice drifted down from above.

'Come aboard, dear lady, come aboard.'